Jumping for Charlotte

Alexander Engel-Hodgkinson

JUMPING FOR CHARLOTTE

ISBN 978-1-989331-14-9

Cover art by Alexander Engel-Hodgkinson

Published by
Dark Brothers Incorporated

PARENTAL ADVISORY

'Jumping for Charlotte' contains some strong violence and profanity, sexuality, and mature themes intended for readers aged 14 and up.

AUTHOR'S COMMENT

This was a difficult one for me to finish, but I'm glad it's finally done now. I'm satisfied with it, and I hope you are, too. I wrote this for someone, but they aren't around anymore. It's unfortunate, but such is life, I guess...

Chapter 1: Home

Summer, 2005

Bang.

Simple. You zero in, you pull the trigger and just...

Bang.

Two down. It used to be so hard. Then it got easy. And then it became *instinct*.

Bang.

Three down. Their headscarves stand out against the yellow sand. Black-and-red-striped dots rising and falling behind the rocks. The rattles of their assault rifles echo, only tipping me off to their numbers. Their bullets bounce harmlessly around me. Not even close. Another headscarf surfaces.

Bang.

The headscarf shreds in a scarlet splatter. Some gets on a rock behind the latest skull I've blown apart.

My spotter laughs, watching through his binoculars. "Fuckin' A, you got another one. You're a natural born killer. Sniper, ground troop; doesn't seem to make a difference with you, does it. That one! There. Three o'clock. Three o'clock."

I oblige him.

Another child grows without his father. Another father without his son. Another mother loses her baby to my trigger finger, left cold to the mercy of my spotter's enthusiastic bloodlust, his lack of empathy.

I hate it. Killing men I don't understand, or don't know. I often wonder how many of them feel the same. It's better to think of them as something else, something not human. Makes the pull of the trigger a little bit easier in the moment.

Two months later, I'm back in Cherry Springs, Michigan with nowhere to go. I know one thing: I'm not going back to the Middle East, and I'm sure as hell not going back to the military. No family. Only one friend.

I shouldn't bother him. I should end it now. After the things I've done for my country. "For my country," I spit in disgust.

"Right." Yusef said every war is the same, and at this point I'm inclined to believe him. They told us we were fighting for the safety and freedom of every citizen in the free world. Going out there, taking orders, following them, killing hundreds of men, women, sometimes children. Back home the politicians brag about how they're doing such a good job leading us, fighting the War on Terror. I don't remember seeing any of them out here with us.

The snack machine outside of a gas station restroom drops a bag of Doritos into the bottom compartment. I take it out and leave, continuing my journey up the road until I reach the middle of a truss bridge that crosses a ravine. I lean over the rail and stare out over the vast length of the ravine fringed with lush green boreal trees and brush. About two hundred feet above it, I can easily tell that the water streaming down the ravine's not very deep.

I don't have much to call my own. Just a duffel bag full of clothes and whatever the military let me take home, which wasn't much—a utility knife and a watch. The clothes on my back. A personal Beretta 92F holstered under my left shoulder, concealed by the unbuttoned Hawaiian shirt I'm wearing over a sleeveless top, uncomfortable in this heat. Frayed jeans tightened by a fake leather belt. My wallet with a few twenties, no change in my left rear pocket.

Not much else.

I rip open my Doritos and eat them at a leisurely pace, watching the trees sway gently in the warm breeze, the birds fly in meandering, carefree arcs above the treeline. White clouds rove slowly across the blue afternoon sky. Not a single car passes along the bridge. It's peaceful out here. Just the sounds of nature to accompany me.

With that thought comes another: this is the perfect place to die.

Ten minutes later, I crumple the Doritos bag into a ball and lose it to the breeze and watch it shrink into a fluttering red dot where it is eventually consumed by the trees. Then I lift a leg over the rail and climb to the other side. Both feet touch the edge. Clinging to the rail, standing on the very edge, I look down at the ravine. Its shallow, snaking stream sparkles brilliantly, even from way up here. Its white rocky banks promise a quick death if I land right. I shift a couple feet to the left so that I'm directly above the rocks. The height is dizzying. It looks so small from up here.

Alexander Engel-Hodgkinson

I take in one last breath of the summer air, close my eyes, and release the rail. The breeze carries me out into oblivion. The wind whistles in my ears, and then something screams. My eyes are clamped shut. A thousand different sounds reverberate around me. The air itself seems to pulsate, throbbing. Everything goes wild. Feels like I'm not falling, but spinning in every direction at once. What is this? I scream, not daring to open my eyes. I think of home in the town of Cherry Springs. Anything that'll comfort me, if only for a few precious seconds before the rocks finally hit me.

It's a soft landing in what feels like a flower bed. My body crushes them into a moist cushion of soil. The world gyrates around me; the sky is the ground and the ground is the sky before everything rights itself. My eyes flick open. A violent wave of nausea sends my Doritos clawing back up and gushing out onto the grass. It's short-lived, but I feel the acids in my stomach roiling painfully now that it's empty again.

I fall back, hitting a fence, and slid down to a sitting position, looking around, trying to get a bearing of my surroundings. This isn't the ravine and the bridge is nowhere to be found. Instead I'm sitting in someone's backyard. The back of the three-storey house on the other end of the yard, with its arched roof and fancy hatched windows, is like some kind of vision from my memories. I've seen it before, but where?

I hear a car door slam on the other side of the fence and I climb up the wood panels to peek over the top. I see a parking lot and a street just beyond it, and the back of a building I could never mistake, with its garage door I painted psychedelic swirls on in seventh grade, or the loading dock that leads right to the kitchen, or the two-storey building with apartments on the top floor and Freddie's Diner on the bottom.

"What the hell?" I can barely breathe. How did I get here? Wasn't I jumping off the bridge? Am I dead? I feel very much alive, and sick, and in pain. My gun is still tucked under my arm. I still have my bag.

There's no denying it. Somehow I'm home—or, the closest place to home I've had in a long time.

This is so confusing. I couldn't have walked all the way to Cherry Springs and not remember it. I *know* I jumped off that bridge. I was trying to kill myself. Why aren't I dead? Did something save me? God or something? I was never a believer of any particular religion, but this… whatever the hell *this* is… I can't explain it.

But I'm home now. I start to wonder if I should go back to the bridge, or some other high point, or hell, I have a gun. Why don't I just shoot myself? Why didn't I try that before? So much easier. Faster. I'd like to see whatever force that got me here get me out of a direct gunshot to the head.

I push the thought out of my mind. I have to know what this is. Why I'm here. Because I thought about it? Have I had this strange ability to teleport just by thinking about a familiar place?

What a stupid idea. I've thought about lots of places and this has never happened before. So what the hell is going on?

I climb over the fence, cross the lot, and walk up the alley along the side of the diner to the sidewalk. I enter the diner, a nice, classy 70's style restaurant, but cleaner than a lot of those places were. Right now, the place is empty, which isn't a surprise, as I recall the hours of two to four in the afternoon during weekdays being the dead hours—cleaning hours. A burly, heavyset man behind the counter immediately looks up when the bell above the door chimes, and for a second he squints until he recognizes me, and then they widen with surprise and joy. "Michael!"

"Hi, Fred."

He laughs heartily as he makes his way around the counter and rushes toward me, meaty arms extended. "My boy! What a pleasant surprise!" He embraces me, squeezes the breath out of my chest. When he releases me, he steps back, laughing, almost in tears. He pats my shoulders. "God, it's good to have you back. It's *good* to see you! When did you get discharged?"

"Last week. I was done."

"You going back?"

"No. No, I'm definitely done."

"Come, come." He gestures toward the counter. "I'll make you some food."

Before I can protest, he practically drags me over to a stool and then runs back around into the kitchen. He yells out, "How've you been? You stopped writing."

"I've been okay. Surviving."

"Today is your lucky day, kiddo. I just made a late lunch. Here, hold on." He comes out with a cheeseburger and a side of fries. He sets it down in front of me, grabs a ketchup bottle, and splatters its contents all over the plate. "Drenched in ketchup," he says. "Just the way you like it."

I stare at the fries soaked under a thick layer of red. They remind me of all the matter contained within those bobbing headscarves right before I pull the trigger and spill them into the sand. Thick red splashed across bright yellow. I try not to imagine it, but I can't stop seeing it.

"You okay?" Freddie asks me.

"No," I say quietly.

"What?" He can barely hear me over the radio. He reaches up and turns it down a few notches. "Sorry, son. My hearing ain't what it used to be."

"Thanks, Freddie. I appreciate it. But... I'm not hungry." I gently push the plate away.

Freddie eyes me with fatherly concern. "When was the last time you ate something, kid?"

I shrug. Was it that bag of chips I bought this morning with my last handful of pocket change? Was that this morning, or yesterday morning? Hell, maybe I never even ate it. Maybe I imagined the whole thing. Maybe it was a weird dream. Maybe I was delirious. I haven't had a sound sleep in days. Maybe that's what it was...

"Come on, talk to me."

Beat.

I say, "I haven't been able to look at ketchup and fries the way I used to lately."

Freddie breathes a short, quiet sigh. He looks at me like he understands exactly what I'm talking about. "I'll make you something else." He takes the plate and heads back into the kitchen. "Something less red."

"That's your lunch."

"I don't like ketchup," he replies. I hear him dump the plate in the garbage. "I'll make us somethin' we can both enjoy."

Good old Freddie.

I sit on that stool for a while, hanging over the counter like a dead tree branch. I say nothing because i have nothing to say.

"You have anywhere to go?" he asks from the kitchen over the clatter of dishes.

"A motel room up south."

With an exaggerated groan of disgust, he says, "That's no

good. I got a room upstairs. If you want, you can stick around. Help out around here. Until you find your footing, of course."

I say nothing, but I appreciate the gesture.

"What d'ya say?"

I think it over. Help out at the diner and live in my only friend's room, or spend another hundred in that ratty motel? Do I even have another hundred? "Thanks, Freddie."

It wasn't a hard decision to make. Matter of fact, it was the easiest decision I've had to make in a long time.

"Then it's settled," he says, smiling. "Welcome home."

The room he made available in the two-bedroom apartment above the diner is small but serviceable. For someone like me, it's perfect.

Freddie stands in the doorway as I set my bag on a rocking chair by the window. "You remember where the bathroom is?"

I manage to smile at his joke. "Yeah."

"What's mine is yours, kiddo. Except toothbrushes and other hygienic supplies, of course."

"I gotcha."

"Aw, man," Freddie says as he approaches me, arms outstretched. "C'mere, son."

He embraces me like a man-sized bear, squeezing the life out of me.

After a while, he lets me go, gives my shoulder a friendly slap. "I'll buy you a round, kid."

"You really don't have to."

"No." He sniffs. "No, I gotta. We gotta celebrate your homecoming somehow, right?"

I smile. "Yeah... yeah, I guess we do."

"Haha! That's the spirit. Come on, I know a good place. It's right across the street here."

I glance out the window and barely catch the flickering electric sign a few storefronts down, right on the corner of Wells Avenue: THE LOVE ZONE in dynamic blue letters with crimson edges. I can hear heavy metal crashing inside. It pounds rapidly like a heart going into cardiac arrest. "Uh..."

"It's not a sappy romantic hotspot," Freddie says, sensing (and misreading) my hesitation, "it's anything but that."

*

So we're sitting in The Love Zone, and it's even louder than I anticipated. I expected loud. I just wasn't expecting the decibel levels to be constantly set to 'loud-enough-to-risk-bursting-your-eardrums-every-other-second.' It's less like a small-town bar and more like a neon-soaked rave for heavy metal enthusiasts and millennials still living in the early nineties. Judas Priest blares on the speakers in all its howling, ear-gouging glory, to no one's surprise, since even I'm aware that the owner named this place after one of their songs. What really boggles my mind is how a place like this is able to run in such a small town like Cherry Springs, where the majority of its population is made up of blue-collar middle-agers and old people. Hell, you may as well call this town a retirement community—the existence of an elementary school on the other end of town is barely justifiable.

The female bartender is facing away from us, reaching for a Broweiser beer bottle someone else had ordered with the smooth grace of a dancer, a youthful spring in her step. She pulls back and gives it to a guy a few seats down the counter from me and collects payment, and I can't take my eyes off her. She has this radiance all about her, this strange glow. Everything else in the bar becomes less and less noticeable the more I look at her. I can't quite place what it is about her that makes my heart pound like a jackhammer. Her youthful energy? Maybe it's her soft, gentle face, or her long, silky brown hair, or her big arctic blue eyes; or her sarcastic responses to the swarms of innuendos and sexual compliments thrown her way by seemingly endless throngs of leering, drunk patrons.

The man she hands a beer to shouts over the music, "Thanks, baby." Hands her a twenty. "Keep the change."

"The beer's only six-twenty, though," she shouts. "Are you sure you wanna do that?"

The man smiles. "Consider it an advance payment for later." He winks and throws back a mouthful of alcohol.

Charming. She calmly replies, "Haha, too bad for you, sweetheart: I'm way too much for your sad little wallet to handle." She waggles the twenty at him and throws it in the till, makes change. Cha-ching!

I laugh. I haven't done that in a while.

She notices my reaction and looks right at me. Our eyes lock for the longest moment. Then she smiles. My gut twists in a knot and I pretend I'm nursing an invisible drink like an awkward idiot.

She's approaching and I'm staring at the counter, breaking into a cold sweat. Shit. Shit. Shit.

"A new face! Hello, stranger. I like your shirt."

I gulp. "Th-thanks."

"What can I get for ya?" she asks me.

"Uh," I stammer and can't do anything else. I lower my head and keep staring at the scratched countertop.

She crosses her arms on the counter and rests her head on top, trying to get a good look at my face. Her big blue eyes look concerned. "Hey, you okay?"

Freddie to the rescue. With a hearty laugh and an arm around my shoulder, he says, "Ah, he's okay, just a little shy. He just got back after a long trip from the east. Tired as hell, too, but I dragged his ass down here anyway!"

She laughs and replies over the music, "Yeah, I guess this isn't the best place for someone who just stepped off the bus or the train or... however you got here." She never takes her eyes off me. I don't have to look at her to know that. Still, she keeps talking to Freddie. "He looks like he walked here!"

"I-I took the train," I say.

"He speaks at last," she says cheerfully, standing upright. "What—"

"Hey, honey," a patron shouts from the other side of the counter, "can I get a refill, please?"

"One second," she says, and then she leaves to fulfill that order, and two more from a couple other opportunistic patrons looking to catch another glimpse of her backside while she reaches back into the fridge. I scowl at them. One of them notices.

"Got a problem, friend?" he asks.

I don't answer. I look away.

"Yeah, thought so," he says.

The barmaid brings the man his beer. "Here ya go, Jeff."

"Thanks, love." The man fixes me with a nasty stink eye before focusing his attention on his booze. Whatever.

She returns to me and asks, "Have you decided yet?"

"Just a beer is fine," I say.

"What brand? Broweiser? Cruise Light? Redline?"

"Just Broweiser is fine."

"Just a sec." She turns back around and reaches up inside the fridge, and even I get a good glimpse of her backside. Her ass is like a peach; perfectly curved in all the right places.

Shit. I look away. Trying to be a gentleman here... the better man. Ah, fuck it. What's the point in trying? I'm not a good man to begin with.

She turns back around and snaps the cap off. Sets it down on a Judas Priest coaster and slides it across the countertop into my half-open hand. Our fingers touch; her soft index finger deliberately grazes my thumb as she pulls away. "There you go," she says, smiling.

Freddie leans in. "What'd ya get?" He looks at my beer, then digs out his wallet. "I got this one."

"No, it's alright," I protest, but he won't have it.

"I got this one. Celebrating my boy's return home from the jaws of hell! And a Cruise Light for me, honey." He gives the barmaid a twenty and she breaks change and gets him his beer. Freddie slaps my back and laughs. "Said it's on me tonight, kid."

"Thanks, Fred..."

The barmaid starts to serve a few patrons, leaving us alone. The music starts up again, but it's not as loud as it was before. More Judas Priest, naturally, though I don't know what song is playing. Something from their later years; that's all I know.

"You didn't have to do this for me, Fred," I say.

"Sure I did. Saw you were down. Figured I'd getcha back into the social circles again."

I nurse my beer. It tastes strange; unfamiliar yet... familiar. If that even makes sense. Haven't had beer in a while. Didn't drink throughout my entire tour in the Middle East. Being a sniper, I had to keep my senses sharp. Couldn't afford to let myself get loosened up and groggy by hangovers and the like, because I never knew what the next day would bring. The guys thought that was laughable. Yes, Ted, you never know what could happen during downtime, so I stay off the drink. Somehow I must've known downtime would be all I got when I came back.

So now that I'm breaking the habit of declining anything with alcohol that isn't medical, I can't say I was missing out on much. It tastes worse than I remember. I set it down and look at it. Even the drinks at home look different. Christ, was I out in the sand that long?

"You look tired," she says, startling me.

"What?" I reply, blinking. Snapped back into reality.

"Sorry?"

She makes a small laugh. "I said, you look tired."

"I am. I should probably be in bed right now."

"Yeah?" She says, her smile widening. Playful, even a little flirty. "Got someone waiting in it for you?"

My heart skips, but I keep my cool. "Heh. No. No, I don't."

"Really. That's too bad."

Someone calls her from the other end asking for a third round. She gives me a quick wink and scoots off to serve her customer.

Fred leans in and whispers over the music, "Hey, I think she likes ya."

I say nothing. I like her too. But I doubt anything would come of it in the long run. Just random tension between random strangers. We might never meet again. Why get worked up over nothing?

I force down my beer and speak up: "I should get to bed. I'm exhausted."

"Ya sure?"

"I'm sure. Hey." I give his shoulder a friendly tap. "I appreciate this, Fred. I really do."

"Don't sweat it, kid. Get some rest. Here." He hands me his key. "Don't lock me out, 'kay?"

"Alright. Thanks again."

Her voice roots me to my spot. "Leaving so soon?" She sounds disappointed. Puffs out her bottom lip in an exaggerated pout that is, frankly, adorable.

I look at her. She's hiding her disappointment with a smile that almost convinces me to stick around. "Yeah, I'm sorry. I'm just a little too tired to party tonight."

"Don't apologize, I understand." She pauses. "Say... I never got your name." She holds out her hand. "I'm Charlotte."

I quickly take her hand in mine. It's a soft, almost velvety contrast to my scarred, sandpapery skin. "Michael. M-my friends call me 'Mike.'"

"Well, 'Mike,'" she says, "I hope you have a good night and pleasant dreams." She gives me a little wave, fingers wiggling at me. "Dream of something special for me, will ya?"

I grin stupidly. "Sure."

She giggles. "Bye, now."

The muffled, rapid heartbeat of the Love Zone keeps beating

outside of my window when I walk into the diner and head upstairs. The light from the electric sign shines through the dusty panes of my room, saturating the stillness in dark blues with an otherworldly pink tinge. I can barely keep myself from crumpling to the floor. Knees're too weak to do much else except fall. And the bed's right there, so I let gravity work its magic, and my head hits the pillow.

Charlotte, huh?

Then I fade out.

Chapter 2: Rise and Shine

It's six in the morning when my eyes snap open. I dreamed about those headscarves bursting open again. I heard a child screaming as he tried to reattach his severed arm in the wake of a car bombing. I could see his face—

I sit up. Don't want to think about that right now. Don't need the grief. Just leave me alone.

And I am. Just me and these four walls. They seem closer than they were last night.

Bacon. I sniff the air, and sure enough, I can smell the intoxicating scent of sizzling bacon. I hear the fat and gristle crackling on the stovetop. I get up, get dressed in the same clothes I wore yesterday, and do a quick sniff test on the T-shirt. Smells worse than the bacon—goes without saying. I slip into it anyway because it's the cleanest shirt I brought with me. Didn't have enough cash to hit a coin laundry joint on my way down here.

I follow the aroma to the bar and take a stool. Freddie's busying himself in the kitchen, doing what he does best. He looks up and sees me through the partition window and smiles. "Mornin', sunshine!"

"Morning," I reply quietly.

"Have a good sleep?"

"Not really."

He grunts. Flips an omelet. "That's too bad." Pauses, scrutinizing me carefully. "You ain't got a hangover after just one beer, do ya?"

"Not even close. I'm just tired."

"Figured I'd ask all the same."

"Some kind of joke? When have I ever been hungover after *three* beers?"

"Fair point. I dunno, I just thought—from your letters, I mean, about you not drinkin' alcohol up there…" He's quiet for a moment as he tongs a few ready bacon strips off the pan and drapes four raw strips in their place. A fresh white noise hiss resounds through the window. "What'd you think of that bar?"

"Loud," I say.

"What?"

I raise my voice over the bacon grease. "Loud."

"Yeah, it was. Ain't usually like that. Party night. Completely slipped my mind, the possibility that it'd be that busy."

I say nothing. I stare at the countertop. The surface is scratched, but Freddie keeps it wiped clean so that the morning sunlight gleams off of it with a new car kinda shine.

He comes in with breakfast and sets two plates down on the counter. Starts digging into one. I thank him and start eating. For a while, we're quiet, but of course, Freddie being Freddie, he starts a conversation. He can't stand silence in the presence of company. "Any plans now that you're back?"

"Nothing, to be completely honest with you."

"You can work here if ya want."

"I really shouldn't."

"Why not?"

"Come on, Fred. Me? Work here? I couldn't do that to you."

Freddie scoffs. "It's settled then. You can start in a week."

I sigh. I'm grateful for the big guy's hospitality, but do I really want to burden him any more than I have to? "You've done too much for me already."

"Look at it this way, kid: you work here, you can pay back the room and board."

Makes sense. I give him a quick nod.

"And make a little money on the side."

Now I'm surprised.

He sees it on my face. "Hey, I'm not *that* cheap."

We share a chuckle together and keep on eating. Nobody makes bacon and eggs quite like Freddie.

"That girl seemed to like you."

I almost choke on scrambled egg and guzzle half a glass of orange juice to properly wash it down. My eyes are watering and my face is going red. Goddamn it.

Freddie snickers. "Looks like the feeling's mutual."

"So what? She's out of my league."

"Do people really still say that? Huh." He looks thoughtfully at the ceiling.

I clear my throat.

"You never know till you try."

"I *do* know, Fred, and I'm not about to try."

"She was interested in you. The seed is planted. All's you gotta do is nurture it."

I sigh. "What are you, my mother?"

Freddie laughs. "Father, maybe, in bond instead o' blood. Wouldn't want to see ya live life without a special lady on your arm. Till then, guess I gotta nag ya for her, whoever she might end up being, till she comes around to relieve me of my duties!" He shakes the counter with his belly laugh.

I scoff.

"Look at you, you're a mess. You're a wreck, kiddo. What you need is a nice, hot shower and some clean clothes and some good, old-fashioned food in your belly. Then you need a job. Women don't like deadbeats. Or squatters, in any and every definition of the word. But first, you need a shave. And then—"

"Alright, alright, alright," I exclaim, a bit annoyed, but at the same time I can't help but crack a smile. "Get off my back, you miserable old bastard."

Freddie chuckles and waits until I finish my food in better spirits before he takes both our plates back to the dish pit. He immediately returns and leans over the counter on his elbows, concern on his face. "Any bad dreams?"

"Nothing but," I say quietly.

"Hmm," he grumbles, nodding. "Brutal."

"A little."

"What of?"

"The violence. What else?"

"Don't know what else there could be. All I know's what you said in your letters."

"What I said in my letters wasn't even the half of it. Or a quarter. Hell, a tenth. It was absolute hell, Fred. Nothing compares to it."

"So I heard. But... you're in good company now, in a nice town, in a quiet part of the countryside. Got some rowdy neighbours; s'about it. You're among friends. More perfect than any rehab clinic or trauma center. That's why I'm givin' you a week before you start work. Maybe two if you really need it. Take my advice an' go somewhere quiet. Make a habit of it. Clears your head. Puts you back into regular, everyday routine away from the majority of the town's noise."

"Know a good place?"

"The park. You remember the park?"

"Yeah."

"Yeah. The park. They put in a fountain. Supposed to attract tourists, but I ain't noticed much difference. But it's nice to look at and even better to listen to for a few hours in the summer afternoons. Done it a few times myself. Real nice. Might do you some good."

"I'll keep it in mind."

"Do I have to start nagging again?"

I smirk. Choice is clearly an illusion in this situation.

While Freddie runs my clothes through the wash, I take a shower in Freddie's small, compacted bathroom, complete with a shower stall that's almost as clean as the countertop downstairs. It's the most refreshing shower I've had in a long time. Something about it energizes me; I almost forget about the hollow pit in my chest for a while as the steaming water rinses over me. By the time I'm out, Freddie tosses a new shaving kit into the bathroom and 'suggests' I shave my unkempt stubble. I shave and trim my hair afterwards and look at the result in the mirror. I look like a new man. Well... I don't look like I just stepped off a five-month stint in the gutter. It's something, I guess.

Then I heed Freddie's advice and go for a walk in my clean clothes that smell like lilacs and honey. I steal a quick glance at the Love Zone at the end of the street thinking, for some reason, that I might see her. Of course I don't since she worked the night shift. She's probably sleeping right now.

The soft breeze blows through my hair and caresses my scalp like a mother's gentle hand. The familiar streets are busy, but quiet. A lot has changed since I left, but much of it still remains the same. Some new shops replace ones I barely remember, sitting next to shops I remember from my high school years. The gas station across the street from the post office isn't there anymore; just a paved lot remains, which I find a bit strange. Still. So many memories of these places; of going by them with my friends during lunch break or after school. A calming nostalgia, with a twinge of sadness. I miss those days. Things seemed to be so much easier back then. I don't remember worrying about anything all that significant when I was in high school.

People don't look scared here. They're comfortably going about their lives. The whole town pulsates with a carefree vibe that I never could find anywhere east no matter where I went. It's nice here, nicer than I deserve. I haven't felt this good in a long time.

Eventually I find the park and discover that it hasn't changed much. Sure, some of the trees are taller, the gardens are twice as big, the vines crawling up the gazebo have since wrapped themselves around the roof; and there's the fountain Freddie mentioned this morning—a stone angel stands mightily in the center of the pool with his wings spread out, dumping an endless supply of clear water from a vase. Old-fashioned cobblestone surrounds the pool and branches out into narrow, winding paths that vein the entire park.

I sit down on a bench in front of the fountain, close my eyes, and take in the sounds: the rustling of the trees, the white noise of water pouring out of the angel's vase, the occasional running footsteps of playing children as they chase each other. Freddie was right. This is nice. Easy to lose track of time.

Too easy.

"Fancy meeting *you* here, stranger."

Startled, my eyes snap open and glance up at her face. She looks different in the natural sunlight. She's even more radiant with a disarming smile that could warm anyone with a beating heart. "O-oh," I stutter.

Charlotte giggles. "I'm sorry. Did I wake you?"

"Wake me...?" I check my watch. Two hours had passed since I sat down. Holy shit. "Uh..."

"You looked pretty serene there. I almost didn't notice you. But then I was like, 'hey, it's that handsome new guy with the fancy Hawaiian shirt I met at the bar last night.'"

"Yeah," I say. 'Handsome,' huh?

"Michael, right?"

"Yeah. Or uh... 'Mike' if you prefer."

"Hm. I thought about it. I think I like 'Michael' a bit better. It suits you more than 'Mike'."

"Does it?"

"It does."

"Oh."

"You feeling better today?"

"What?"

"You didn't look so good last night. Tired after a long trek home?"

"Something like that."

"You look better." My heart skips at the compliment. She smiles. "I see you shaved this morning."

"I cut myself while doing it."

"You're a little too handsome for me to notice a tiny shaving cut," she says, as boisterously blunt as she was last night. My heart races as she leans closer, studying my face. "Can't see it."

"I, uh... well... I do try to keep up appearances every now and then."

She straightens her back. "Keep it up an' you'll have the ladies lining up at your door in no time."

I chuckle. "I'd be happy with just one."

I see a flash of approval on her face. "You seem the type."

I'm starting to sweat. This strange scrutiny is something I was never used to. I know she's fishing for information about me; considering me. Or maybe she isn't and I'm just over-thinking things. Either way, I'm eager to get off this topic. I don't think we'd be a good match, anyway. "So uh... come here often?" What a dumb thing to say.

"I walk through here every day on my way to work."

Interesting. "You're going to work already?"

"Yeah... night shift and then an afternoon shift right after. Not fun. You can tag along if you want." She flashes me a hopeful smile. "There won't be any loud music playing at this time of day."

I give her my best smile in return. Feels awkward. Probably looked awkward, too. If it did, she didn't show me a reaction. "Maybe later."

"Alright," she sings, walking by me, swaying her hips. "Don't be a stranger, now."

And like that, she's gone. I'm sitting on the bench, unable to calm down now that I've seen her. A chance to talk to her in a quieter environment, huh? Sounds nice... but I don't have any money.

Chapter 3: Back to the Love Zone

The doorbell announces my return to the diner, prompting Freddie to peek up from behind the counter. The hopeful look on his face tells me all I need to know about his suggestion—he knew what he was doing. "You sneaky son of a bitch," I say with a grin I can't hide.

He straightens up. "I don't know what you're talking about," he replies, feigning innocence. He starts wiping the countertop with a rag without taking his eyes off me, giving me a look that screams 'oblivious' but isn't the least bit convincing.

I reach the counter and deliberately smear my palms across its surface. "Yes, you do. I'm not stupid. You knew she'd be there, at the park, and lo and behold, there she was."

"Oh? She was there? Huh! What a surprise! So how'd that go?"

I chuckle and heave a sigh. "She invited me over to the bar. Guess she wants to chat while she works."

"Hey, that's great!"

"Eh... sort of."

"What d'ya mean, 'sort of'?"

"I'm broke..."

"So? A woman worth your time wouldn't care."

"All the same, I don't want to go there and just loiter around the bar, soooo..."

"Soooo..."

"So."

"*Soooooo...*"

"I need to borrow some cash."

"Aha! *There* it is." He slaps his hand down and laughs. Drifts toward the cash register. "Now why should I lend you money?"

"You started this, that's why."

"No idea what you mean by that."

"You can't fool me, old man."

"You're already sounding better than you were this morning."

"You're avoiding the subject."

"Alright," he says, punching open the register. Hands me a

twenty. "Don't spend it all in one place."

"No promises." I take the cash and pocket it. "Thanks. I owe you one."

"I think this makes three now, actually."

We exchange smiles that only old pals could throw at each other—Christ, what would I do without him—and then I rush out the door.

I walk into the Love Zone and there are only two patrons sitting on complete opposite ends of the bar. It's a lot quieter than it was last night; the electric humming of the refrigerators behind Charlotte are the loudest things in the place, drowning out the country station playing quietly on the radio. She's on a stool behind the tap, scribbling into a black sketchbook. When she spots me coming down the ramp, she beams and sets her sketchbook down. "Hello, stranger."

"Hi back at you, stranger," I reply, adopting a stool in the middle.

"What'll it be?"

"Same as yesterday."

She fixes me with a coy smile, raises an eyebrow. "Do you know how many 'same as yesterdays' I get on a daily basis? And I just met you, too..."

Duh, idiot. She's a busy girl who serves hundreds of customers every day. Why would she remember you? I'm about to apologize, but before I get the chance, I'm silenced by her grabbing a Broweiser out of the fridge, snapping the cap off, and emptying it into a glass. I look at her, surprised. "Oh."

She tops it off with a lemon slice. Her slender index finger pushes down on the peel until the rim cuts through the flesh up to the bottom. A small citrus drop streaks down the side and beads when it touches the perspiration rimming the base of the glass. Satisfied, she says, "Some extra flavour, from me to you."

"Thanks. What were you drawing?"

"Oh." She draws a thin spike of her behind her ear bashfully. "Just.. a little something to pass the time."

"Can I see?"

She takes a moment to visibly contemplate. Then: "Okay. It's not much, but... here." She lifts it, opens it so that neither of the other patrons can see what I can see: a highly detailed, stylized sketch of a voluptuous young woman straddling the back of a fire-spewing wyvern, spreading its massive, membranous wings. It's not photo-realistic, but it could easily pass off as something a professional comic book artist or storybook illustrator could have done.

My eyes are wide without me realizing as I take in every detail, every masterful stroke in her artwork. "That's absolutely outstanding."

Shyly, she shuts the book and sets it down behind the counter. "I-it's, uh, you know, it's a start. Thanks." She's blushing. It's adorable.

She clears her throat loudly and regains her straight, confident posture from before. "So what brings you back to town?"

"Freddie. That's about it."

"I've eaten breakfast there a couple times."

"Good, eh?"

"Oh, yeah. Love the bacon. His spaghetti and pizza isn't bad either."

I sip my beer. Still doesn't taste great, but I brought this one on myself.

"How long have you known him?"

"Freddie? A long time. Since I was a kid."

"Aww. And you came back for him."

"He's like a father to me."

She smiles warmly.

I think about all the times Freddie was there for me. When that gets to be too much, I think about the first time I met him.

I was twelve, maybe thirteen. I remember the day well because it was the day my mother got the phone call from her supervisor informing her that she'd been fired. Too many sick days. She had depression, or something, I don't know. I was too young to understand, but she was in bed a lot, and rarely smiled anymore. She always looked exhausted. The day she got fired, she broke down and cried, wondering how she was going to take care of me, talking about how we were going to lose the house and wind up on the street. Couldn't sell her paintings. Not enough to earn a living. We weren't going to last the month. I couldn't stand it. Couldn't stand in the doorway to her bedroom watching her sob into her blanket, apologizing and begging me to forgive her.

"I'll be back, Mom."

"Please don't go. Don't leave me too."

"I'm not going far, Mom."

"Michael, please..."

"I promise, Mom. I'll be back really soon."

"Where are you going?"

"To the store."

"Which store?"

"I don't know yet. But I promise I'll be right back."

A flash of doubt. "Sure you will."

"You'll see. I'll bring something back."

"Whatever... if you want to go, I can't blame you. Your mother's a wreck."

"Don't say that, Mom..."

The tears came back. "You deserve so much better."

"I'll be back, and then we'll hang out or something, Mom. We'll do a puzzle or, uh, watch a movie?"

"Sure... fine."

I left. I went around town. I only had three dollars in my pocket, but I felt a strange determination to find something to cheer her up. Nanaimo bars were one of her favourite snacks, so I searched every window of every bakery and diner for them until finally I caught sight of a Jenga tower made of Nanaimo bars on a countertop platter stand in Freddie's diner. I went inside, went straight for the platter stand. Freddie was thinner back then, maybe in his thirties. He stood behind the counter watching my approach. With a cheerful smile, I remember him saying, "Well, look what the cat dragged in! What can I get'cha?"

I was just tall enough to reach the platter. I scooped all the change from my pocket and scattered it across the counter toward him. "Whoops! Sorry!"

Freddie was more confused than anything else. He tried to catch the coins as they rolled and bounced and twirled around. Meanwhile, I was making off with the whole platter. "Hey, wait! Hey!"

Made it three blocks before he caught up with me. He didn't tackle me down or kick my feet out from under me. All he had to do was reach out and grab my shoulder, and I stopped. I didn't want to drop the platter and I didn't want to fall. So I stopped and looked up at him, and to say that he looked annoyed would be an understatement, although I wouldn't go so far as to say he was full-on pissed off.

"What was going through your mind there?" He asked me.

Now it was my turn to bring out the water works and endless apologies, along with the classic "Please don't tell my mom" and the equally classic "I don't wanna go to jail."

Freddie wouldn't hear it. "You didn't answer my question. Quit crying. Stop it. What's crying gonna do for you now? Nothing."

I kept on sobbing.

"Give me one good reason I shouldn't tell your mother."

I couldn't give him one.

"Yeah. Thought not. Give me the food."

I obeyed.

"Let's get back to the restaurant, kid. We're gonna call home."

"We uh... we don't have a phone."

He looked at me, incredulous. "You don't have a phone?"

"It was cut off."

"Do you have a house, at least?"

"Sort of..."

"What d'ya mean, 'sort of'? You either have a house or you don't, kid."

"We probably won't have it much longer."

"I see. What do you think I should do, then? Huh? Call the cops?"

I started to panic again. More tears welled up in my eyes. "Please, no. I'm sorry."

"Why'd you do it?"

"My mom was sad. I just wanted to cheer her up."

"You think you stealing food would've cheered her up? You think that'd make her proud?"

"No, but..."

"But?"

"I didn't have enough money."

"If that three dollars you threw at me was all you had, you're correct."

"I'm sorry."

He seemed to be considering something. "Your mom home?"

"Yes."

"What about your dad?"

"No."

"He at work?"

"No."

He probably decided it was best not to try and get me to clarify on that because he immediately changed the subject. Probably assumed the worst. "You shouldn't be stealing, kid. Come on."

"It won't happen again," I tried my best to reassure him, if nothing else to get my ass out of the fire.

"Yeah, yeah, yeah; you're sorry, you'll never do it again." He sighed. Looked at the platter. Lifted the lid off and offered it to me. "Take one and get the hell outta here."

I gave him a look of utter confusion and disbelief.

"Go on, before I change my mind."

I reached for one. He withdrew the platter slightly, and I knew then that he had more to say.

"But the next time you show up in my restaurant, for the love of God, kid, *buy* something. A dessert, a meal, I don't care; just don't go stealing things that people worked hard to make. You understand?"

"Yes, sir."

"Take one." His voice was gentler now. Guess he'd calmed down. And hell, it was just one Nanaimo bar out of sixteen. He didn't seem to care about just one.

I tentatively selected one off the platter and he snapped the lid shut and asked for my name. "Michael," I answered.

"Michael," he repeated. "Mine's Freddie. I own that restaurant. You need anything and you're short on cash, or you just want a job—when you're a little older, of course—come on over. I'll help you however I can, but you gotta promise me you'll never steal again."

"I won't."

"Promise?"

"I promise."

"I catch you stealing again, the deal's off. I'll kick your little ass, I promise you."

"Okay."

"Got it?"

"Yes, sir."

"Good. I'll hold you to it. Got it?"

"Yes, sir."

"Not allowed to break your hands." He chuckled. Even back then, I didn't think he would've been capable of that degree of violence. He wasn't an intimidating man in the violent sense. But he was a figure of authority, as all adults were supposed to be for kids my age, and that was intimidating enough at the time.

"Go home," he said. "And stay outta trouble, you hear?"

"Yes, sir." And then I ran all the way home, protecting the saran-wrapped Nanaimo bar in my hands until I reached the front door. I burst inside, rushed up the stairs, and found that my mother's bedroom door was closed shut. I knocked on it, giddy with the aftershock of being caught and the lingering fear of the consequences that never came combined with the anticipation that I'd get to see Mom smile again, if only for a minute or two.

No answer. I knocked again. "Mom, I'm home."

No answer. "Mom?"

Must've been sleeping. I shrugged and went downstairs. Left the Nanaimo bar in the fridge. Hydro was still on for a while longer, at least.

"Anyone home?" Charlotte's voice yanks me back into the present.

"Huh?"

She giggles. "I think you zoned out there for a second."

"Oh. Sorry about that."

"It's okay, don't worry about it. You've probably got a lot on your mind, don't you?"

"I'm always thinking."

"A thinking man, are ya? We don't get a lot of those in here." She chuckles and sips some red liquid topped with a layer of ice through a straw. "What were you thinking about?"

"Lots of things," I reply, staring at the strange, bright red liquid. "Like how the gas station changed places since last I was here. It used to be on the other side of town, across from the post office. And uhh, oh, yeah, the uh... the book store closed down."

"The book store didn't close down. It moved, too. Right next to the library. Weird choice if you ask me."

"What happened to the gas station?"

"Some psycho blew it up two, three years ago. The whole block had to be evacuated. Scary times."

"Yeah, that sounds scary." Small town like this, I wouldn't expect something like that to happen here. But then again, maybe that's the problem.

"What's that?" I ask her.

"This?" She lifts the glass of red liquid. "I call it 'Diabetes in a Cup.'"

"Seriously?"

"I only drink one a month because of how much sugar's in it."

"What's in it? Besides sugar." I crack a smile.

"Uh, club soda, grenadine, some special cherries, and you know, ice to keep the sweetness from being totally overwhelming." She raises the glass for me to see, indicates the dark bed of cherries at the bottom of this strange, blood red cocktail she's made for herself.

"You serve that, too?"

"No, no. I make it for myself. Homemade recipe."

"Can I try it?"

"I dunno... got any heart problems?"

"No."

"Sugar content problems?"

"Not that I know of."

She thinks for a beat. Shrugs. "What the hell." So she makes this 'Diabetes in a Cup' for me. Dumps a handful of sweet cherries into the bottom. Scoops up half a glass of ice from the freezer, pours club soda into it and then saturates it red with a hearty dose of grenadine. Then she sets it on a separate coaster beside my beer and waits.

I immediately try it, feeling her eyes on me while I do. The ice rolls over my upper lip as I suck in my first mouthful of it, and holy shit, she wasn't joking when she said it was sweet. It's almost too sweet. It's like drinking cold, thin syrup with a strong, punchy tang. It's hard for me to describe, but one thing's for damn sure: it tastes good.

"Wow."

She beams. "You like that, do ya?"

"Yeah." I sip it again, savouring the taste. "Wow."

She giggles and takes another sip from hers.

"You don't serve this to anyone else?"

She scoffs. "Hell no. Last thing I need is a guy keeling over from a heart attack in here. I kinda need this job, you know?"

We share a laugh.

A new patron walks in from outside and orders a poutine for himself and a glass of Cruise Light to indulge in while he waits, prying Charlotte away from the counter for a while. I sit in silence for the time it takes her to heat up the fryer and dunk a load of frozen fries into the boiling oil and prepare cheese curds and gravy.

It's nice here. For a while, I forget that I'm depressed and haunted by my time in that eastern hell. All I can think about is her and the way she is, and how good she looks behind that fryer; the pose she makes, her posture, the concentration on her face...

Damn, it's been less than two days and I'm already gushing over this woman. What'd I tell you, Michael? It won't work. You're a broken toy fresh out of the junkyard and back into the toy box for no explainable reason.

And like that, I fall back into my usual depressive slump until she returns with her customer's poutine and then skips right back in front of me.

"What's wrong?" She asks.

"Huh? Sorry?"

"You look down," she says with visible concern. "Did that drink make you sick?"

"No, no, nothing like that." I finish it off and look at the cherries on the bottom.

"Here." She sticks a straw into my cup, impales a cherry on the end, then raises it to my face. "Eat up."

I give her a look, then shrug—what the hell, why not?—and eat the cherry off the end. It's cold and has lost some of its flavour to the drink, but it's still juicy, if a little mushy now.

She drops the straw into my glass and leans back, smiling. I don't notice that I'm staring at her until she chortles and asks, "What?"

"Uh, nothing."

"Nothing, huh?"

"Nothing at all."

"Uh-huh. Uh-huh."

A familiar potbellied patron takes a seat just a few stools down from me. He looks like he'd recently crawled out of a dirty basement after living in it without a shower or any kind of personal hygiene for two years. His thick, scraggly beard had dried old food and leaf crumbs in it. A logger, I guess, and not a very hygienic one.

"Hey, sweetheart," he leers, "why don'tcha shake that ass for me while you get me a beer, huh?"

"Hello, Jeff." Charlotte's tone is polite, but her words are biting: "Only 'shake' you should be getting ought to have some protein in it, slim."

I hide my smirk behind my beer, making a show of sipping from the bottle.

"Oho, snappy!" He says. He slaps a five dollar bill flat on the countertop. "Cruise Light, babe." She gets it for him and makes change from a ten. "Keep the change. I'm feelin' generous today."

"Thanks."

The guy looks at me. Eyes full of contempt. Don't know why; it's not like I did anything to him. I set my beer down and look back at him. That's when he asks, "What're you lookin' at?"

"I'm looking at you," I reply. "You're looking at me, so I'm looking at you."

"We gonna have a problem?"

"Why would we? I don't have a problem with you."

"Jeff," Charlotte says in a warning tone.

"Les keep it that way." He steps off his stool and heads for a table by the jukebox.

"Agreed," I say quietly, looking at Charlotte. I can tell this isn't the first time he's tried to pick a fight with someone.

She rolls her eyes. "Ignore him."

"Way ahead of you."

She smirks.

"Do you like this job?"

She nods her head 'yes,' still smiling, and whispers, "No."

"Guess there aren't many other opportunities down here, huh?"

"Nothing that's any more or less appealing."

"You could work at Freddie's."

"I dunno. I'm not that good at cooking."

"But you're good at the till and you can talk to customers pretty well."

"I can insult them well enough. I don't think Freddie would appreciate my snappy comebacks over there. People who eat at Freddie's don't come here very often, and when they do, they don't stay long. Some guys eat all their meals here and stay hydrated on our alcohol. Sad, lonely, angry men and washed up women. Everyone's looking to have a good time and forget about it, too.

People like that don't eat in a classy joint like Freddie's. It's just the way it is. I'm too accustomed to the guys who're after my tits and my ass. I mean, I know they're good qualities, but damn. At least I know how to knock 'em back into line without laying a hand on them, you know? I insult a customer behind Freddie's counter, and I'll be out of a job in no time."

"Selling yourself short, I think."

"You think so?"

"I do. I know you're nice."

"Eh. When I can. It's not always easy."

"I know that."

"I'll be outta here sooner or later anyway. Preferably sooner."

"Where to?"

"Haven't decided yet. Wherever life takes me, I guess."

"What if life takes you to the city?"

"Then I guess that's just where I'll end up. Whatever happens, happens. What about you? Anywhere you'd like to go? Any special place in mind?"

I shrug.

She chuckles and leans against the counter. "You have no idea, do you?"

"Whatever happens, happens," I reply.

"You like that, huh?"

"It's a good philosophy. Carefree. Easygoing."

"That's how I like it. Too much stressing makes your hair fall out. I like my hair a little too much for that."

"But aren't you stressing about working at Freddie's? How you'd act?"

"Well, yeah. I wouldn't have as much freedom at Freddie's, like I said. I don't have to put on so many filters in here. Over there, I'd have to worry about it more. You get it now?"

I nod. "Yeah."

"Besides," she adds, folding her arms across her chest and leaning back on her stool almost too carelessly for my liking, "I know you just want me there so you can have me all to yourself."

I choke on my beer and start coughing. Some of it dribbles down my chin and I try to wipe it on my sleeve in embarrassment.

She laughs and grabs a few napkins. "Sorry, sorry. Couldn't resist." She dabs my chin before handing me the last of them and waiting until I'm good to talk again. "You still alive?"

"Yeah," I croak.

"Caught you off guard there, didn't I?"

I nod again. "Th-that's not why I suggested it, I just... uh..."

"I know."

"I just thought it'd be a nicer environment."

"I know, I was kidding."

"You know? Like a more stress-free, friendly place."

"You need to lighten up."

"Yeah, you got that right." I finish my beer.

"Want another one?"

"I'm kind of curious about the poutine..."

"Damn it, Michael, I just shut off the deep fryer," she exclaims, with a joking tone in her voice.

"Oh well."

"More work for me." She glances at the clock beside the till. "And another five hours to go. Goody."

Jeff messes with the jukebox. Selects *Sunshine of Your Love* by Cream, and that's exactly what plays, and all I can think of is Robert De Niro and how cool he looked when that song played in *Goodfellas*. Christ, all I wanted to be was a gangster like De Niro, back when I thought being a gangster was cool. Then after a while, I thought just being De Niro was cool enough, gangster or not.

So I emulate the same pose he struck in the movie when the song started playing, with one arm resting on the counter and an orange-flavoured sucker between my fingers as a substitute for a cigarette. "Tell you what."

She looks at me, interested.

"I won't make you make me lunch if..."

"If?"

"You let me take you to dinner sometime."

Her eyebrows rise. Genuine surprise on her face.

My brain is screaming WHAT THE FUCK ARE YOU DOING?

"Oooh, a negotiator, ehhh?"

"I prefer the term 'extortionist.' It's classier."

She laughs hard enough to nearly fall off her stool. Grabs the counter's edge and rights herself at the last second. "Whoop!"

I maintain the De Niro Pose, giving her my best smile with the sucker held just an inch from my face.

She looks at me again, amused eyes flicking from the candy to my face. "You're a Scorsese fan, aren't you?"

Saw right through me. My shoulders slump. "Yeah..."

"Caught red-handed," she says.

I show my palms. "You got me."

"Still," she says, stirring her drink, "that's an interesting proposal..."

"You don't have to go with it. I was kidding."

"Oh, no. You're not getting off that easy. You're in too deep now."

"Am I?"

She nods, eyes narrowed into mock predatory slits. Whispers, "You are."

"Should I be scared?"

"Terrified."

"What if I'm not?" You're getting yourself way in over your head, buddy.

Another one of her mischievous smiles creeps up. "Let's not get ahead of ourselves just yet." She winks. Takes another generous sip from her weird diabetic cocktail. "Let's get to know each other a bit before we form a suicide pact together, hm?"

My heart skips. I almost think she's serious. One look at her eyes tells me the opposite, though, and all alarm bells go quiet. A classy enough lady with a sharp wit and a dark sense of humour on top of that. Nice. "Sounds like a plan."

The phone rings, startling me. Rings again. She picks up. "Love Zone, Charlotte speaking. Uh-huh? Uh-huh. Alrighty, I'll meet you back there." She hangs up and glances my way. "New shipment is in. I'll have to tend to it."

"I'll be here when you get back."

"You don't have to waste your whole day in this place just to talk to me, Michael."

I'm about to protest, but I remember something—an old dating tip from one of my sniper pals in the CIA: "Trying to woo a lady's like trying to find a good target with your rifle. Shooting a guy out in the open's easy enough... after a while, it gets old fast. The ones that stick with you... heh... those are the ones that gave you the biggest challenge, hiding behind walls, in houses, underground, behind cars. Same goes for women, man. Let 'em shoot you too soon, they'll move on faster. Make 'em work for it, well... you've got a chance."

Of all the places to get relationship advice, I get it during Operation Anaconda. Makes sense. Morbid as hell, but it makes sense.

"Matter of fact," I begin, "I just remembered, I offered to start work with Freddie soon. Gotta start learning it sometime, right? Earn my keep."

"Already at it just a day after hopping off the train, eh? Impressive."

I finish my beer and step off my stool. "Call you later?"

"Just swing on by whenever you like. Or sit in the park again. I'll find you."

"Oh, you will, will you?"

"You can't hide forever."

I pop the sucker in my mouth and cock my eyebrows at her. "I don't hide. I seek."

She laughs. "Get the hell outta here!"

Chapter 4: After Hours

What a woman. I didn't even have to talk to her long for me to forget the majority of my problems. They just went away, and she slipped right in their place to brighten up my world like a ray of sunshine stabbing through a floating blanket of storm clouds.

My dark, dark world.

It's sunny outside, but it may as well start raining because the minute I'm out of the Love Zone and a few doors down the street, everything comes rolling back in. The depression. The creeping anxiety. Feels like I was dropped into a different era when I walked out of that bar. It all feels different. Alien. People on the sidewalks don't notice me. Drivers in their cars and pickups and the occasional minivan drive by me like I'm not even there. Like I don't exist. Suddenly the world feels empty, and yet, it feels like it's way too full and the walls, the old buildings with faded murals and cracked paint and dusty old brick; are all closing in around me.

Damn. A date with Charlotte. It's not gonna work out. She'll see through me like she saw through the De Niro Pose and she'll know how much of a fucking wreck I really am in no time. Should've left it alone. Should've kept my distance.

I scuff my feet across the street and up the sidewalk. Patrons are starting to fill up the diner when I arrive. Freddie notices me, smiles, waves, then the cheerfulness slowly disappears when he reads my mood. I head for the door leading to the stairwell and he follows me behind the counter, matching my pace. Still, somehow he manages to get between me and the door before I get there. "What's wrong?" He keeps his voice down, lower than the clacking of cutlery hitting plates and grinding through food all around us. It's no one else's business but ours.

"I'm tired."

"Did something happen?"

"Yeah, I uh... I got a date."

"Well, that's great!"

"Yeah. Great."

"What's the deal? C'mon, son. You know you can talk to me."

"Later, okay? I think I just need some sleep or something."

He nods slowly. "Alright... alright." He pats my shoulder. "Get some rest, kiddo."

He steps aside. I head upstairs to my room and the first thing I do is look out the window. There, just a few storefronts down south from my room on the opposite side of the street lies the Love Zone bar, dull and lifeless during the day, occupying its own dirty corner. I pull the blinds down and sit on the edge of the bed. The springs groan under my weight. My bag's on the floor. I reach down and unzip the front pocket, take out my gun. Check the magazine. Loaded. Pull back the slide. Chambered. Put the gun to my head. Eyes shut. Heart races. Tears welling behind my eyelids. Finger twitches as it slides around the trigger. I inhale. Exhale. Breathe in. Breathe out. Suck in my last breath. Heartrate spikes. Finger tightens.

Charlotte.

Bang.

Freddie stands over my body, unable to take it. The last person still alive that he considered family just blew his brains out above his diner. This room will never be the same, and neither will he.

Shit.

I throw the gun on the floor and just breathe and sob and wish I wasn't such a coward. Maybe I'm keeping myself alive for Freddie. Maybe for Charlotte and the potential future we might, or might not have. I couldn't say for sure. I don't know why I didn't pull the trigger. I should have. All the people I killed, the kind of person I am... I should have. I don't deserve their kindness or their hospitality. If Charlotte knew what kind of person I was, would she still be interested in me? Unlikely. She'd probably think I was a psychopath or worse.

And what if I succeeded? What would they do then? Would they care? Charlotte probably wouldn't, anyway. I just met her. To her, I'd just be another nutcase with emotional problems that walks into that bar and never comes back.

Freddie would, I guess, but he'd move on after my brains're washed off the floor. One less thing to worry about, after all.

I look at the gun. Pick it up. I ought to try again. Get it over with in a flash instead of prolonging it with months of countless disappointments.

JUMPING FOR CHARLOTTE

So why don't I?

I ask myself that same question for an hour, crying the whole time.

Suddenly I'm awake and it's night-time and Judas Priest's *Electric Eye* can be heard all the way from down the street and the sign's blue and red lights flash brightly against the walls of my room like Willy Wonka's psychedelic nightmare. Shadows and headlights strobe across the flickering red and blue neon ceiling above me.

Christ, how long was I asleep?

I glance at the digital clock. Quarter after seven. What's it matter what time it is, anyway? I'm not doing anything worthwhile for at least a week.

What if she moves?

The thought suddenly pops into my head and my heart spikes. I hadn't thought of that. What if I never get my chance? What if she quits the Love Zone and leaves town? What if I never see her again? Worse, what if I spook her so bad she leaves and never comes back?

Straighten yourself out, man. You're ridiculous. Get yourself something to eat.

I tuck my gun in my bag and walk over to the bathroom and clean myself off before I head to the kitchenette for something to eat. I slap some egg salad into a sandwich and eat it in the living room while I watch some sleazy old movie playing on cable. I hardly pay attention to it, lost in thought; thinking about Charlotte and Freddie and the future. Do I have a future? If I do, is it worth living long enough to see?

Gotta quit thinking like this. It's not healthy. Oh, but I deserve it, don't I?

I try to focus more on the movie. It's one of those 'women in prison' films that used to be so prominent back in the 70's and 80's. Linda Blair's in this one. Jesus. She's really grown up since *Exorcist*. Sometimes it's hard to watch. Sometimes it isn't and it's just dull. An hour later my eyes sting with fatigue and my eyelids get heavier every minute. I don't fight them.

My eyes snap open to the door slamming behind me. I whirl and look up at Freddie as he kicks his shoes off and tosses his apron onto the outer partition that surrounds the kitchenette. He looks exhausted, still manages to crack a smile when he notices me looking at him. "Hey, kid."

"Hey."

"What'cha watching?" He walks around the couch and plops down beside me. He and I both observe the grainy picture on the screen, with the occasional flicker as two women speak to each other about things neither of us care about. "Looks old."

"Probably is. I just woke up to it. No idea what it is."

"You're on the late-night channel." He chuckles. "I wonder why..."

"What're you implying, eh?"

"Nothing, nothing at all."

I chuckle. "Hey, it was the first thing I got when I turned on the TV, so..."

He clears his throat, exaggerated and loud. Doesn't need words to tell me to shut up when he's got this. "Why were you so down earlier?"

"I was just tired."

"Didn't seem tired to me. Well... you did, but it didn't seem like that was it."

"It's nothing."

"Nothing is 'nothing,' kid."

I can feel him looking at me, prying for answers. I don't give him any. My face is a blank slate.

"If you don't wanna talk about it right now, that's okay. Just don't bottle yourself up. It's unhealthy."

"Do you think I'm okay?"

"What?" He looks at me, confused.

I don't look at him. I stare at the floor. Can't stand looking at him right now. Almost like I feel unworthy or something. "Do you think I'm an alright person?"

Freddie doesn't say anything for a while. When he finally says something, it's: "Do you think I'd let an indecent person live in my apartment? What's with you?"

"I've done things, Freddie. Back east. Horrible things." My voice cracks. I clear my throat. Blink back the tears. "Do you know what I see when I look at fries and hamburger soaked in ketchup? Because I don't see that. I don't see potato slices or... or hamburger meat. I just see blood and brains and pieces of the heads that used to contain them scattered all over the fucking place."

Freddie stares at me.

"Kids, Freddie. Some of them were kids. Kids with rifles, kids with, with... with those jackets, brainwashed, blowing themselves up—"

He sets a hand on my shoulder. "Michael," he says, his tone firm but understanding, "that's enough."

I sputter, "Why?!" Now I can't stop the tears. "Do you have any idea what I did down there?"

"You did what you had to do and that's all there is to it. Nothing more, nothing less. Fact of the matter is, it happened, and there's nothing you can do that can change that fact." He keeps talking over my blubbering. I bury my face in my hands and keep on crying. "It was you or them, kid. There was nothing else you could've done. You listening? Only thing you can do now is move on with your life. Put it behind you. The people you killed, you killed quickly. You know that, don't you?"

"Yes..."

"Right?"

"Yes," I say louder.

"Right. Don't beat yourself up over the fact that you killed them. You had no choice. Instead, take comfort in knowing that they didn't suffer by your hands."

Somehow that doesn't help ease my pain. Neither does the big hug he gives me when I break down.

Chapter 5: Eavesdropper

I decide to stay home the next day. I once heard that if you make yourself seem too available, your chances of success go down, and I'm not about to get cocky just because I scored a date right off the bat. "It's like a game of tag," one of my sniper pals had said; "just don't leave all the chasing to one side or else it'll get boring. Chase, catch, release, get chased. Keep the back-and-forth momentum, just don't end it too soon, and don't force it to continue."

What the hell was his name again? We talked so often, but come to think of it, we only exchanged names once, and I'd forgotten his name a long time ago. He didn't forget mine at the time. He probably doesn't remember me now anyway, if he's even still alive.

Damn it, what was his name?

I lean against the back of the couch. Linda Blair's on TV again, this time in *The Exorcist*, cussing in ways that shocked people thirty years ago but wouldn't turn many heads nowadays. I'm not really watching it. Just passing time. Making noise. Sometimes noise is the only thing stopping me from being completely alone for the day. Nothing else to do. I don't want to go to the park just in case Charlotte ends up taking that route again, and... well...

Linda's head spins around on the TV screen.

I guess I feel the same way. All this thinking is making my head spin. I have all day to think. Mostly about her, and how just thinking about her smile seems to brighten up the room little by little despite the curtains drawn over both windows flanking the TV in the corner.

The phone rings. I answer it and Freddie asks me to help him with something downstairs. Suspecting another matchmaking setup like the park 'recommendation,' I ask why. "New shipment arrived," he answers. "Could use a little help moving the food off the truck."

Fair enough. "I'll be right down."

"Thank you."

I hang up.

*

"'Why?'" Freddie laughs from behind the stove as I enter the kitchen. It's spotless, as expected, with only a few tough grease stains on the fryer and the stove. He's got an omelet cooking in a skillet, which he holds by the handle with an oven mitt. "'Why,' he asks! Didja think I was gonna pull another fountain stunt on you?"

"That's exactly what I was thinking, actually."

"Cheeky little shit."

"I learned from the best." I smile as I head for the rear loading dock in the vestibule beside the walk-in fridge where a trailer sits open and docked to the platform. Two guys in grey jumpsuits roll across a ramp with beverage cases on hand trucks. Both steal fleeting glances at me, I figure in greeting; eyes shaded under the bills of their caps as they push the drinks into the walk-in. Something about them makes me feel uneasy, so I watch them until they disappear behind the walk-in's door, and listen to Freddie complimenting them, "For new guys, you two ain't bad at all. First day on the job, right?"

"That's right," one of them replies.

"Guess it ain't too hard to push food and drinks around a kitchen, but hey, I once had a guy spill a thousand dollars without even reachin' the bottom of the ramp, so... you guys are a blessing."

The shorter guy laughs at that as he guides his now empty hand truck back up into the trailer. He notices me watching him and his grin is instantly replaced by a poker face. That's not weird at all...

"He sounds like a real idiot," the other guy replies from the fridge.

Inside the trailer I grab a hand truck, stealing another glance toward the short guy as I pull it away from the wall and start stacking bundles of soda cans on it.

Freddie's still reminiscing, talking more to himself than anyone else now: "Had another guy start driving his truck with the shutter still open! Not sure how much money he cost the company, but it must've been a lot because I never found the body after that." He cackles at the joke he made of his memory.

The two workers' pacing compliments each other's. While one unloads in the walk-in, the other's busy stacking more bundles onto his hand truck. The ramp is just wide enough for the two of them, and they pass each other up and down that thing without missing a beat. Hard to find a break between them without getting in their way. May as well try to—

"Don't worry about that," the tall guy says as he ascends the ramp and stands his empty hand truck against the wall. He reaches for mine. "I'll take it from here."

I step aside and watch him take it down the ramp. I feel like an idiot. I'm only in the way up here, so I hop down and slip back into the kitchen. Freddie's just setting the fresh omelet on a plate. "Done already?"

"They seem to have a handle on things," I reply.

The shorter guy says, "The gesture's appreciated, though."

"Glad to hear it." I can't shake the weird vibe I'm getting from these two. "Where're you guys from, if you don't mind me asking?"

The short one says, "Winnipeg."

"New York."

"Nice," I reply. "I'm from Ontario myself."

"Beautiful province," the short one says, "but it doesn't compare to Winnipeg. I always feel nostalgic for Winnipeg, man. But Ontario? Eh. It's got a nice countryside and Toronto's okay, I guess, but it just doesn't feel the same to me. No offense."

"None taken. I hardly remember it anyway. Been living here in Michigan since I was twelve."

"That right?"

I nod and glance at Freddie. He seems surprised by my social behaviour. Well, I don't blame him. I'm just as surprised as he is. But I need to know what it is about these guys that bothers me. "So, uh. Been in town long?"

"Not long."

"A few weeks."

"Few weeks," the short one echoes his partner with a nod.

"How do you like it?"

They exchange looks, as if they seem to know I'm suspicious of them. The tall one shrugs. "S'alright. Small and quiet town for the most part. Not much to say about it, honestly."

"Yeah." The short one nods again.

"What'd you say your names were?"

The taller one chuckles. "We didn't, but since you asked, the name's Timothy. Timothy Moon."

"Mason Hopper, at your service." The short one does a mock

salute.

Freddie butts in: "Eh, Michael, let's leave 'em to their job, huh? They got a schedule just like we do, right boys?"

"Yeah."

"That's right." The two get back to work, muttering to each other as they return to the truck.

"What was that all about?" Freddie asks.

I shrug. "I don't know. Listen, I'm gonna head out. You need anything?"

Freddie shakes his head. "You don't start for a few days. Enjoy your freedom while you still can." He grins.

I grin back. "Thanks, Fred. I'll be back in a couple hours, tops. Hey, huh..."

"What?"

"Is my baby still in her crib?"

It takes him a second to get what I'm referring to. "That dusty old thing?" He scoffs. "Couldn't bring myself to throw out a classic now, could I?"

I smile.

The attached garage facing the rear lot behind the diner has been providing shelter for my '77 Mustang II Cobra II with a hatchback ever since I left for the Middle East. I remember wanting one of these when I was a kid, even when most of my peers said it was garbage; and at nineteen, I got my wish after saving three grand from the diner and graduating high school with at least a B in every subject. Freddie pitched in the other two thousand, and the rest is history.

After throwing up the shutter, I see a familiar straight path along the side of the diner straight out to the parking lot, now with more weeds and patches of grass than before. I turn to her, then, reach over and pull the dusty old tarp and let it fly into the wall, revealing the beauty sleeping beneath it. The fluorescent lights above my head reflect off its night-black divided by white dual racing stripes running the length of the car with a polished sheen. My baby's looking as slick as I left her.

I have to fumble around for the keys, checking racks and boxes and drawers until finally, I find the old evil smiley keychain under a folded newspaper in the work bench drawer. I take a moment to stare at the hateful little thing; its faded yellow, round head and nest of orange, spiky hair; black dotted eyes furrowed in a nasty glare while its pitch-black, half-circle grin takes up the whole bottom half of its cartoonish face. My keys jingle under it. What was I thinking when I bought this thing?

I'll throw it out later. Right now I'm too giddy with excitement, finally reuniting with my car after so long. I hop in and shut the door, shut out the world, and take in the deafening silence, just me and her. The air is stale with that lingering new car smell. Every rustling noise my clothes make when I rub against the red vinyl seats is louder than a buzz saw in this enclosed space. A glance at the pair of fingerless motorcycle gloves on the passenger seat tells me that nobody else had breathed in this car while I was away. The gloves' worn black leather caresses the rough skin of my hands as I pull them on. Clench my hands into fists a few times, feeling the stiffness built in them from the gap in time squeak softly away. I slip the key in the ignition and start it up. She roars to life as she shakes awake all around me, vibrating my very core. I pat the steering wheel—so familiar, yet so... alien to the touch. But it all comes back in a flash when I grip the wheel and shift gear. I take a deep breath—be still, my heart—and I floor the gas. She screams. She lurches forward, rockets along the side of the diner. I'm thrown back in my seat as I throttle it into the parking lot and peel out. Right across from me is the loading dock. I steal a quick glance and see that the delivery boys haven't left yet, right before my hellion and I screech out into the street for a round-the-block joyride.

I park on the curb just a few doors down from the rear parking area. I snap open the glovebox for a notepad and pen, remembering I'd left some clutter before I went overseas. I grab the notepad—and a roll of twenty-dollar bills. Score! Completely forgot about my old backup stash. I tuck the roll in my pocket and then write the names down on the notepad: 'Timothy Moon, Mason Hopper.'

Another twenty minutes and I catch the delivery boys' truck pulling into the street from my parking spot. They stop at the lights. I wait until a couple cars go by me before I pull in behind them, eyes on the truck. What the hell are you doing, Michael?

I don't have to follow them long; they pull in around the corner across the street from the Love Zone, parking on the edge of a gas station parking lot. I check my gas: half full. Decent, but I guess I could use a top-up and occupy myself so that I don't raise any suspicions. I'm just an ordinary citizen gassing up his luxury car.

As I drive around them into the forecourt, I notice they're staring straight across at the Love Zone, chatting about something. They're definitely eyeing the place. Petty criminals, maybe? Planning on robbing the bar? Strange that they would want to do that when the gas station is right there, though, so maybe it's something else.

Maybe I'm just being paranoid.

I park beside the pump and start gassing up. Lean against the side of the car, casually watching the ten-foot truck as it sits idly under the station's sign. The driver named Timothy gets out and crosses to the station's convenience store. Mason rolls down the passenger window and lights a smoke.

I turn my head away from Mason as he walks by, and then watch him enter the store. I'll have to go in there at some point, and it's not like I can gas up forever. Last thing I want is to run straight into him inside the store. If nothing else, it'd be awkward. Might even deter him from doing... whatever it is I think he might be doing. I don't even know what he's doing, or why I'm following him, really. Instincts? Come on. The guy might've given me weird vibes, but is that any reason to stalk him and his pal?

Maybe I'm just being overprotective.

They stopped in front of the bar, for Christ's sake. Staking it out? I don't know what for. Maybe that's a good enough reason for me.

And with that thought in mind, I glance over at the bar just as someone steps out onto the fenced-in patio. It's Charlotte. Of course it is, and she's the only one on that patio, flanked by two outdoor tables with stools and parasols providing shade from the sun. She's looking fantastic in a spaghetti strap sleeveless tank top under an unbuttoned, translucent white blouse, and a skirt. I take in the sight of her for a moment, seeing how radiant she looks, even in the shade, before my eyes dart over to the truck at Mason. He's watching her intently—so intently that he forgets he's holding a cigarette until it shrinks and burns his fingers. Maybe I'm not being so paranoid...

Charlotte's completely unaware, leaning her elbows on top of the patio's wooden perimeter fence with a cigarette of her own. Huh. Didn't know she smoked. She doesn't smell like a smoker. A wisp of smoke slithers from between her lips and lashes out at the sky as she watches the clouds, seemingly oblivious to her surroundings and to the men watching her, me included. The breeze whips her lustrous chestnut hair up in an oceanic wave around her round head, her gentle face…

I hook the nozzle and screw the cap back on. Car's full. I take an anxious glance toward the convenience store and catch a glimpse of Timothy in line with an armful of snacks. I grab a squeegee and start running it across my windshield until finally Timothy's on his way out and I'm rushing my way in to pay. I beat a teenager with headphones over his ears by two feet and tell the girl behind the register which car I'm paying for. She takes her time running the payment through, and I'm anxiously looking outside in time to see the ten-foot truck starting to move. The attendant gives me my change and my receipt and I book it out of there, hop between the pumps, and climb into my car. By then, Charlotte's heading back inside and the truck's going southbound out of my field of vision. I'm not too far behind it.

So now we're on the highway with nothing but countryside and the odd gas station or roadside shop and diner blurring past us, and I'm beginning to wonder if these guys have noticed me yet. I'm the only car behind them right now, trying to keep my distance without going below the speed limit or making myself too obvious— a hard task, considering the roaring engine of the Mustang. Not exactly the best car in the world for tailing someone. Only advantage is the back of the truck has no rear window for them to easily turn their heads and look through, and I can hide in the blind spots of their side mirrors, but that can only take me so far. If they think they're being followed, there's no hiding from them long.

Eventually they turn onto a dirt road leading to a ratty old warehouse that probably hasn't seen a human footprint in thirty years or more. All the windows are boarded up with rotting wood and the walls are thickly veined with bulging vines and moss. A few old trees stand mightily around it with large overhanging branches.

I keep going straight, letting them drive solo down that road, watching them until corn stalks from the neighbouring field hides them from my view. Next corner takes me to the opposite side of the cornfield. I pull over in the ditch and get out. Tuck my pen and notepad in the pocket of my jeans. Damn. Now that I think about it,

I left my gun in my bag...

You're getting a little ahead of yourself there, Michael. Jesus.

I descend the gravel slope, hop the wire fence into the cornfield, and start wading through the stalks. They're tall, strong, some covered in webs, others fine and leathery. They're taller than me by about a foot. Pushing through them proves to be tiresome in no time because I'm breaking a sweat and seriously considering just heading back home and calling it a day. What the hell am I doing out here, anyway? All this effort because of a stupid hunch? God knows I'm paranoid, but this is something else.

I break through the other side of the field and I see the warehouse plain as day. There's an excavator and a six-foot-wide by four-foot-deep pit near it, but I don't see anyone else around. I take a moment to catch my breath, soaked in my own hot sweat, the summertime sun beating down on my wet hair like it's the last time it'll get the chance to do it. My heart's pounding, probably from the workout. Who knew pushing through a cornfield could be so damn exhausting?

The door to the side of the warehouse is wide open but the windows here are boarded up, too. Could be convenient. I dart across the gap, feeling exposed, feeling like I'm back in the desert where a sniper could cut off my run at any given second. When I reach the doorway, I peek inside and find nothing. It's just an empty storage room lined with empty shelves. Creeping inside proves to be slightly difficult because of the patches of broken glass scattered about the cracked concrete floor. The air is musty and thick with dust. It would be quiet if not for the voices coming from the wall in front of me.

Voices!

The wall's made up of old rotten planks. Plenty of little spaces between them to look through, and once I navigate my way across the telltale field of glass, that's exactly what I do.

Three men and a woman are talking to Mason and Timothy in the largest section of the warehouse. Gun lockers line the wall across from where I'm sitting, with a table between us.

"...jumped the gun in #504,569," the woman was saying. Scarlet hair styled in a permed femullet. A noticeable scar frames the entire left side of her intensely curved face. Angry green eyes with an otherworldly shimmer. She has a shotgun slung across her back, and her outfit looks like a bizarre cross between something from *Road Warrior*, with lots of leather straps and armour pads of some kind, and an S&M stripper. She doesn't look like someone who occupies planet earth, in any case; by far the most unusual of the group. "Fucked up big time," she said. She's chewing something, gum maybe. I can hear it smacking in her mouth when she talks. "One of you assholes got'chaselves killed."

"Yeah, right." Mason scoffs.

"I'm not in the mood," Timothy says. "Sarge, she's at the bar. Saw her taking a smoke break on the patio."

Charlotte! My heart skips. So they *were* watching her! But why?

A man standing against the wall in a cornflower blue dress shirt and black pants, scarlet-red tie, glances at the weirdly dressed woman, then at Timothy and Mason. "And Michael?"

I freeze at the sound of my own name. What the hell is going on here?

"Working at the diner, like most of the others."

"You deal with them yet?"

"No, we thought we'd report back, just in case there was a change of plans or somethin'."

"He a jumper?"

"Dunno. What does Yusef's report say?"

Yusef?! Sadness stabs me in the chest at the mention of my friend's name. This is getting too damn confusing. How do these people know Yusef? What's he got to do with any of this?

The businessman says, "Insufficient data. He never got to finish his report."

"Well isn't that a damn shame," the woman says, though she doesn't seem too broken up about it. The mockery in her voice instantly pisses me off, but I remain in my hiding place, silent.

The businessman tells them, "as far as I know, there's no change of plans. You should've killed them both when you were in town. We'd be leaving now if you had."

I should've taken my gun with me.

One of the other men, this one an Asian with two guns holstered under his armpits, about as immaculately dressed as his superior, speaks up: "With all due respect, sir, after the incident in #504,569, I don't think a direct confrontation would be wise. Michael's paranoia is still at its peak, even though he is in no perceived danger. He still realized far too quickly that we were closing in on him in '569, and by then Charlotte had only been dead for ten minutes. He had no way of knowing that yet."

The businessman grunts. "Thank you, Chow."

Chow. I file it away in my memories. Mason. Timothy. Chow. I write the Asian's name under the other two in my notepad, writing lightly so that no one can hear my pen scratching across the paper. Then, just for future reference in case I can't get everyone's names, I write at the top of the page '5 M, 1 F.'

A man in a suit that's several shades of black speaks behind the woman: "I find that getting Michael alone, and hitting him first and fast, from the shadows, tends to work best." His face is plain and unassuming; he looks like any random person you'd see on the train, but something about him creeps me out. "With Charlotte, at least the ones in the five hundreds, you can deal with her in any method you please. They aren't very fast, and they don't suspect a thing in a quiet town like this. Hell, I've killed most of them behind the bar. Women in this town even walk the alleys in the middle of the night. Tells you something about the neighbourhood, doesn't it?"

The woman sneers. "Good way to get raped by a creep like you."

"Zona," the businessman snaps, "that's uncalled for."

Zona. What the hell kind of name is Zona? I jot it down under Chow's name.

"Whatever, Sarge," Zona says. "Are we just gonna ignore Hunter?"

"No," the businessman replied. "Hunter? It's been an honour."

Timothy says, "What?" As if realizing something, he staggers back and shouts, "No! No way!" He's about to make a run for it. Zona's shotgun doesn't let him get far. I jump at the sudden roar of the blast and watch in shock as Timothy hits the floor.

"So long, partner." Zona sounds a little regretful now. So she *does* feel. She passes a stunned Mason, pumps a shell out of her shotgun, and delivers a final shot to Timothy's head.

They keep on talking after that. No one seems outraged by the murder committed before them. It takes me a few minutes to get over what just happened, or to at least move my hands again. I write 'HUNTER' next to 'TIMOTHY' and then cross them both out. Then I write 'SARGE?' under 'ZONA'. Now I just need the names of the man in black and this 'Sarge'.

The businessman sighs and lights himself a cigarette. He sucks the toxins in silence for a while, staring distantly at Timothy's corpse. In the meantime, Mason pulls up a folding chair and sits far away from his dead companion. Zona taps her foot impatiently, shotgun resting on her shoulder. Chow whispers a prayer for the dead. The man in black does nothing but stand there, staring away from me.

Finally, the businessman says, "Zona, you and Chow keep an eye on the diner. From now on, don't let Michael out of your sight. Reeves, do the alley thing at the end of her shift. Make it quick."

"What about Michael? Shouldn't I kill him first?"

"If the opportunity arises, Zona or Chow will take care of that."

"Of course." So his name is Reeves… I quickly write it down. As I do so, Zona adds, "If he hasn't bolted already."

Mason, apparently nervous, chimes in: "He doesn't suspect a thing. We were just there. He went joyriding in his car. A really nice one."

Chow and Reeves exchange looks that strike me as peculiar. Chow asks, "Mustang II Cobra II?"

Reeves sounds hopeful: "Or was it a '68 Pontiac?"

Mason chortles, agitating them.

"Come on!"

"Spit it out, damn you."

"Cobra II," Mason answers.

Reeves swears and hands Chow some green. Can't tell how much it is from here. All I know is that they've got some weird continuous betting pool running between them.

The businessman continues to address Zona and Chow. "Kill them both if you catch them together. I don't want their deaths spaced more than five minutes apart from each other, understand?"

Mason asks, "What about me, Sarge?"

"Your task here is done. Go to '571. Should be a cakewalk since Michael apparently shot himself in his room last night."

What?

"Charlotte still has the afternoon shift, so just walk into the bar, shoot her, make it look like a robbery, I don't care. Just make it quick and report back here."

"Yes, sir."

JUMPING FOR CHARLOTTE

They file out of the warehouse, leaving the 'Sarge' all alone. I listen to engines start and tires grinding in the dirt, and I wait for them to fade into the distance. I never take my eyes off 'Sarge' as he remains seated, dragging leisurely on his cigarette, as if in contemplation. He keeps on staring at Timothy's body and I wonder if he's feeling any remorse about it. I'll just have to ask him.

Chapter 6: Interloper

He doesn't look armed, so I make my move, swinging out from around the wall I was hiding behind and shooting straight for him. 'Sarge' looks at me in shock, eyes going wide, cigarette falling to the floor. Then he leaps out of his chair and dives for a cabinet by the door, throws it open, takes out a pistol—

I slam into him, body-checking him against the cabinet. I grip the wrist attached to the hand holding the gun, and my other hand grabs him by the shirt and I spin forcefully, hurling him around. His feet hit the chair and he trips and falls over it, tumbles across the ground toward Timothy's body. The gun clatters away. A Beretta M9. I snatch it up and point it at him before he can get to his feet.

When he sees the gun he freezes.

I unload my questions into him, finger on the trigger. "Who the hell are you people? How do you know Yusef? What do you want with me and Charlotte?"

"Easy, kid," he says, taking a breath. He rises on one knee, shows me his palms. "Take it easy."

"Answer my fucking questions!" I yell. "What the hell is going on here?"

"Something you shouldn't even be aware of," he tells me. "Something a whole lot bigger than you."

"Are you going to kill Charlotte? Are you going to kill me?"

"Yes and yes." At least he's honest, I guess. He seems calmer now that the initial shock of my entrance has worn off. He seems like he's in total control of the situation, even though I'm the one with the gun. He sits himself on the floor properly, crossing his legs. "As for *who* I am, my name is Sergeant Jameson Armitage."

I glance out the nearest window into a dirt lot where what looks like a sixth-generation four-door Impala sits on its own. "What the hell is going on?"

"Just some maintenance."

I look at him. "Maintenance?"

"Yes. A quick clean-up, so to speak." He builds a tent with his fingers, setting his elbows on his knees, leaning forward. The position looks odd to me. "I can imagine this is a bit of a shock to your system. It sure shocked the others."

"What others?"

"The other Michaels, of course. The other Charlottes, too. And hundreds of thousands of others I've had to work with."

"Work with…?" I take a second to figure out what he means, connecting it with the conversation I just listened in on. "You mean eliminate."

"Yes."

"Why?"

"Why eliminate?"

"Yeah."

"The same reason this poor soul was taken out of the equation," 'Sarge' says, indicating the body lying beside him. "To keep things tidy and organized. To limit chaos. Synchronization to avoid catastrophic implosion."

"I don't understand."

"I didn't think you would."

"You're trying to kill Charlotte."

"We've established this, yes."

"And you're trying to kill me."

"Yes." 'Sarge' sounded a little impatient.

"Maybe I can persuade you not to." I cock the pistol's hammer back for dramatic effect. A punctuation. The look on his face tells me he understands.

"Unfortunately, that's not how this works. See, you can kill me, sure, and I'll die, sure, just like Hunter here had to be killed because you killed him first. Killing us here won't put a stop to your problem. If we fail, others will come to finish you and Charlotte off. It's better if you let us do you in quickly and humanely."

"Quickly and humanely, huh?" I sneer at him. "Bullshit."

"We're just doing our job, kid. It's nothing personal. We don't like it either, and we certainly don't revel in the suffering of others." He broke the tent to shrug, palms up. "But somebody has to do it. It may as well be us."

"I won't allow you to."

"None of you ever do."

"What's that supposed to mean?"

"Are you familiar with the concept of alternate realities, Michael? Parallel universes?"

I give him a confused look. My brain's racing for possible

outcomes to this conversation. Just what the hell is he getting at?

"We're jumpers, Michael. We go from universe to universe to universe, fixing things, keeping things in line, maintaining order and consistency within this great expansive multiverse. It's no fun, and it doesn't feel like our efforts affect the outcome very much, but I'm sure you know how narrow-minded the powers that be upstairs often are." He chuckles dryly. "Every time you make a conscious decision—or, I guess *any* decision, for that matter, you create alternate timelines, each one following a different outcome. Like a ripple, if you will—"

"Okay, shut up. Just stop. Just… *stop*. That's a load of shit."

"No, it isn't."

"Here's how it's going to go," I tell him, "You're going to call your followers and you're going to go back to whatever weird church or cult thing or… or whatever the hell this is, and you're never going to step foot in this town again. You're going to leave Charlotte and I alone. If I see you again, I'll kill you."

"Well, see, that's the problem right there," Armitage says. "We're infinite. You can kill me if you want, but another one will jump in to finish the job. Not the prime, but you know, someone will. And let me tell you something, my friend: if you spare me here and now, I'll call the others as soon as you leave this warehouse, and I'll tell them exactly where you are… long before you get the chance to save her. They're already on their way back into Cherry Springs… what are you going to—?"

I don't need to second-guess anything. I shoot him between the eyes and I bolt out of the room before his head has the chance to touch the floor. They'd already be halfway to town by now, and I don't know when Charlotte's shift ends. Cutting through the cornfield back to my car, my mind's racing. Whatever this is, it's big, and in some weird way they think they've done it before. I don't understand it. Multiverses? Dimension jumpers? It's crazy. But Armitage seemed so damn sure he's killed us before. Charlotte and me. They talked like I was already a thorn in their side, even though I knew nothing about them. They were so damn sure of it, too. Mass hypnosis, maybe? A shared delusion? Has to be. What they're talking about is fucking impossible.

I went home first, briefly, dodging Freddie's questions as I race upstairs and retrieve my pistol. I'm in and out in two minutes, maybe less, and then I reach the Love Zone and occupy a space closest to the sidewalk in the parking lot across the street. It's on the corner of the town's main intersection, with the Foodmeistro grocery store on the other side, across from the gas station I stopped at earlier.

I pull the keys out of the ignition and stare through the chain link fence at the bar across the street. The afternoon sun is starting to hang heavy over the horizon, not quite setting, but about to. The façade of the bar looks darker now, its dusty red bricks taking on a salmon pink shade before the electric sign above the door switches on. Shadows set into its old town-style niches and arches with smooth familiarity, creating thick black outlines. Judas Priest roars inside, rumbling out into the street through its open doorway. Pedestrian/patron traffic is steady. The streets are in constant motion as office workers rush to get home and factory workers come looking for drinks to end a long day with.

My Beretta 92F is now loaded and tucked into the front of my pants with the safety on. I had stored away two spare magazines with a hunting knife under the driver's seat—now I was tucking the mags into my pockets and slipping the sheathed knife into my sock under the leg of my jeans. Armitage's M9 is now in the glovebox.

The big neon sign flashes on, bathing the car's interior with aquatic blues and hot pinks, overpowering the custom blue neon trimmings of the round gauges on the dash. I glance up over the steering wheel at the bar again. Women laugh and men chatter and shout loud enough for me to almost make out what they're saying if not for the fact that every outside sound is suppressed by the windows surrounding me. Sitting alone in my Mustang II, I have time to think, time to plan a strategy, then plan a backup strategy for it. I think about all the possible outcomes that could transpire if I walk into that bar and if I don't want in at all. I don't know how this weird situation—whatever the hell it is, exactly—will end, but I know for a fact that if I don't enter that bar, there's a good chance that Charlotte will be murdered.

I open my door, letting in a world of noise, step out and slam the door shut. Wait for a beaten pickup to rattle by before crossing the street, slipping into the crowd gathered outside the Love Zone. The rapid pounding of drums reverberate my core, feeling like secondary heartbeats in my ribs, as an electric guitar tears into my ears. The laughter and chatter almost drowns out the music. I scan the tables. Everybody's having a good time; the boys from a local factory bitching about all the little inconveniences that had occurred during their day on the job; women giggling, talking excitedly to one another about various things, two in the back kissing while their fellow lady friends in the booth whoop and cheer. Turning my head to the other side, I see a group of college kids playing pool. I look forward, searching behind the bar, and I see Charlotte safe and sound, running around to serve a multitude of customers with the help of an older-looking blonde woman with a smoker's cough.

Relief washes over me to see Charlotte alive and oblivious to the danger she's in. But then, that could be a problem…

She sees me and beams, like I'm the best thing she's seen all day. She waves me over. "C'mon, Michael, don't be shy, now." She turns to the blonde woman and I barely make out what she tells her: "This is the one I was telling you about."

"Ooohhhh." The blonde lady looks me up and down as I approach, and suddenly I'm feeling way too shy about being here. I feel like everybody in the bar's noticing me for the first time, and not just the servers. She seems to approve, giving Charlotte a nod. "Handsome catch." She gestures toward an empty stool between a slumped man in a business suit and Jeff, who's glancing over his shoulder at me with that contemptuous glare of his. Great. "Got a stool right over here for ya, honey."

I take the stool, doing my best to ignore Jeff's eyes as they bore into the side of my head. I barely have the patience for his shit. "Broweiser, please."

Charlotte gleefully pours a glass for me, ice clinking as the golden-brown drink splashes down the cubes, and she pushes a lemon slice on the rim for me, same as before, winking at me. "Knew you'd be back today."

"Oh, yeah? Why's that?"

"Just a feeling." A patron calls for a refill. "Don't go away, now," she sings, and then she's gone down the length of the bar.

I nurse my beer, straining to hear her talk above the loud din of the other patrons and the roar of the music, inconspicuously glancing to and fro for any faces belonging to the weird characters I spied on earlier. I begin to wonder if they're aware of their superior's death yet, or if they're maintaining radio silence until the job's done.

I realize then that I've been shaking. I hadn't shot anyone point-blank in a long time. I've had to before, but in most ops, my position was limited to that of a sniper. I didn't look into Armitage's eyes when I killed him. I didn't linger. Maybe that's what made it easier—the urgency to be elsewhere, to be here with Charlotte.

I look over my shoulder at the ramp leading outside as someone stomps down the hollow incline and looks around. I watch him closely, taking mental note of his short brown hair, brown eyes, casual wear—Hawaiian shirt, ripped jeans. Then the girls at the booth in the far corner, with the two girls who were making out earlier, wave at him and call him over. "Hello, ladies!" he shouts over the noise, sounding like he's already tipsy from some other bar. He's not a threat.

I turn my head back to Charlotte as she opens the fridge and reaches up for a Cruise Light. Gives me a quick wink and returns to a different patron a few stools down with a playful sway in her hips, which makes me smile through the intense stress I'm feeling.

I can still feel Jeff's persistent glower attempting to burn itself into the side of my head, so I give him a look. A hard look. A 'fuck off or I will kick the shit out of you because I'm *not in the fucking mood*' kind of look. After a few seconds, he looks away and throws back his beer.

My gaze returns to Charlotte, watching her every move. I can feel my anxiety growing in the pit of my stomach like a vicious parasite. Feels like I can barely keep the few sips I've swallowed. Even now, when all I can think about is the incredible danger she's in, she has this strange, unearthly glow about her...

Focus. Sweep the room again. Every face. No one looks like they shouldn't be here. Expressions, mannerisms, gestures, all directed toward anyone and everyone in the bar with the kind of comfortable familiarity that could only be found in a small community like this one. There are a few faces I recognize, from a time before my departure far east, though it doesn't seem like I left much of a lasting impact in their lives, as no one else seems to have noticed my return.

There's Martin from the corner store a block from here, probably still working the afternoon till. He barely gives me a glance before going right back to talking to some girl I don't recognize, a cute blonde. Then there's Eddie and Jane, obviously lovebirds in their sixth year now—hell, maybe they've married since I last spoke to them.

Charlotte's voice snaps me out of my thoughts. "Earth to

stranger."

I whirl back around to face her. She grins patiently at me. "Uh... sorry," I say.

"How far out were you?"

"Sorry?"

"You looked like you were in another dimension," she tells me, "what one?"

"This one. Was just cruising down memory lane."

"Good memories?"

"What?"

She leans closer. I can smell her shampoo, orchids, as her tundra-cold eyes sparkle wondrously under the ceiling lamps. "Good memories?"

I shrug.

"Lamenting an old girlfriend?" She gives me a sly smirk. Somehow it makes her look even younger than... hey... I don't even know how old she is...

"No, nothing like that. Just saw a few faces I recognize before I left. Don't think they recognized me. Not like we were close or anything, you know?"

"I think so."

"So how long have you lived here?"

"Three or four years." Someone calls her for another Broweiser. "One sec." She serves her patron quickly, collects payment, runs it through the till, and then returns to her spot across from me. She notices the sour look on Jeff's face. "Playing nice, Jeff?"

"What?"

"You playing nice with my new friend here?"

"Sure, sure."

"Lighten up before I spank you." Her words are humorous, but her face says otherwise. Perfect deadpan delivery.

"No way," Jeff says, "I'm out," and he leaves, waddling up the ramp with half a bottle of beer held by the neck at his side.

I chortle at his reaction. She giggles. "Like that, do ya?"

"Not the spanking, just... just his reaction there..."

"I haven't had to actually do it... *yet*."

I look at her and she laughs. I force a laugh in response. Her smile fades a bit, just enough for me to see that she knows something's wrong.

"So, what's up?"

"Huh?"

She tries again to speak over the music. "I said, what's up?"

"Nothing, really." My mind races to find a witty follow-up, something she might find funny or flattering, if only to loosen up some of the tension in my muscles. I know they're around here somewhere...

"The sun is down, the moon is up, and yet somehow you're still brightening my day."

She flashes me a playful smirk. "That was awful."

I shrug, trying my best to maintain an air of confidence. "It was worth a shot."

"Well, it's the thought that counts, doesn't it?" She shows her index finger and thumb with an inch gap between them. "Off the mark by this much."

"That so?"

She lowers her hand. "Yes."

I smile at her and she smiles back.

"Refill!" someone shouts down the bar.

The older blonde woman passes behind Charlotte and sneers playfully, "Get to work, you lazy bitch!"

Charlotte returns the tone, grinning from ear to ear. "You first, you old sow!"

My eyebrows are raised. When Charlotte sees my reaction, she laughs. "That's Bertha."

"Oh."

Another patron at the other end of the bar calls for another Cruise Light.

"Don't go away." She heads over to serve her customer, leaving me alone to glance around the bar again, searching for any of those weird people I saw in the warehouse. All these faces in the crowd... newcomers and the departing all mixing together. They could be anywhere among them.

I recall two of them being assigned to watch the diner. Shit. That means they know I'm here. The unusual woman named Zona and the Chinese—I think he's Chinese—gunman known as Chow. The bell tower of the old firehouse overlooks the town just a block away from the diner, just up the street from the bar. It would be easy to scope the surrounding area with a rifle up there, if only I had one. They could be hiding in the parking lot, or watching it from some other vantage point, or worse: *two* different vantage points.

The one called Reeves is waiting until Charlotte's shift ends... she's been here since... well, I don't know. It was around one in the afternoon when I was following Mason and his dead friend at the gas station. She was working then, taking a short break. It's five past seven now. Her shift is almost over.

"I'm back!" She returns with a theatrical flourish that instantly makes me laugh. She looks slightly embarrassed when the other patrons look at her and shrugs them off, deciding, I guess, to ignore them. "Miss me?" she asks.

"Of course."

She beams.

"Can I ask you something?" There's a way to ask these things without sounding like a creep. I'm not entirely sure how to ask her and avoid alarming her at the same time. But I have to risk it if I want to keep her safe. "What time do you get off work?"

"Hmmm." She smiles coyly, moving forward, crossed arms resting on the bar. "And why would you like to know that?"

"Well, I," I stammer, "I was wondering if you'd like me to drive you home."

"Really." Her eyes stare straight into me, unblinking. I can't tell what the hell she's thinking.

"You know, just a courtesy. I mean, I'm not trying to do anything; if you don't want me to, that's fine, I understand. You barely know me and all. I just thought—"

She chuckles. "You're cute when you're nervous."

"Oh... I am?"

"Yes." She leans closer. I can smell her perfume again. I keep my eyes up despite the tempting cleavage provided by her tank top. "I didn't know you drove."

"H-had a car in storage while I went overseas."

"What kinda car?"

"'77 Mustang."

"Ooh," she coos. "You're a Mustang man."

I nod. "I am."

"And you want to drive me home in your Mustang, stranger?"

"If you want."

"Just the two of us alone in your fast car?"

My heart starts pounding. "Of course."

She says, as quietly as possible without being drowned out by the music, "I get off at eight."

My heart leaps. "Oh."

She gives me a playful wink. "It's up to you."

"Oh, I want to. Definitely."

"Good."

I have less than an hour to find Armitage's men. I can't let them find her. "Where's the bathroom?"

She points to my left. "That-a-way, good sir. Down the hall."

"Thanks. I'll be right back."

"I'll keep your seat warm." She winks at me. Oh, man.

I slip off the stool and weave my way through the crowd into a narrow corridor. Up ahead is the side door to the patio, which is propped wide open by a cinderblock. To my left is a doorway to a small storage room. To my right, the women's restroom, and then the men's at the end next to the patio entrance. I fly right out onto the patio, pass a couple tables where indifferent patrons chatter over the loud music, and hop the fence. I make a beeline back to the parking lot across the street and get into my car and drive the hell out of there. Somewhere within a block radius of the diner, two of Armitage's goons are waiting for their chance to kill me. I take the car around the blocks surrounding the diner at cruising speed to avoid any unwanted attention. Last thing I need is a cop pulling me over right now.

I don't see them anywhere. There's no shady van parked on the side of the road or in an alley. No suspicious persons hanging around the rear parking area. I can't see the rooftops or too many windows from the street, but I'm sure they're in one of those buildings, looking through one of those windows, or they're on a rooftop. I go around and peer intently down the alley behind the bar, but I don't see Reeves. Nothing. Not a damn thing. They could be anywhere.

Or maybe they got wind of their superior's fate and called off the mission altogether.

No... even if it were that simple, I can't let my guard down.

Chapter 7: Drive

I return to my parking space in front of the bar and get back inside from the patio-side entrance. I find my stool unoccupied and I gratefully reoccupy it.

Charlotte seems to have noticed my return immediately, even from the far side of the bar. "There you are." She moves a stray hair away from her eye, behind her ear. "Was gonna send a search party. Maybe a diving team."

I chortle and flash her a reassuring smile. "Can't get rid of me that easy. Not without a few drinks."

"Well, if you're driving me, I can't get you drunk yet, can I?"

"No, I guess not."

"I'll whip up something for you." I watch her prepare a Diabetes-in-a-Cup with the grace of a skilled pro. She places it on a coaster in front of me in less than a minute, taking away my half-empty Broweiser. "That oughtta keep you going till morning."

"Thanks." I sip my drink, glancing anxiously at the digital clock next to one of the overhanging TVs. Ten to eight. "What'll I be doing till then?"

"Till when? Morning? Hmm." She rotates her head, bouncing animatedly on her shoulders, smiling. "I'll play you some songs."

"Play me some songs?"

"Yep."

"With what, a piano? A guitar?"

"A guitar."

"So you draw…"

"Mhm."

"…and you play guitar?"

"That's right." She draws back shyly, tucking stray hair behind her ear. She's blushing, trying not to look too shy about me putting her talents front and center. "I only know a few songs right now. Old ones."

"I would love to hear you play."

"Yeah?"

"Yeah. Yeah, I would."

"Maybe after a couple of drinks. At least then I'll have an excuse for striking the wrong chord." We share a laugh.

"Refill!" someone shouts.

Charlotte glances up and realizes Bertha's serving a platter of drinks to the college kids around the pool table. "Dammit," she says through grit, perfect teeth, "had to be somebody to get me in my last ten minutes."

"I'll be right here," I tell her, raising the Diabetes-in-a-Cup in a mock salute. "I'll hold down the fort."

"I expect the cannons to shine by the time I get back," she quips, and then she gets up to serve her last customer for the night.

When her shift ends, Charlotte and Bertha head off to the side to count their tills and organize their tips while two girls show up to work the night shift. While they're doing that, I bring the car out front and head back inside to make sure nothing happens to Charlotte, even if she'll only be out in the open for a few seconds. Of course I glance around the street for anyone suspicious, and find nothing out of the ordinary. They're damn good at hiding, I'll give them that.

When she finally gathers all her tips in a baggie, which she puts in her purse, and returns the till, she grabs my arm and smiles at me. "Shall we depart, stranger?"

I smile back, doing my best to hide my anxiety. "We shall, milady."

She laughs at that and I lead her out to the Mustang, which I left rumbling idly on the curb. "Oooh!" she coos excitedly. "It's beautiful!"

"Like it?"

"Love it!"

I open the passenger side door for her and she hops right in, her index finger stroking my chin as she lowers herself into the seat. "You're such a gentleman."

"I try." I shut the door once her hands and feet are clear, and hurry around the front, jumping in behind the wheel. "We're off." I floor it and the Mustang roars in our ears, blasts off the curb and shoots up to the intersection, much to Charlotte's surprise and delight as she grips the door handle so hard I'm afraid she might break it. I take a left turn. She hoots as the car peels onto the highway sharply. As the car picks up speed to over a hundred, she presses herself into her seat, chest heaving sensually in her top, her open blouse wrapped around her arms, giving me a better look at her bouncing cleavage. It's hard to look away, especially when she's worked up like this, making sounds that strike an almost seductive balance between nervous laughter and excitement.

"Oh, God! Haha…!"

"Want me to slow down?"

"God, no," she yells over the engine's near-deafening roar. "Faster!"

I throttle it. The car lurches into one-twenty. Charlotte whoops and laughs. I check the rear-view mirror and see a van following behind us, keeping its distance, and I wonder if it's *them*. If it is, I can't let them find out where she lives…

"Want me to take a detour?" I ask Charlotte.

"Oh, where to, stranger?"

I give her my best mischievous smirk, cocking an eyebrow for dramatic effect. "It's a surprise."

She responds with a playful grin. "Well," she says, "you already took a wrong turn back there."

"Oh, I did?" I'm genuinely startled by this.

"Yes, you silly man. I live in the opposite direction. Remember the park?"

"Oh… right."

"Keep going where you were going."

"You sure?"

She nods. "I'm curious about wherever you want to take me."

I steal another anxious glance in the sideview mirror. That van's still on us. I don't want to go too fast just yet, in case there are any traffic cops hidden off road, but hell, I *need* to lose them somehow.

"Where *are* you taking me, stranger?"

I look at her and note a thin—*very* thin—sense of unease behind the playful look in her eyes. Oh, shit. She's starting to think I might be a creep, or worse.

"There's this spot. Uh, a… like, it's secluded, I guess? Off the highway, a few kilometres away. My mom used to take me out there for picnics. It's a picnic spot, but it's also a good spot to be alone. I used to go there when I needed a few hours to myself, watch the sunset. I was thinking… it might be even better if I shared it with someone. You know the park up there?"

"Moosehunt Park?"

"That's the one."

"It's been ages."

"Do you want to? If you don't, that's okay, we can just drive around…"

Her unease begins to fade when she sees how awkward I'm getting. She shakes her head. "Show me your special spot."

I look at her and stifle a laugh. "Do you… do you know how dirty that sounds?"

She giggles. "Sorry. Sometimes I guess I have a dirty mind. Especially when I get excited."

"You're… you're excited?"

She nods slowly. "Mhm."

I keep switching my eyes from her to the road, back to her again. "Is it the car?"

She laughs, looking bashful. Is she blushing? "I like fast cars, and I like you. It's a winning combination." She makes an exaggerated shrug. "Sue me."

I chuckle. "I think i-it's obvious that, uh… that I like you too." My eyes dart to the set of headlights in the sideview mirror. The van is still there…

She tells me, "That was obvious from the very minute I looked into your eyes, Michael."

My head swivels in her direction. I can feel my cheeks flaring. "Really?"

"Oh, yes."

We're approaching an intersection about twenty yards ahead. The light turns yellow. We have a clean getaway. I gun it and Charlotte gasps and giggles again. We roar across the intersection just as the light shines red. We roll along a gentle curve going ninety-five and climbing, yellow barrier signs flashing by, my eyes watching the van's headlights disappear behind streams of east- and westbound traffic before a line of pine trees obscure the intersection from my mirrors entirely. I glance around ahead of me with a desperate need to find a road, any road to turn on to to ensure the loss of our tail. Charlotte's enjoying the speeds we're reaching and surpassing. Thick pines fly by us on both sides, the grey-brown bark and dark green spruces blurring in the white light of my Mustang's high beams. We pass one-thirty. Still climbing.

"Hooo boy!" Charlotte cheers. In my peripherals, I catch her shapely legs squirming together, inadvertently pulling her skirt up her peach-coloured thighs. Her hands grip the sides of her seat. "Mmm," I hear her purring turn into a sexy moan. Oh, Jesus. My heart pounds in my ears. I tear my eyes away just for an instant look into the mirror. Nothing yet.

Then I spot a backroad and slow the car down so I can make the turn, and take it. Gravel rumbles and pebbles pop as they strike the Mustang's underbelly. The car rocks a bit as we grind down the backroad through a narrow aisle of pines. A sign up ahead warns us of roadblocks. The road bends away from sight of the highway and I almost breathe a sigh of relief, though now I have a new problem: I have no idea where this particular trail goes. Still, I follow it as if I do, just to keep up appearances with Charlotte.

"Is this the part where I get murdered and fed to some rabbits?" she asks good-naturedly.

"No, no," I tell her, "the raccoons might make faster work of you out here." She chortles. I add, "And if the racoons don't, the lions and tigers and bears will."

"Oh, my." She laughs. I don't catch even a hint of tension in her tone. She seems laid back, relaxed, like she's actually enjoying herself here with me.

"I wouldn't wanna kill you," I tell her. "Who the hell would want to do that to a kind soul like you?"

"'Kind soul,' huh? I'm afraid you don't quite know me *that* well yet."

"No?"

"Not yet."

"I don't think knowing you for very long is a requirement to determine that."

"Oh, really?"

"Yeah."

"What makes you think that?"

I gave her a genuine warm smile. "I can just tell, you know?"

"That's cheating."

I suppress a laugh. "Oh, is it?"

She grins at me. "Yes, yes it is."

"Okay, fine." I look forward again. Even with my headlights at maximum, the dense blackness of the forest seems to be closing in on us, swallowing us. The breaks in our conversation are almost too much combined with that darkness, so I switch on the radio. Bruce

Thorogood plays his version of *One Bourbon, One Scotch, One Beer* to us. We rock through a particularly rough patch that throws us around in our seats, the left side tires dipping into a muddy puddle and ramping back up to level terrain jarringly.

"Fun fact," I say, trying to ignore the impatient prying in her twinkling eyes. "This car is a '77. And this song, uh, this song was also recorded in '77." Finally I muster up the courage to look at her. She's unwavering. Still waiting. Not at all falling for my distraction. "Cool, huh?" I ask feebly.

She folds her arm across her chest and cocks an eyebrow, making an exaggerated frown.

"Sure is nice this time of night, huh?"

"Oh, no," she says, "you're not getting out of it *that* easily. You're in too deep now."

"Oho, am I?"

"*Yeah*, you are!"

"Alright, alright." I take another moment to focus on navigating another rough patch in the path, which gives me a chance to think of a way to convey what I'm thinking. "Well... I think... it's just the way you are. The way you present yourself."

"The way I present myself?"

"Yeah, like... I can tell it's not a façade, you know?" I keep my eyes on the trail. I don't think I would've been able to look her in the eyes right now anyway. "If it was, we wouldn't be out here. I can just tell which people are real and which ones aren't. If you know where to look, how to find it, it's easy. Sure, I-I don't know you *that* well yet, but I've seen enough of you to think, 'wow, I wouldn't mind getting to know her more.'

"And you? What do you think about me?"

"Hmm?" She shuffles her feet, letting her skirt slide up her thighs just a little bit more.

"How do you know I'm not some weirdo, or a psycho murderer or something... or..." my tone drops a decibel when I think about the odd person I've encountered since my return from the Middle East—people who looked at me with contempt, judging me for all the murders I've committed. Just today, I killed a man and witnessed another murder. If I found the others, I would have killed them without hesitation, just to protect her. It kills the joyous mood I was in just a few seconds ago. "...or some crazy, PTSD-ridden maniac who can never stop killing?"

Something about her voice is soft and sad. "Michael…"

I don't make eye contact with her out of shame, maybe.

"I wouldn't be in this car with you if I thought any of those things about you." She reaches over and touches my thigh, making me jolt; despite my initial reaction, she doesn't remove her hand. "I think you're a wonderful guy. I don't know you that well, either. But I know you're a good man."

"But how?"

"Because you don't give me any 'bad man vibes.'"

I almost smile. "'Bad man vibes'?"

"That's right. I don't get those from you. You're sweet. You're awkward. You stepped out of your comfort zone just to try and connect with me. You'd be surprised how long I've been waiting for somebody to do that."

"Do what, exactly?"

"*Talk* to me. And I don't mean like those jackasses at the bar, or a cashier at the gas station or something. I mean, like, a genuine conversation. You actually have something to say. You have things on your mind—not all of them good, I know that much, at least—you know what I'm trying to tell you?"

"I think so…"

"So chin up." She pinches my chin and smiles. "You haven't struck out yet."

"'Yet.'" I scoff, force a smile in her direction. We reach the end of the trail and stop at the edge of a dark road. A sign up ahead reads 'MOOSEHUNT PARK – 5 KM.'

"Yeah, you're off to a better start than anyone else who tried, to be perfectly honest with you."

"Really?"

"Mhm."

We're sitting there. I haven't made the turn yet. "So… you want to see that spot?"

"Possibly more."

My heart leaps and I look at her. She smiles. Even in the poor lighting of the Mustang's high beams reflecting off the sign across the road, I can see that she's a little flustered, but confident at the same time.

"Mind you," she adds quickly, "I don't normally… you know, do anything on the first date. This would probably be my second exception."

"You mean…?"

"Yes. Does that bother you?"

My heart pounds. "No, ma'am."

She beams. "Good. You want to?"

I take a moment to breathe. I can't stop my eyes from looking over her legs to her torso to her breasts as they slowly rise and fall with her steady breathing, to her face, which wears a hopeful expression. Her eyes seem bigger than they are in the dim lighting of the sign's reflection, twinkling like stars. There's a shyness in them that I find unbelievably adorable.

I answer quietly, "Yes, ma'am."

She runs her hands up and down her exposed legs and inhales deeply, pushing her shoulders forward and then leaning back, straightening her back against her seat. She breathes a long sigh and smiles at me. "Lead the way, stranger."

<u>Chapter 8: Paradise</u>

The picnic spot is a grassy plateau surrounded by a dense family of pines and cedars, overlooking a valley resting far below filled by the Township of Herman, a fishing port on Lake Huron. Tonight, despite the bright gold aura enveloping the town's antiquated grey buildings, the stars in the night sky twinkle brightly and unobscured above Herman's electric skyline. Beyond Herman, Lake Huron ripples gently against the shoreline, a dark blue and vast entity that goes on farther than either of us can see, peacefully guarded by a 19th century lighthouse jutting high above Herman's tallest building. The picnic spot slopes steeply up from a dark, fenced-in boat cemetery, though it can't be seen from our viewpoint and doesn't hinder the sight.

Paradise by the Dashboard Light by Meat Loaf plays quietly on the radio, as if the radio jockey predicted this moment between us. Charlotte's leaning over the glovebox, taking in the bright vista of the valley.

"It's beautiful," she breathes.

"Not as beautiful as you." It blurts out. I can feel my face turning red. She's looking at me. I can feel it.

"That's cheesy as hell, Michael." She's laughing.

Gotta own up to it. I shrug, giving her a winning smirk. "It had to be said."

"I can always tell when you're trying to put up an act. You're very easy to read."

I falter. "I am?"

"Yes," she says. "But that's okay."

"It is?"

"Yes." She presses a forefinger to my lips before I can say anything else. "Shh."

I mumble something.

She takes her finger off my mouth. "Hmm?"

"I wasn't lying. Y-you know, when I said that."

She turns in her chair toward me, burying her shoulder into the seat's vinyl cushions, lolling her head against the rest. Shifts her hips, brings her knees together, up against the gear shift, getting comfortable. Her eyes are half-open, brimming with ease and excitement. She breathes a light sigh, loud in this tiny car, even over the music.

I look at her carefully, taking in the full sight of her, the way she's totally loose, not a single tense muscle. The shadows cast from the dashboard console's neon lighting bathe her smooth, delicate face in complimentary teal. Neither of us wants to turn away from the other's gaze. We're locked in. The air between us seems to crystallize, the tension electrified.

She's been staring at me for a while now.

I can't take my eyes off her, either.

"I can see paradise by the dashboard liiiiiiggghht!"

"'Ain't no doubt about it,'" she said, perfectly synchronized with the song's lyrics, "'We were doubly blessed.'" She giggles, leans toward me. My heart's beating so hard I feel like she could hear it. Her forefinger drifts away from my mouth as her other hand comes up. She cups my face in her hands and gently pulls me closer to her as she rises toward me.

Our lips touch. Warm, mushy, wet... our lips part for only a second and reconnect; our tongues explore each other. It's a strange, squirmy sensation. I reach back for the gun tucked in my pants and quietly drop it to the floor and kick it under my seat. She tastes so good, and feels even better, that I take her in my arms and drag her to my side. She melts against me, legs curling over my lap, and then she straddles me, tilts my head back—

She bumps the horn, startling us both. We share a laugh. I recline the seat back. She lies on top of me, hands pressed down on my chest for a moment, then caressing my shoulders. I feel her grinding on my crotch, making me harden, and she encourages my growth with more pressure in her thrusts. My hands glide over her hips, under her shirt...

We break apart to breathe. She stares into my eyes, sucking her bottom lip. We're both breathing hard. "You like that?" she asks me.

"Yes," I whisper. This doesn't feel real anymore. My hands reach back down and grab her shapely ass and pull her down against me. Feels like my pants can barely contain my hardness at this point, and judging by the look she's giving me, she's aware of that fact. "We've only just met."

"I'm okay with waiting, if that's what you want..."

"No, I'm just making sure you're okay with it."

She gives me a reassuring smile, and then an even more reassuring kiss. "How's that for okay?"

"Better than okay."

"Okay."

I taste her again. She settles her body over me, thighs locking me in. My fingers trickle up the small of her back. She moans into my mouth and shudders. It's such a subtle yet unmissable reaction that excites me. My hands become more possessive and she becomes more willing to my touch, tasting each other's lips even as my hands run up her thighs under her skirt and caress the soft fabric of her panties. I can feel her dampening the crotch of my pants, and then her hands shift away from my chest and fumble with the zipper of my jeans and reach inside to grip me. I jolt, startled by her newfound eagerness.

"Sorry."

"No, don't be."

My pants are dragged down to my knees. She accidentally hits her elbow against the horn and giggles. "Goddamn it."

I take hold of her again, arms wrapped around her torso under her top, my lips gently brushing above her cleavage. She throws her blouse into the passenger seat and shoves me back down in my seat. Leans back and straightens as much as the roof of the Mustang will allow; she's still hunched as she lifts her tank top from the bottom up over her head. Her breasts roll out before me. She throws her top across the dash and pulls her hair behind her back, watching my reaction to her exposure—and liking it.

"Jesus." I barely say it before she falls on top of me again. Her hard nipples tickle me through my shirt. I cup her soft breasts. My thumbs tease her. She moans again. She gives me a flustered smile and it's the cutest damn thing I've ever seen. I peel my shirt off and she helps me get it over my head, and throws it aside. She unclips her skirt and lets it fly with a playful flick of her wrist.

She looks like an angel with the golden glow of the port town's aura outlining her naked body through the windshield. Her dark brown hair radiates with an ethereal shine. She smiles bashfully, turning slightly away without averting her eyes from me. "What're you staring at?"

I lean closer. She hesitates only a moment. I pause, watching her. She hovers toward me. I frame her face delicately with my hands and kiss her.

"Ready?" she whispers, and I nod. She reaches down, grips me, guides me, and lowers herself on me with a deep sigh. I'm engulfed and squeezed in her tight warmth. She grinds on me, biting her lower lip, eyes closed, hands pressing down on my chest again. I watch her in awe, loving the way her breasts swell toward me between her arms almost as much as the terrific sensation she's giving me below. She pauses, biting her bottom lip, tightening around me, and I feel a sudden gush that forces my hardness out of her and splashes all over my legs.

"Fuck!" she gasps. "Oh, God." She looks down at my skin glistening between her legs and chuckles with embarrassment. "Sorry."

I lean forward and kiss her, my right hand guiding my hardness back inside her and my left hand on her hip, gently lowering her back on it. I kiss her. She breathes into my mouth and pulls away slightly, her lips brushing against mine as she continues to grind on me. She can't seem to stop herself at this point, and that's more than fine by me. "W-we're making a mess in your car."

"It's okay," I assure her, taking hold of her hips and thrusting upwards. She grunts and leans back, hands reaching behind her, gripping the steering wheel. Now she's bouncing on me, her wet skin clapping against mine. God, she feels like heaven. I look into her eyes as she rises and falls in full view, arching her back; they're boring into my own, watching my every little reaction to her body as she does what she wants to me. There's almost something primal about the way we're going about this, exploring each other as we go along, throwing ourselves into each other.

She's so goddamn beautiful.

I don't know how long it's been since we got here. I finish for the second time—narrowly avoiding the risk of impregnating her on the first date both times—and now she's lying on top of me, her head resting under my chin, her hot breath tickling the hairs on my heaving chest, our sweaty skin sticking together. The windows are all fogged up. The interior of the car feels like a sauna. Rolling down the window would let the bugs in, but hell.

It really was a taste of paradise.

Chapter 9: An Interruption

"I'm not usually that easy," she says, seemingly to herself. "This is the first time I ever slept with someone on the first date."

"If it's any consolation, it's a first for me, too."

"First time having sex?"

"On a first date, yeah."

"But not in general?"

"No, I've... I've had sex before."

"I could certainly tell. I'm probably not the first woman you've had in this car."

"It was a long time ago. I was a kid then." I hold her a little tighter. "It was nothing like this."

"What *was* this?"

"It was special."

"Was it?"

"It was." I kiss the newly disheveled hair on her head. "But maybe... if you want... we can take this a little slower. Before we get too far ahead of ourselves. A few more dates. A movie, perhaps. A lot of long talks about nothing in particular. Boring couple stuff, you know? Taking the time to really get to know each other, because... well, I'd like to get to know you for you. Not just as Charlotte, the sexy bartender with the bouncy personality—"

She scoffs. "Oh, stop."

"—but also the real Charlotte. The one no one else gets to see. And you know, I'll be an open book. As open as I can possibly be. I just... I know things won't be perfect... but I want us to be comfortable with each other."

"Hm." She traces a forefinger along my collarbone. "I'd like that. It sounds nice."

I smile. "And I still owe you a dinner."

She gives my shoulder a playful slap. "Yes. Yes, you do.

"You know what else I want?" She looks up at me.

"What's that?"

"I really want this to work."

"Me, too. I could use a feel-good summer."

"Well," she continued, "it's off to a damn good start, isn't it?"

I laugh and she does too. "Hell yeah, it is. What about you?"

She grins. "Could be worse."

"D'aww."

"I'm teasing."

"I know."

She glances at the clock in the dash. "Jesus. It's 11:30."

I look at the clock, confirming her statement. "Getting late."

She lifts herself up, her still-hardened nipples grazing my sweaty chest. "Take me home, stranger." She leans forward and kisses me one final time before rolling into the passenger side and beginning the awkward search for her clothes.

I watch her for a moment before I lean forward and pull up my pants. "Is my shirt over there?"

She purposely flings my shirt into my face and giggles. I give her a roguish smirk and get dressed. "Ready?"

She's looking at her reflection in the rearview mirror, adjusting her hair. Fully dressed. "Yes, sir," she breathes. Something about her delivery of her response turns me on again.

"I love it when you call me 'sir'."

She chortles and punches my arm.

I feign agony. "Oh, God, ow." I turn the key, which is still in the ignition, and the engine sputters and roars to life.

Suddenly the car is filled with white light. We're blind. Something comes up and rams into the trunk, slamming Charlotte into the dash while hurling me across the wheel. The car lurches toward the cliff. Charlotte screams. Terrified, I look into the rearview mirror.

The van from earlier backs up and starts for us again, bearing down on us like a predator, and smashes into the rear, throttling us in our seats. I floor the brakes, which doesn't do much, and then shift gears and floor the accelerator, trying to force our way backwards. The rear tires rip into the dirt in the opposite direction of the van, fighting its bulk. The van's grille seems to be stuck to my smashed back fender as our bulky attacker slowly forces us closer and closer to the steep incline ahead.

"Michael!" Charlotte screams.

I look at her. She's in hysterics, no sign of the confident, humorous woman I just slept with in sight. No surprise there. Oh, but it pisses me off. These bastards are gonna pay.

I hit the brakes again. The Mustang slides forward as the van gains traction. I shift gears, watching the edge of the cliff disappear from my frontal view. Nothing but the blacked-out boat cemetery below. The van backs off a few metres and roars straight for us again. I watch it in the rearview mirror, my hand working the stick into forward gear, heart pounding in my brain, adrenaline spiking as it comes down on us for one final push—and then I floor the accelerator and the Mustang shoots forward. I jerk the wheel left and the Mustang swerves sharply, rear end skidding over the edge. For a moment the rear tires aren't touching earth as we careen out of the van's path.

Van's going too fast. Its driver hits the brakes, but too late. The van flies out into the night, dips forward into the slope with a deafening crunching noise. The rear doors swing upward and come down; the van topples down the slope, pieces of it flying in all directions. Eventually it plows through the chain link fence and blows through the hull of a rusted yacht. It explodes in a ball of orange flame, lighting up the boat cemetery. Secondary explosions from inside the van blast its walls and the boat apart.

The car stops spinning with my side facing the steep drop. I watch the crash, and I know for a fact that no one could've survived it. That means two or three of *them*—it had to be *them*—are out of the picture. But that could still leave at least one more...

Charlotte trembles uncontrollably beside me, tears streaming down her face. She can't even bring herself to speak. Breathing heavily, the few syllables of noise coming out shaky and unintelligible.

I reach over and grip her hand. "Charlotte, i-it's okay, it's over—"

She throws herself onto me, arms wrapped tightly around me, and cries.

Police arrive and take our statements. The picnic spot is illuminated by the blue and red flashes of their cherry lights. I hear an ambulance and a fire truck approaching the burning wreck below. Since they were called, I'd moved the car toward the edge of the forest where ramming it would be next to impossible. I knew no one else would try that tactic again, but my paranoia was through the roof.

"Probably some kids," the cop, an Officer Willard, tells me. "Had a white van reported stolen two days ago. Wouldn't surprise me if it's the one burnin' down there now."

"Assholes," Charlotte snarls, now holding a lit cigarette between her middle and index finger, "what the fuck did we do to them?" She seems like a different person right now, all fear replaced with fury.

I choose my words carefully. "You don't think we were purposely targeted, do you?"

"Do you have any reason to think so?"

"No, none that I can think of."

Charlotte takes notice of Willard's eyes shifting to her. "I deal with a lot of stuck-up bastards at the bar. N-none of them have the spine or the lack of brains to try something like this, though."

"Then it was probably spur-o'-the-moment. They saw you two out here and thought they'd try to run you off the cliff. Wouldn't be the first time something like that's happened, if you can believe that. That's why there aren't any houses right at the bottom there. Just a bunch o' boats. Mayor said he'd put up a fence to prevent nightly passage for vehicles, but I guess that's yet to happen." Officer Willard shrugs, takes a long look at my car. "1977 Mustang. Nice."

He turns back to us. "Nothin' to worry about now. No one could survive a fall like that. I'll call ya if I need another statement, but I don't think that'll be necessary. Drive safe, alright? Here's my card." He hands me two contact cards with his full name on it: John T. Willard. I give one to Charlotte and she takes it. "Call me if you need anything," Willard tells me.

Charlotte and I thank him and bid him good night before I slowly drive back out onto the road. The journey home is done in silence, with Charlotte smoking and sniffling occasionally in the passenger seat. It isn't until we get back into town when we feel like some dangerous presence has been lifted from us. By then she's smoked twelve cigarettes.

"You sure know how to show a lady a good time," Charlotte jokes, though her voice is trembling too much to sell the humour in it. "Never had a date end like that before."

I scoff humourlessly. "Yeah."

She gives me directions block by block until finally, I stop in front of her house. It's two storeys, an old-fashioned country home, with a wooden fence around the backyard. How a single woman like her is able to afford a place like this is beyond me.

"Look, I'm sorry about all that," I tell her. "I... Jesus, I don't know what the hell to say. I'm just… I'm sorry."

She touches my chin and gently pulls my face toward her. "It wasn't your fault, Michael. It's over now, isn't it? At least now I know you're capable of thinking fast in a dangerous situation."

"Got my time overseas to thank for that." I sound regretful, and in a way, I kind of am. But I know that if it weren't for my training, we would've most likely died back there.

She gives me a reassuring smile. "The safest place for me to be is right beside you." She kisses me gratefully, and then kisses me again, pressing harder, more passionately, arms strung around my neck. When she releases me, she whispers, "Won't you walk me to the door?"

"Yes, ma'am." I get out, and as I step on the sidewalk, she climbs out of her side and walks around the car. Locks her arm in mine and leads me up the steps of her front porch under an outdoor light above her door. The lights are out inside.

"You need me to stay? Just in case?" I realize what I just said and quickly add, "N-not in the same bed or anything… just… you know, I'll take the couch, keep watch over things while you sleep."

She smiles and embraces me one final time. "I'll be fine. I'm a big girl." Another kiss. "Call me."

I watch her get her keys out of her purse and unlock the door, slowly drifting back toward the stairs as I do. "Okay. I'll call you tomorrow. Uh, what time is good?"

She's almost got the door open when she turns to me and shrugs. "Lunch. I'm off tomorrow. Gimme a call then. I don't think I'll be sleeping for a few more hours after… after *that*." She sighs. "So I'll be sleeping in for sure. Noon. Call me at noon. Cheer me up with a joke first thing."

"I will."

She opens the door. "Good night, Michael."

"Uh," I suddenly exclaim.

She pauses, stares at me curiously.

"I just realized, I don't actually *have* your number."

"Oh? Oh. Here. Hold out your hand." She takes out a permanent marker from her pocket and writes her phone number across my palm. Holds up the marker. "Never leave the cave without it."

"Did you just—?"

"Yes, and I have no regrets." She manages a small smile.

"Good night, stranger."

"Good night, Charlotte." I start down the steps. She closes the door when I reach the sidewalk.

Then I hear a muffled, metallic clanking sound coming from inside the house and turn back around. The lights are still out. My heart sinks. No. *No!* What if…?

"Charlotte?" I watch the windows. The darkness persists. No lights are switched on. More alarmed now, I hop back up the stairs. "Charlotte?" The frosted glass window in the door doesn't show me shit, so I try the knob. Unlocked. I open the door and peek inside. No sign of her. I step inside.

A shape in my peripherals sets my reflexes in motion. My arm throws up and hits something. A loud metallic clang rings above my head. The mirror on the wall beside me shatters, dusting the coats on the nearby rack with flying glass. I whirl, punching my assailant in the chest. Another shot from his silenced pistol puts a hole in the wall. I grapple him. We spin around the foyer. Another shot goes wild. I take hold of his gun arm and hurl him through the doorway. He somersaults across the porch, nearly falls down the stairs. I finally get a decent look at him—the one named Reeves. He leaps into a squatting stance, levels his gun—

I kick the door shut and lock it. He fires two shots through the wood. Both miss me. Another bullet screams through the frosted window past my head. I hear another shot and the lightbulb outside tinkles loudly as it's put out. Fragments of glass clatter on the doormat. The front porch is blacked out. Reeves is now concealed under cover of darkness. I hear him clamber off the porch and run along the side of the house.

"Charlotte?" I stagger in the dark, groping for a light switch. Every moment that passes in silence adds tremendous weight to the growing pit in my stomach. "Charlotte?" My hand discovers a light switch. The living room's ceiling fan drones on, blades spinning clockwise, lamps dousing the room in easy white light.

Charlotte's lying on the floor just a few inches from where I'm standing. Her eyes stare lifelessly at the ceiling. Crimson rivulets of blood leaking from the side of her head. It's pooling across the floor, dark against the pinewood panels she's splayed across.

I do not move. A minute ago, I was assuring her that everything would be okay. I kissed her good night. Now she's…

"Charlotte," I mutter dumbly. I collapse on my knees. I can't feel my legs. My hands reach for her but stop midway. I can't touch her. This isn't real. This isn't...

Real... but she's here... lying here...
Dead... on the floor...
Here... but...

Chapter 10: Gone

Seems like hours have passed by. Reeves never came back. The shock doesn't quite wear off, but my instincts take control. I search the premises, both for a phone and a clue as to how Reeves got in. I find the clue first—a hole had been punched next to the lock in the screen door leading to the rear patio and garden. I find a mottled patch of duct tape with glass shards on the sticky side. A crude way to break a window without making much noise, or a mess. Reeves knew what he's doing, and he's done it well.

I find the phone on an end table by the couch and call the cops. I can barely choke out the words to the dispatcher. "I-I'm reporting a murder." I give the dispatcher Charlotte's address. The dispatcher tells me to wait there. I hang up and obey her command.

Two black-and-whites arrive on the curb somewhere in the following ten minutes; an ambulance shows up one minute later. The three officers who enter—one of whom is Willard—are suspicious of me at first, but act sympathetic as I tell them what happened. I tell them everything except that I know the man's name, or the alias I'd heard earlier; and of course I leave out any mention of Armitage and his followers.

"Seems you've had a busy night," Willard says.

"You could say that." My tone is neutral. At this point, I'm past fighting back tears, instead fighting my heavy eyelids and weariness. Yeah. It's been a long night, alright.

"You understand I can't pass this off as coincidence anymore, right?" Willard continues, maintaining a sympathetic tinge to his words. "The van incident just an hour earlier and now your... well, this. Someone was gunning for her. Any idea who?"

I shake my head.

Willard takes a step forward, his piercing green eyes studying me. "Now... you're *sure* about that?"

"Yes. I just met her not too long ago." Come to think of it, I didn't know her all too well. "Doesn't make it hurt any less."

"I understand, buddy. I understand. You mind if we search your car?"

"Am I a suspect?"

"Look at it from my point of view. You were with her when two people in a van tried to run you guys off a cliff—now, granted, you were in the car with her. Still. And now, just an hour later, you call in a homicide, which you witnessed—"

"I heard it. I didn't see it."

"Okay. Calm down. So you heard the shots, right?"

"Suppressed shots."

"Silenced, huh? How—"

"The movies aren't accurate. Even with a suppressor, a pistol shot is pretty loud."

"You have experience with firearms?"

"Yes. Military training. Some combat."

"You're a vet?"

"Just returned from my latest tour in Afghanistan."

"Oh. Oh, I see. Well, thanks for that."

I shrug.

"Still, I'll have to search your car, man. Or I can get a warrant—"

"I have a gun under the seat," I tell him.

The other two officers behind Willard standing on either side of Charlotte's body stop what they're doing and look at me. Willard doesn't move. His face doesn't seem to react to what I tell him.

Willard asks, "Why do you have a gun under your seat?"

"Just where I keep it."

"What kind?"

"Pistol. Beretta 92F." I quickly add, "You'll find a permit in the glovebox." Shit. The glovebox. Where Armitage's gun is. *Fuck.* "I also have another gun in there."

The cops don't take their eyes off me for a second.

"I found it on the side of the road. A Beretta M9, I think. I spotted it on the highway when I was driving earlier today. I was—"

"Why didn't you report it?"

"I was *going to*," if you'd let me finish my goddamn sentence, "but I got distracted."

"I see."

"Okay." Willard looks at me expectantly.

"I don't care if you search it," I say, slowly reaching into my pocket and handing Willard the keys.

"Cartman," Willard says, tossing the keys to the nearest officer, who leaves the house with them.

"I wish I had it on me."

"Wouldn't have saved her, if things went the way you say they did. There was nothing you could've done, man."

"She…" My voice cracks. Tears seem to explode behind my eyes. I shake my head, blinking furiously. I have to sit down on the couch and bury my head in my hands. Can't hold it in anymore.

"Just knew her a couple days, huh?"

"You don't get it. There aren't many people who treated me with the same… the same kind of… I don't know how to describe it. She was different."

"I think I understand, man." Willard touches my shoulder sympathetically. "I'm sorry. We're gonna have to take you down to the station to get an official statement. Let the investigative team do their job. I'll drive ya."

I need another minute, and take it, sobbing on the couch. The tears just won't stop.

"I'm sorry. We gotta go." Willard takes hold of my arm. I rise and walk out with him, wiping my eyes on my sleeves.

Officer Cartman pulls out of my car just as we descend the steps of the front porch. "The gun was where he said it was and so was the permit."

"And the other one?"

"All checks out."

Willard stops for a moment, still gripping my shoulder. "You mind if we take it down with us to the station? Just gonna run some quick tests, is all."

"Yeah, whatever." I sniffle.

I'm loaded in the back seat as two more cruisers arrive, these ones black and unmarked. Cartman and Willard climb in the front. Willard drives. Cartman has my gun in a plastic bag and the M9 in a separate one. Christ, I'm a suspect.

And to make things worse, I never reloaded the M9 after shooting Armitage.

Five blocks up the road, a right turn past Freddie's diner, a left turn around the corner, a block up the road to a 24-hour doughnut shop—Willard taxies into the parking lot and starts for the drive-thru. "Michael, right?"

"Yeah."

"Want a donut, Michael?"

"No."

"Coffee?"

"No."

"You sure? My treat."

"I don't want anything. Thanks."

"Fair enough." He orders a medium triple-triple with espresso for himself and Cartman; a double chocolate doughnut and an apple fritter. He goes through the drive-thru. Pays at the first window, gets his stuff at the second window, and hits the road again. "I'm really sorry about Charlotte, Michael."

"Yeah." I'm staring out the window. The lights of the cop shop are just up ahead; it's an old building with steel framing and partitioned windows. We fly by it. My eyes follow it until they can't anymore, a sinking feeling in my stomach again. I glance forward and catch Willard's eyes watching me in the rearview mirror.

"You're really something, Mikey. Mind if I call you Mikey?"

I say nothing, watching them, braced against the seat. I'm not cuffed, which I think is strange now, if they're about to do what I think they're about to do.

Willard takes my silence with a grain of salt. "Mikey, Mikey... you pissed off the Agency, my friend. Did you think it was just Armitage and his team? The Agency dispatched six teams to deal with your case. *Six*, man. You're an anomaly. A major complication."

"Why are you people doing this to me? Why Charlotte?"

"Because she's dead, man. It's a cleanup job, that's all. Balance, you know? Organization."

"You're starting to sound like Armitage," I growl.

Willard's eyes shoot up at the rearview mirror at my reflection again while Cartman looks at his partner. "You *talked* to Armitage?"

"Yeah," I snarl, "right before I blew his fucking head off."

"Zona and Chow... Armitage, too. Well, damn. Racked yourself up one hell of a body count, didn't you? That's too bad. I liked that one."

Cartman mutters, barely audible: "No wonder the Agency's pissed off."

"You haven't told me why."

"That's just it, man, I did. Just now."

I'm confused. "What the hell are you...?"

"She was dead before we got to her. In neighbouring dimensions. The Agency likes to keep things neat. They don't like when someone dies in one reality and lives in another closely related reality. Makes it hard to keep track of things, you know?"

More of Armitage's nonsense. I can't believe I'm hearing this shit from a cop.

"You don't get it. I get it. I get why you don't get it. It's a tough concept to swallow."

Cartman turns his head and says to me through the steel mesh barrier, "See, this is our universe. A universe exists for every possible outcome to every decision we make. So, say you're given a choice, like if you want to buy a car. You got a choice between that nice '77 Mustang or a '68 Pontiac. In this dimension, you chose the Mustang, but now *another* reality exists where you bought the Pontiac instead. That opens a whole other cluster of possible outcomes. You get what I mean?"

I run the idea through my head a few times, and then I apply it to other things. Hypothetically, that could mean my mother never committed suicide that fateful day I met Freddie somewhere out there, far away. Or I never left the house, instead opting to comfort my mother—maybe then she wouldn't have killed herself, but then I would never have met Freddie, or I would have met him at a later time, but not under the same circumstances that led to the relationship I have with him now. Christ. It's a lot to take in. But I think I get it. "So," I say, after four minutes of silently thinking it all through, "that would mean that for every dimension Charlotte dies… it would create another reality where she survives."

Cartman grins at me, flashing slightly yellow teeth. "Right! That's right." He says to Willard, "he catches on quick."

"Uh-huh."

I give it a bit more thought. Something about it causes anger to boil up inside me. "Then this whole endeavour is pointless. If she's just going to live on in a different reality, what the hell is the point? No matter what you do, there will always be two realities where she survives everything you bastards throw at her."

"Look, I don't make the rules, I just follow 'em," Cartman tells me.

Huh. Not even the peons know how to explain that one.

"But the rules say you gotta die, too, Mikey," Willard says. He shakes his head sadly. "You've died a few times along the way, apparently. You've been lucky so far—just the other day, I hear you shot yourself in your room. Freddie was devastated, you know. Inconsolable. I felt so damn sorry for the poor guy. And tonight, tonight you *both* died when Zona and Chow pushed your car down that cliff. It's really easy to tell sometimes, especially when certain subjects are constantly avoiding death—because there will always be a time when they weren't so lucky. You know what I'm sayin'?"

Cartman chimes in: "We don't do this because we enjoy it or anything like that, Mike. To be straight with you, we hate this job. It's ghastly. It's ugly. It's miserable. But it's gotta be done. Somebody has to maintain order in this crazy multiverse we live in. May as well be us." Cartman sips his coffee. "Just wanted you to know that... we don't hold anything personal against you. You just happened to draw the short straw in the existential cup of straws, or... or whatever."

"'Existential cup of straws,'" Willard repeats slowly, unimpressed. "What the hell is that, Cartman?"

"I'm tired, okay? Christ."

"But it doesn't make any goddamn sense!" I shout at them. "Why would anyone think they can control something like that?"

"Like we said," Willard says calmly, "we don't make the rules. We just follow them."

We're surrounded by pines and maples now. Cartman rolls down his window and empties my Beretta into the trees as we pass them by. He pulls his hand back in once it's empty, tucks it back into the plastic bag he'd put it in earlier, and peels a rubber glove off the hand that fired the gun, abandons it to the winds whipping past the car. He mutters something like "Chow has a good eye for guns, I'll give 'im that."

"Yeah," Willard says.

"What about the silencer?"

"Shouldn't be hard to come up with something when we get back."

"Alright."

I growl at them, "You people are insane."

"Tell me something, Mikey," Willard replies, "is it really insane to try and prevent the multiverse from overloading itself? Do you *want* all possibilities of reality to fold in on themselves? Last thing we need's a paradox, man, let me tell ya. Nothing makes a reality implode faster than a paradox. I never had to deal with time traveling cases myself, but I've heard stories, and man, they aren't pretty.

"You know what *is* insane? Willful ignorance, or worse, cognitive dissonance. You know what cognitive dissonance is?"

I glare at him. Somehow Willard gets the right answer out of that, because he continues like I had confirmed my knowledge of the subject. "It would be insane to carry on while the multiverse multiplies by infinity, infinite times, every second, without guidance, and expect nothing bad to happen from that. Maybe not right away. Maybe not in twenty million years. But *eventually*, something will happen. The constant natural equation will hit a snag. The flow of time and space and reality will jam up. Everything will derail. We're here to make damn sure that doesn't happen. Scary when you think about it, huh? Ever see a universe derail, Mikey? Of course you haven't, because it hasn't happened yet. Do you know how many times earth has had an apocalypse? How many times has the world ended? A lot, but it could've been a lot worse. If it weren't for us, humanity would have gone extinct decades ago. Can you guess when the last time the world ended was? The sixties, man. The early sixties. S'long time ago. You know why? Because of us. We contained it to just a small handful of realities. But it could've been worse. Lucky they got Arkhipov on K-19 beforehand. No doubt influenced his decision during the Crisis."

Cartman slaps his partner's shoulder. "Come on, you're giving him too much. Look at him. You're frying his brain. He's gonna die in a few minutes anyway. What's the point?"

"I guess you're right." We drive on in silence.

For a while.

There's something else on Willard's mind. I can tell by watching him in the rearview mirror that he's dying to get it out. Finally, he does: "You know how many times Charlotte's died in the past few months?"

I don't answer.

"A lot. She died a lot. Too many times. I'm gonna level with you, Mikey: she would've died a whole lot less if it weren't for you. You jumped so many goddamn times, across so many goddamn realities, that you tainted them. You involved them. What the hell were we supposed to do? Let the respective narratives of every separate Charlotte get tangled up?"

"Murder's murder no matter how you justify it," I tell them.

"Ha!" Willard sniggered, glancing at his partner. "That's a riot, coming from you."

"I know."

"What's your excuse, then?"

"I have a goal, same as all murderers. Like you, I have a job to do."

"And that is?"

"To protect Charlotte."

"But why? You've known her for what? A week? Less? It varies depending on the dimension. Damn-near impossible to keep track of all the timelines."

"It doesn't matter anymore." I feel a painful twinge in my chest, tightening. I fight back tears as the fresh image of her corpse flashes through my mind for the millionth time. It happened so fast. They were waiting for her. They took her from me. Now they're trying to tell me more of her exist? Bullshit. I'm not cuffed. As soon as I'm out of this car, I'm going to kill them both if it's the last goddamn thing I do.

After a long pause, Willard says quietly, "You're right. It doesn't." He sips his coffee.

Chapter 11: Water Under the Bridge

It's almost 1:00 AM when Willard takes a side road through dense forest and stops in the middle of a remote bridge. We're in the middle of nowhere. Crickets chirp loudly in the brush. The night air is cold, nipping at the hairs on my arms. I can hear my heart's rapid-fire drumbeat reverberating in my ears. Cartman covers Willard, gun drawn, as Willard lets me out of the cruiser. I'm instructed to walk slowly to the railing, which I do. As I stand over the rail, I see a river flowing steadily in the opposite direction under my feet, skirted by white beds of stone jutting up at the sky in jagged points. An old quarry by the looks of it. The calm hiss of the river compliments the crickets somehow. Nature in perfect harmony.

I feel the muzzle of Willard's gun brushing the hairs on the back of my head. I turn my head—

"Don't look at us," Willard commands. There's something in his voice that tells me he's not enjoying this. He almost seems to be holding back.

So it's difficult for him. Good.

"Just say what you need to say to whoever you need to say it too," Willard says. "God, or Allah, or Mary, or Buddha, or whatever you believe in. And please don't make any sudden movements. I don't want you to suffer. I mean that. Just one shot to the head. You won't even feel the bullet, alright? Quick and painless. Quick and painless..."

I look down at the dark waters. The sharp rocks tinged grey-blue in the dim, pale light of the stars glittering above. Willard's gun tingles up the nape of my neck.

Suddenly I reach back and grab hold of his wrist and yank his gun and the hand gripping it forward over my shoulder. A shot barks from the weapon into the dark trees beyond the rail. Cartman yells. The muzzle flash leaves white dots in my eyes. Willard stumbles against my back. I'm still gripping his wrist. Another shot fires from the gun, wide above the dark treeline. Willard begins to struggle. I whirl around, my free arm jabbing an elbow into Willard's ribs. Then I place my free hand over his, squeezing my forefinger into the trigger guard with his own. Cartman freezes, looking shocked. The gun goes off. The bullet glances off the hood of the cruiser just inches from Cartman. The close call throws Cartman into a panic. Despite Willard's efforts, I fight him off, trying my best to aim the gun at his partner, who looks scared and lost, trying to figure out what to do with himself. I squeeze his finger down. The gun shoots again. A split-second twitch sends the bullet wide. Not too far off. Cartman dives behind the cruiser. Fuck.

"You son of a—" Willard grunts as he awkwardly reaches around, trying to grab at my face. I stab my elbow into his ribcage again. He jolts painfully. Another shot is fired. The cruiser's windshield spider-webs in the far side.

Willard kicks behind my left knee. I collapse on one knee, sliding down his front. I reach up, grab hold of his jacket, and tug hard, using my fall to flip him over my head. He pitches forward, gun arm twisting in my grip, snapping, gun flying out of his fingers. He slams down on his back. The gun lands beside my right foot. Willard immediately sits up, reaching for it. I drive my heel into his collarbone, feeling the bone shatter under my shoe. He falls on his back, wheezing. I snatch up the gun and put two in Willard's chest. He falls flat.

Cartman springs up from behind the cruiser. Fires. I see a flash. I hear the bullet whistle by my ear. I'm acting on sheer instinct. Adrenaline. I unload in his direction. I barely have time to look before I confirm the kill.

The slide locks back. Empty.

Confirm the kill. That was always a rule in close combat—I didn't do much of it, but I knew men who died when they neglected to confirm the kill. "Always confirm the kill," they said.

Cartman is definitely dead. His left eye is pulverized. His blown-open left carotid gushes blood onto the road, darkening the dirt and filling in old tire tracks.

A scraping noise behind me. I whirl around just as Willard rises to one knee. He sees me and lunges, eyes wild, teeth bared in a snarl. I hurl the empty gun at him and it cracks him in the jaw, throwing his charge off-kilter. He staggers forward into my extended heel. He buckles, stomach folding inward. I step back and try to deliver a right hook to his jaw—miss—he arcs back suddenly, drawing his Taser. Shit. He glares at me, Taser poised, knees bent slightly, shoulders hunched forward. His breath is ragged. I can see mushroomed brass peeking brightly through the holes in his uniform shirt. A vest. Of course he's still alive. His ribs are bruised, or cracked. Maybe.

"Come on, Mikey," Willard rasps, "it shouldn't happen like this. Quick and painless. Water under the bridge."

"Yeah," I reply curtly, "Right."

Keeping his eyes and his Taser on me, he stoops down, picks up the pistol I threw at him, rests it in the nook of his arm, straining against what must be agonizing pain in his broken collarbone; ejects the spent magazine. He shoves a loaded one from his belt home and the slide snaps back into place. He points the gun at me, tucks the Taser back in its holster. "I don't want you to suffer, man." He glances over the hood of the cruiser. From his spot, he can just barely see Cartman's head lying in the dirt. "Cartman?"

No answer. I can see the pain in his face. He knows what happened, but he can't believe it. Not yet. "Cartman?" He shifts toward the cruiser just enough to see over the hood to confirm his fears. "You killed my partner."

I say nothing, doing my best to hide the small pang of guilt I feel for him. It's a case of them or me.

Rage flashes in his eyes. "Son of a bitch. You son of a bitch. Get to the rail. Get going, goddamn you."

"What the hell have you got to be so mad about? You people hunted the woman I cared about all night long, preaching to me about maintaining the goddamn universe and that it wasn't personal... now that I've killed your partner, it's personal."

There's understanding partially hidden in the mask of rage he's wearing. He knows exactly what I'm talking about. "That's just the job I was given, Mikey. I told you I don't enjoy it. I don't do it for fun. I do it out of necessity. What the fuck is *your* excuse?"

"Same thing," I answer, "necessity."

Willard's keeping his distance. He knows better than to get close to me now. The beating I gave him shook him up. He can't hold his gun steady. My chances of surviving this are still slim. "Look," I say quietly, "it doesn't have to be like this."

"It can only go one way," Willard replies. His breath shudders as he speaks. "A bullet in your head's the only way, Mikey. I'm sorry, man, okay? I hate to be the one to do this, but I have to. Just the way it is."

"You know as well as I do that I'll get away. If not in this reality, then another one."

"We'll corner you then, too."

This is getting frustrating. "Don't you get it? It's pointless! There will always be an outcome where I survive an encounter with you people, whoever the hell you really are. And that's if—*if* what you're telling me isn't just complete bullshit made up by your cult leader or… or whatever the hell all this is."

His gun wavers for only a second. "Maybe in another reality. But not *this* one." His fist shakes as he strains to squeeze the trigger. It throws off his aim. I pitch into a roll as he fires and the bullet punches through the cruiser's windshield. I'm up and on him in half a second, tackling him against the rail, grabbing hold of his gun arm again. Willard throws a knee into my hip. I push forward—too hard, in fact, because we both feel gravity pulling us over the rail. My heart lurches as we spin through the air, locked in our violent embrace as we plummet to the river. A myriad of images flicker through my mind, cycling at light speed; Freddie at the diner, Charlotte's smile behind the counter in the Love Zone, her house—

Something flashes like a neon strobe light around us. Bright purple, blinding ropes of white light coiling in an alien space. A chorus of unintelligible screams and sounds that are so foreign that I can't accurately describe them. Electronic whooshing in my ears as beams of light swirl around in a dizzying vortex, each colour appearing to have its own unique voice or sound that would be strange on its own, but all at once it's a deafening assault on every one of my senses.

Just like before…

We hit earth. Grass? Willard cushions my fall. I hear his bones crackling and feel his chest flex inwardly under my weight as a rush of air explodes from his lungs. He flails, mouth agape, wheezing. He dropped the gun. No thinking, just desperate panic. I act on instinct again, tucking my arm under his jaw and heaving all my body weight into his neck until it snaps. He gurgles and dies beneath me. His body seems to deflate as his muscles slacken. My head's so light I'm surprised I managed to do it. Feels like all my weight is shifting in every direction. I roll off of Willard and feel a sudden burst of sickness, so I scramble on my hands and knees right before a jet stream of vomit burns up my throat and sprays into the grass. I heave a few times before it stops, sucking in air when I can. My lungs blaze. I look around desperately, so goddamn disoriented.

Can't stay up on wobbling, matchstick legs. A bird bath spins into my field of vision. I scramble toward it and look at the clear water reflecting the starry night sky and suck in a mouthful, swish it around, spit it out into a bed of orchids. I swallow the next mouthful of water, grateful that birds haven't shit in it. It tastes fine. Refreshing.

The nausea starts to fade. My vision gradually stops spinning as I rest on the grass that tickles my wrists. Grass...

I take in my surroundings. I'm in a yard—backyard. Flowers line a wood-paneled fence that surrounds me, boxes me in. I turn my head and look at the back of a house. Something about it is familiar. There's a deck, a screen door. No lights are on. Then something hits me. It's Charlotte's house. I squint. There's a hole in the screen door. I crane my neck. It's night. The stars shine brightly. Crickets sing in the bushes. Something scurries in the branches of a maple tree towering over the fence from the next yard over.

What the hell is going on?

I test my legs. They're still unstable, but I can stand now, at least. I rush over to the gun lying in the grass and pick it up. Willard only fired five shots, I think. I frisk his body and find two more magazines in his belt and pocket them. Then I hunch over and cross the yard to the stairs of the deck. Stretching my neck, peering across the deck at the hole in the screen door, trying my damnedest to see inside. The window reflects the stars, blocking my view of the inside. Damn.

Something groans around front. I duck down and crawl toward the gate beside the house. Slowly, quietly, I pull the latch and peek through the crack. I see my car out front. I see Charlotte step out. My heart almost explodes. What the fuck is going on?! She's alive? She's alive!

And then I see the driver appear from around the other side of the car—*another* me!

She locks her arm in my counterpart's and leads me—uh, him?—up the steps of her front porch. I hear myself say, "You need me to stay? Just in case? N-not in the same bed or anything... just... you know, I'll take the couch, keep watch over things while you sleep."

This is... I can't even begin. Where *do* I begin? I'm watching myself talk to Charlotte, who *isn't dead*. What...

That means…

I leave the gate unlatched and return to a squat at the foot of the stairs, once again looking up at the hole in the screen door. Quickly, I ascend the stairs and stay close to the wall, eyes locked on the door. When I get there, I cautiously peek around the jamb inside. These damn stars aren't doing me any favours. The splintered glass reflects them in odd spectral patterns.

I hear the front door open. Streetlight filters in. For a brief second, I see the outline of Reeves' face in the light reflecting on the glass before he ducks away. Have to think fast.

The solution doesn't take long to enter my mind.

I smash the butt of my gun against the cracked screen door, shattering it. I hear Charlotte's startled yelp as glass shards trickle loudly to the floor. She screams. I hear my own voice shout her name, but it's not from my mouth. I fire two shots into the kitchen cupboards, which I can see. The door slams shut. No more light from the streetlamps. I hear metallic clanking in quick succession from the darkness. Two bullets whiz out across the deck. I hear Charlotte in hysterics from the front of the house and my counterpart yelling for her to get down. More streetlight slices through the darkness. I chance a look inside and see Reeves framed in the front door. I can't see his gun so I know it's raised and pointed forward at my counterpart and Charlotte. Not again.

I leap into the kitchen and open up, riddling his back with two quick shots. He jolts and then collapses in the doorway. Charlotte's still screaming. I don't know what my counterpart's doing. Would I go back to the car for my gun? Would I try to take her back into the car and drive away to safety? What if I tried to be the hero and rushed in to neutralize the intruders? I would have known that these Agency guys, or whatever they are, would be behind this.

One thing I *do* know is that I can't chance an encounter with myself. Not like this.

A door slams on the curb. Then another door. The Mustang's engine roars and the tires squeal as my counterpart whisks her away. Good man.

Confirm the kill.

I cross the living room, entering the foyer, Willard's Beretta trained squarely on Reeves' back. He's sprawled face down, legs in the foyer, upper body on the front porch. I eject the spent magazine, slide in a fresh one and put another bullet in the back of his head just in case.

Now what would I do? I almost want to jump for joy. Charlotte's still alive! I saved her twice tonight. I couldn't save her before, but now this… this is like some kind of second chance. Then that would mean that everything—or almost everything—that Armitage and Willard told me had at least one layer of truth to it.

Would I take her home? I guess I would. Where else would we go?

Suddenly I get a sinking feeling in my stomach.

Shit.

The cops.

Chapter 12: My Own Guardian Angel

This is so goddamn weird. Just an hour ago, I was sitting in this room staring at… at her. On the floor.

Now she's alive. Still. Don't really know how the hell I should feel about this. About her. About any of this. I keep glancing at the floor in the foyer, expecting to see her body lying there,.

I consider waiting for this dimension's Willard and Cartman to show up at the house after the inevitable report. No doubt my counterpart would have called them again after this, or Charlotte would have.

I decide against sticking around and start running up the street in the direction of my place.

Now I'm cutting through the park, taking the same route Charlotte takes to work. Willard's gun is tucked in the waistband of my pants. The night air is cold, nipping at my sore throat. This is nothing compared to running in hot sand under the scorching desert sun while weighed down by equipment and gear back east. By the time I get to Wells Avenue, I'm out of breath and my legs are weak and I'm perspired. Freddie's diner is just down the street, half a block away from the corner. The lights are on. A police cruiser is out front, unoccupied. I just know that Willard and Cartman are inside talking with Charlotte and my counterpart. Possibly Freddie too. Poor guy's probably worried enough to lose half the hair on his head.

I dash across the street and take cover behind a battered late-eighties Plymouth parked on the curb two doors up from the diner. Sticking to the walls, I advance, drawing my gun from my waistband. I reach the edge of the storefront windows and peek inside. Charlotte's the first one I look for and I find her sitting down on one of the counter stools looking frazzled with her head leaning against her arm, which is propped up on the counter. My counterpart is doing his best to console her on the next stool over, but, well, I was never too good at that sort of thing. He looks so damned awkward from where I'm sitting. Damn. Do I really look like that all the time?

Shake that thought. This isn't about you. Well, not quite.

I steal another grateful glance at Charlotte, relieved to see her okay. Willard and Cartman are speaking to them, standing with their backs facing the front windows. Freddie is standing with rigid shock a few paces away from my counterpart, wide eyes sticking to the cops like glue. He's hanging on their every word, taking in every answer to every question. It's too bad I can't hear them.

My counterpart and Charlotte exchange looks. At this point, she looks exhausted and fearful. My counterpart's wearing a mask of dread—I know damn-well it isn't for himself but for her. He knows everything I know except that Willard and Cartman are bastards that can't be trusted. They get up. The cops turn and head for the exit, and my counterpart follows them with Charlotte, gripping her hand.

No, no, no, no, *no*! You idiot! You're leading her to her death! "Shit!" I hiss under my breath as I delve into the shadowy niche between the diner and the barbershop, avoiding the cops' paranoid eyes as they open the back door for their unsuspecting pair of victims. I watch in horror—*real* fucking horror as they climb into the cruiser. Willard shuts the door behind my counterpart and gives Cartman a nod. Cartman acknowledges as he opens the front passenger-side door.

No.

I lurch out of the alley, take a bead on Willard, and open fire. Three shots slam into Willard. He crumples against a lamppost. I fire again, burning a red dot into his cheekbone as he slides to the sidewalk.

Cartman squats. I beeline between my Mustang parked between the cruiser and the Plymouth, and immediately nail Cartman to the inside of the passenger-side door with two consecutive shots in his throat. The window pops when his head smacks against it, leaving a red circle on its fractured surface. He teeters on his side in a heap. I can hear Charlotte screaming in the back seat and I look and see my counterpart trying to shield her with his body. His eyes are wide in disbelief and fear—*real* fear this time. And when he registers who he's looking at, he starts to look utterly confused.

"No!" Freddie bellows as he bursts out onto the sidewalk. "Michael! Michael!"

"I'm here, Fred. I'm here."

He stops in his tracks. He can see the couple in the back seat.

He can see me standing on the other side of the cruiser. He can't seem to wrap his head around it, either. I don't blame him. "What...?"

"Fred..."

"Who... who are you?"

I can hear Charlotte wailing in the back seat. At her wit's end, no doubt.

"Fred, there isn't any time."

"Who the hell *are* you?"

"We have to go, Fred. Get in the other side."

"What the hell is... is *this*? Oh, my God. You killed cops. Michael, why—?"

"I can explain, Fred, but we *have* to go, *now*!" I shout. I slap the roof of the cruiser. "Now, Fred, come on! Get behind the wheel!"

Freddie hesitates, unsure of what to do, how to process this.

"Goddamn it, Fred." I kick Cartman's body off the door and drag it further out onto the road. Then I circle round the front of the cruiser and grab him by the sleeve. "Please, we have to go. They're coming!"

"Who...?"

I have no hope in dragging him off the sidewalk. He's twice my size and three hundred pounds. "Fred, we need to get out of here! Trust me on this, okay? Trust me. Just trust me, we gotta go! I know how crazy this all looks, I know."

He's staring at Willard's corpse. "Yuh-you... you... you killed..."

"I know I did. It was them or us, Freddie. They already tried to kill me."

He glances down at the gun in my hand. I take note and tuck it into my pants with the safety on. He almost seems too dazed to move. "Let's go, Fred. Come on." I extend my hand. "Come with me, Fred."

He finally moves—unsteadily, looking pale, bewildered. I guide him around the cruiser, as he's not really fit to drive, and he climbs into the passenger seat. I run back around, double-checking Willard's body as I curve around the open door. Definitely dead this time, if the ugly exit wound in the back of his head is any indication.

I slide in behind the wheel and start the engine. Charlotte and my counterpart are looking at me in terror and disbelief. I turn my head and look back at them. "H-hi. Everything's going to be okay." Really? 'Hi'?

"Michael?" Charlotte doesn't know what to do or how to do it. Her tearful, frightened eyes constantly switch between my counterpart and I, trying to figure out the difference between us. My counterpart's gripping her tightly, protectively. I'm wish I knew how I'd react to seeing someone who looks just like me in his point of view. My circumstances in the backyard weren't as extreme or as sudden as this.

"What's going on?" Charlotte asks. "Who are you?"

"Whoever you are," my counterpart says before I have a chance to answer her, "whatever this all is…"

"Relax," I tell them as I take the cruiser off the curb, "I'm on your side. Now, this is gonna sound crazy, Michael—" feels weird to say that to myself "—but I think at this point we should level with her."

He's about to protest, the bastard. We make eye contact in the rearview mirror. He understands. Good.

"Michael? Michael, what is this? Who is he? Your twin? Do you have a brother or something? Why did he kill those cops? Oh, Jesus, God. He killed those cops!"

"Relax," I reply, as calmly as I can, "I know how insane this all is, Charlotte. I didn't believe it myself until half an hour ago. Jesus Christ, this *is* insane." I swerve to the right. The police car slews around the corner of the Love Zone and shoots down the highway.

"Careful, careful," Freddie gasps.

"Alright, you listening?" I glance at them in the rearview mirror. "Hey! You listening?"

They flood me with affirmatives.

"Good. Okay." I take a deep breath. "Armitage wasn't lying. All that talk of parallel universes a-and some kind of crazy agency trying to maintain it all in some weird orderly fashion that—that makes no sense whatsoever… it was all true! It wasn't bullshit! Jesus, I sound like a nutcase."

"What the hell are you talking about?" Charlotte demands. There's that spark again, a no-nonsense fire peeking out from a gentle, and right now terrified demeanour. "Parallel universes? That… that doesn't exist! It can't be real!"

"For every decision we make, a universe is automatically

created for each and every possible outcome," I explain. We pass the 'YOU ARE NOW LEAVING CHERRY SPRINGS' sign. "An hour, more two hours ago, Zona and Chow tried to run us off the cliff. I'm asking you, did they try to do that with the van?"

Charlotte seems to have been taken off guard by the question.

"Yes," my counterpart answers. He's starting to really believe.

"Same thing happened in my universe. I managed to trick them into driving off the cliff. As far as I know, neither one survived the fall. I took her home. Reeves was waiting for her in her house... he'd broken in through the screen door and... he killed her." I gaze into Charlotte's eyes in the rearview mirror again as she stares at me through the mesh barrier. It's still so strange, though relieving, to see that she's okay.

"I wound up here by accident," I continue. "Those cops, Cartman and Willard, they were in on it. They tried to kill me. We fell off a bridge and... and somehow, I wound up in your backyard, Charlotte. I can't explain it. I don't know what the hell—or *how* the hell it happened. It just... *happened*! And then I heard you two out front. Christ, I couldn't believe it. I still can't. I knew Reeves was in there waiting for you, so—"

"Wait," Charlotte intervened, "the shooting, that was you?"

"Yeah. I'm sorry I scared you, but it was that or let you die again. No way in hell was I going to let you die again." I glance at Freddie. He's staring right at me, trying to process what I'd just told them. "You okay, Fred?"

"It's... it's definitely you. You're him... but... you're not *him*..."

"Parallel universes." I shake my head slowly, watching the road. "I thought it was all bullshit until just an hour ago. Now my eyes are wide open."

"This is insane," Charlotte says. "Please, just let me out. I can't do this."

My counterpart reaches over to console her. She recoils. "Don't! Don't touch me!"

"None of us have any choice, Charlotte," I tell her. "I'm sorry. These people aren't going to stop."

"Why?! What do they want?"

"They want to kill us. Plain and simple."

"But why?"

"They think they're cleaning up the multiverse."

"Multiverse?"

"Uh, like…" I pause, straining to find a simple explanation for such a high concept in a short amount of time. "Like an existential cup full of straws, except the straws are each their own universe and we drew the short straw." I frown. For fuck's sake.

"That doesn't make *any* sense whatsoever!" She turns to my counterpart. "Are you in on this? What kind of bullshit prank is this? This isn't funny!"

"It's not. It's not a prank," he says.

"Where are we going?" she asks.

"I don't know," I answer. "Somewhere they won't find us for the time being."

"Pull over," she demands.

"I can't."

"Pull! Over!"

"I can't! You have to believe me; you're safer with either of us than by yourself anywhere else! They're trying to kill you. They're trying to kill *all* of us! They think if parallel versions of ourselves die than *we* have to die, to preserve some kind of fucked-up status quo or something. It doesn't make any sense, but goddamn it, they believe it, and that's the scary part. That's the part that we should all be taking seriously. I already watched you die once tonight and I am *not* doing it again!"

She falls silent, her mouth slightly agape. Maybe I was a little too harsh. Fact of the matter is, I really wouldn't be able to handle seeing her die again. A bright soul like her should be allowed to shine on for years to come. No way in hell I'm going to let some weirdly misplaced organization put a premature end to her light.

I won't let them take her from me.

Chapter 13: Night-Time Encounter

I chance a drive to the old abandoned warehouse where I'd shot Armitage. Can't chance a loop back into town for the Mustang. I remember seeing an Impala parked there and wonder if it's still in the same spot now that its owner has been dead for several hours.

"Where are we going?" Charlotte asks, her voice wavering.

"Ditching this car," I answer truthfully as I follow the dirt path up to the side of the old warehouse. "We can't drive a stolen cop car on the highway." Keeping my eyes sharp for any figures hiding in the shadows, I slowly take the turn into the rear lot. I glance over at Freddie and then look back at my counterpart. "Watch the corn."

My counterpart understands. Freddie looks perplexed. "For suspicious activity," I elaborate for him. He nods with understanding.

The Impala's still there. A four-door sedan, '81 or '85. Hard to tell. The year doesn't matter. It'll do.

The lot and the warehouse and the cornfields are shrouded in darkness. The stars seem to have dimmed in the night sky. There could be assailants everywhere for all I know, watching us, waiting for the word of a superior to take us all out.

"I'll be right back." Gripping Willard's pistol, I step out of the cruiser and quickly check inside the warehouse. It's almost pitch-black in there, but I can smell the unmistakable stench of death pervading the air. The droning of flies accompanies the smell. Yeah. The bodies haven't been moved. I run back to the car and search the glove compartment and find a small but powerful flashlight, return to the warehouse, and shine its beam inside. The white light plays over the corpses of Hunter and Armitage lying in stale pools of their own blood, bloated by the heat and pale as snow. It's an eerie sight, and the smell and the flies make it worse. I scan the area, shining the beam wherever my eyes and my gun's sights go. They fall upon a table where a small object shines in the light. Upon further investigation, I find what I'm looking for: keys. I snatch them up and turn toward the exit—the gun case glints dully in the light, housing a couple of M4 carbines and a bolt-action scoped rifle. Upon closer inspection I determine that the rifle is a Savage

Arms 25 Walking Varminter, matte black finish, with detachable box magazines loaded with .204 Ruger rounds in the second drawer below the cabinet. Could be useful. I hurry out of the warehouse into the open air with the keys.

The cornfield surrounds us. It's alive with the cacophonic chirping of crickets and the occasional rustling noises whenever a soft breeze picks up. Freddie, Charlotte, and my counterpart are still in the cruiser, watching me test the keys on the Impala's driver-side door. I get it open and then pop the trunk; run back inside to retrieve the rifles and several box mags of ammunition for each and drop them into the trunk and shut the lid. Then I hurry over to the cruiser, opening the rear door for Charlotte and my counterpart to get out. "Let's go. Fred, you too."

My counterpart steps out, looking apprehensively at me and the warehouse. I can read his expression perfectly—no, I don't want Charlotte to see what's in there, either, and she won't.

Freddie rises on the other side of the cruiser, looking around at the endless rows of shadowy cornstalks. He turns his head and watches me interact with my counterpart without so much as a word between us, and says, "It's strange."

My counterpart follows my stare and looks at Freddie.

Freddie goes on, "This is something I never thought… was even *possible*. But there are *two* of you. I'm seein' it with my own eyes and I don't believe it."

"It's a lot," I agree, "I'm trying to—"

As soon as Charlotte gets out of the car, she bolts for the cornfield. No hesitation. She's a survivor, alright.

"Charlotte!" I cry out after her and my counterpart and I give chase. "Charlotte, wait!"

She runs as fast as her legs can take her, galloping desperately for whatever sanctuary she supposes the cornstalks will provide from this weirdness. My counterpart catches up to her and throws his arms around her and she screams, struggling in his arms. She throws her head back and shrieks in terror. "NO! NOOO! LET ME GO! LET ME GO!" She flails wildly, her elbows knocking against the side of my counterpart's head, but he perseveres.

I run around to face her, the gun tucked back in my pants, my palms showing. "Charlotte. Charlotte. Calm down."

"NO! Let me go! You can't take me like this! I can't do this! I can't!" She breaks down into a sob, sagging in my counterpart's arms. It kills me to see her like this. I can't blame her. How could I? "I don't know what's going on anymore," she whimpers.

"I know, Charlotte. I know. It… it's a complicated thing. I don't know much more than you do. But the important thing is to stay calm, okay? That's how we survive—"

Something crackles in the direction of the cornstalks. It's so loud that for a split second I think it's distant thunder. Every muscle in my body goes rigid. A cold claw grazes down my spine as I turn the flashlight's beam on the stalks and search them. A sharp snapping sound cuts through the air. The crickets' lively choir falls silent. Something's moving in there. We all hear another snapping of twigs in there, followed by rustling noses. I see the tops of a couple stalks swaying a few rows back. I draw the gun again and hold it forward. I whisper urgently to Charlotte and my counterpart, "Get in the car."

By now my counterpart has released Charlotte, who stands fearfully between us, big blue eyes watching the stalks intensely. I ask her, "Can you drive?" When I get no immediate response, I reach out and touch her shoulder gently. Her head jerks in my direction as if I've startled her. I repeat my question.

"No," she says.

I toss my counterpart the keys. "Go. Take her. Now."

The other Michael doesn't waste any time. He takes Charlotte's hand and runs to the Impala while I watch the stalks move as whatever's in there comes closer. I gradually back-step toward the Impale. I hear my counterpart urge Freddie into the car. I hear the engine turn over once before starting. The headlights flash on, dousing higher beams on the stalks, illuminating a third of the rear wall of corn bordering the lot, revealing that more of them are moving. There's more than one. Ten or more.

I turn and start for the Impala when a figure standing in my peripherals locks my legs in mid-step. I whirl, pistol rising—

"Not another inch." Reeves has the drop on me with a suppressed pistol, standing just outside of the Impala's high beams, the light casting deep, angry shadows across his front. "I'm getting tired of chasing you across time and space, Michael. I'd hoped to prevent another pursuit over here. Seems my significant other's home visit wasn't as fortuitous as—"

The cornfields roar and the stalks spit tongues of flame into the lot. My instincts kick into high gear as booming gunfire pounds my eardrums and I hunch over and zigzag toward the Impala's passenger side. My counterpart pushes it forward and swerves around me, providing cover. Freddie's screaming my name from the front passenger seat. Charlotte's wailing in the back.

Reeves pirouettes in front of the Impala as dirt geysers erupt around him. Pieces of him fly off, vanishing in a swirling dust cloud. Nothing hit the car, just him, precise and merciless. He hits the dirt and the gunfire stops.

I throw open the rear door and hurl myself into the back and scream, "DRIVE!"

My counterpart floors the gas. The Impala blasts through the dirt, fishtailing around Reeves' fallen form. Charlotte grabs hold of me, fingers digging into my shoulders, and I wrap my arms around her in a hasty attempt to comfort her, whatever good it may do. By pure chance my eyes flick up and see a human-shaped blur standing in front of the stalks. It appears to have red and blue skin. The fading brightness of the Impala's headlights glinting inhumanly in the figure's eyes as it watches us leave. I hold Charlotte close to my chest, feeling her tremble violently in my embrace, but my eyes are busy trying to focus on the figure in our rear window now, and just before we reach the warehouse corner, I see more of them emerging from the field, disappearing as the Impala slews around the corner and bolts straight for the highway.

After about an hour's drive, my counterpart turns off the highway into a parking lot paved with weathered slabs of cement that time and constant use have separated. The two-storey motel is a shadow of its glory days; paint peeling, rails along the wraparound balcony on the second floor rusted brown, and only half the letters on the neon sign towering over the roadside ditch working. A generic motel in desperate need of maintenance. The kind of place I think would fuel the imagination of any horror fan who found themselves looking for a cheap place to sleep during their travels.

The other Michael drives around the L-shaped building to the rear wing, out of the desk clerk's line of sight in the check-in office, and turns off the engine. By now, Charlotte's calmer, fighting fatigue from an extremely taxing—to say the least—day. I'm stroking her hair, which seems to help. "I'm sorry," I whisper in her ear.

Her body presses against me. She breathes deeply, then

exhales slowly, still trembling. "It's okay. Well," she quickly corrects herself, "It's *not*, but… you," she jabs her forefinger into my chest, "you have some explaining to do, mister."

I can't help but chuckle. "Yes, ma'am."

Freddie gets us two rooms, each with two double beds, and suggests we clear things up before we decide on who sleeps in which room.

Once Freddie registers our rooms (both on ground level, in D wing—rear—facing a field of tall grass) and gets our keys, he leads us to one of the rooms and starts boiling water in the electric kettle provided on a writing table beside the television set. As he lines double-layered paper cups in a straight line on the table, he says, "Now, Michael, i-if you could shed some light on this whole insane situation, that'd be appreciated."

"I don't even know where to start," I admit.

"Storytellers usually start at the beginning." He turns to face me, glancing at the second Michael, who's sitting in a chair by the window. He's just drawn the curtains. "When did this all start?" As he speaks, his voice gets louder, "You're barely in town, not even a full week, and then you go from telling me you've got a date to tellin' me someone tried to kill you and Charlotte here to *shooting a pair of cops in the street in front of my diner*! In the same day!"

"Freddie—"

"Were you involved in something shady before you got into town? D-did someone follow you from the Middle East? Yeah. Are there a bunch of Afghan terrorists hell-bent on revenge or something? Or maybe if we wanna get *real creative*, it's your old unit that feels you betrayed them? Or what? What the hell happened?"

I look at Charlotte. She's sitting on the edge of the double bed closest to the bathroom, looking tired and frazzled.

"Don't look at her," Freddie chides me, "she's not the reason we're in the mess."

I snap at him, "Bullshit."

"How?"

"They were after *her* to start!"

Charlotte looks up at me, eyebrows furrowed in confusion. "Me?!"

"How would you even know that?"

My counterpart butts in, "The guys who came in this morning. Remember them? Something about them felt very off, especially when you told me they were new and they confirmed it."

"So? They were new. They delivered food. So what?"

"So I followed them," I tell him.

"What he said," my counterpart interjects, "I also followed them to that warehouse we just left."

"You were there earlier?"

"Yes."

"So you know who shot at us and killed that guy?"

"No."

Freddie pulls a cheap office chair out from under the table and sits in it. The chair squeaks and groans from the strain his weight puts on it. He sighs heavily. "Who was that guy? He had a gun on you."

"His name was Reeves. He was part of an organization that can—apparently—cross over into parallel universes. He was the only one I missed in my universe, but I rectified that the second time around. But I guess the other one followed me over here." I pause, studying the looks on the faces of Freddie and Charlotte. "I know how crazy it sounds."

"Do you?" she asks.

"Yes. I'm telling you, they were crazy. They said... they said... what did they say... oh, yeah: they said Charlotte died, but in a different reality, and they were cleaning up all the other realities by killing all the other parallel versions of her, or something close to that effect. And they wanted to do the same to me. They said I shot myself." I scoff. "Obviously I didn't. I wouldn't be standing right here if I did."

"Okay, so how did you find that out?"

"Right. Okay. So I followed the delivery guys to that warehouse and there were a few others there with them. Looked like radical militants or something. I don't know."

"So you *are* being chased by terrorists," Freddie says, adding a sarcastic, "That's some great news right there."

"I don't know them. They're not Middle-Eastern, anyway."

"But they *are* terrorists?"

"If they are, they're not spiritual ones. Didn't seem to have any political leanings. They just talked about this multiverse bullshit."

My counterpart says, "The leader's name is Armitage. *Was* Armitage. I thought they were part of some weird cult. I uh... I overheard them talking about it while I was eavesdropping in on their conversation."

My counterpart and I exchange looks. Stretching the truth a bit there. I guess when I think about it, I wouldn't want to straight-up tell my date and my father figure that I executed a man in cold blood. The thought puts a knot in my stomach regardless. Christ, that's going to eat at me for a while. But do they really need to know that?

Charlotte asks, "Was this before or after you asked me out?"

Michael and I answer in perfect sync: "Before."

She considers us both, pondering our answer. "I see..."

Freddie's eyebrows reach his hairline. "*You* asked her out?"

"Yes," I tell him, and he almost smiles, but before he can say anything else, I continue my story: "I got back into town as fast as I could. I didn't want to let her out of my sight. I couldn't find any of them, but I knew they were in town, so I wanted to get her out of town, you know, without resorting to kidnapping.

"It's lucky I managed to bring myself to ask you on a date," I say directly to her.

She manages a half-smile. "See, now that just makes me think you're switching up the timeline so that it sounds like you asked me *before* you knew my life was in danger." Making light out of a life-or-death situation. Nice. I can't help but appreciate the fact that her sense of humour is coming back now that the initial shock is wearing off.

"I'm telling the only truth there is," I assure her, giving her a weak smile. "I didn't want you to get hurt. Or killed."

"Well... I can appreciate that now. I think."

"What about the cops?" Freddie asks.

"They were in on it. They were going to take you—" I point at the other Michael, then at Charlotte "—and you, to a bridge above a river way up in the boonies and shoot you both in the head."

"They said they were gonna take our statements at the station," Charlotte says.

"Yeah," I reply, "I fell for that, too. About half an hour after Reeves killed you. He didn't even wait for me to drive away when I dropped you off at your house."

She stares at me in shock.

"So that was you?" my counterpart asks, "at the house? The shooting?"

"Yeah. I was shooting at him."

"How did you get here?"

"What do you mean? 'Here,' like, in *this* universe?"

Michael nods.

I try my best to remember all the details concerning my fight with Cartman and Willard on the bridge. Everything happened so fast that it's all starting to blur. Too much shit has happened today. "Uh... I... I remember falling off the bridge, but instead of water, I hit grass, and I looked up and found myself standing in the backyard."

I can tell the other Michael is connecting my description of my transfer to the suicide attempt we'd made before this whole mess even started.

Freddie scratches his head. "This is crazy. This is nuts. You tryin' to tell me that there's a portal or something to a parallel dimension at the quarry? It was the quarry, right? The one by the old hiking trails?"

"Yeah. I told you, I know how crazy this all sounds."

"Michael, if I wasn't seeing two of you right now I'd be calling somebody." Freddie rubs his eyes. "God knows who I'd call about something like *this*..."

Charlotte stands up and curls her arms around me, hugs me warmly. "I'm sorry about your Charlotte, Michael. I... I don't know how else to say it. Im sorry."

My chest tightens. My heart feels like it's been stabbed by a corkscrew and twisted apart. I feel my eyes strain as the tears start to come. I take her into my arms again, blinking furiously. She smells as wonderful now as she did a few hours ago, when she was still alive. She feels so real. So alive. So warm. It feels cruel how this has turned out, with Charlotte apologizing to me for failing to protect her from an enemy that none of us can possibly hope to understand. The privilege to be able to run my fingers through her hair again is enough to throw me over the edge. I break down and start to cry. Her hold on me grows tighter, nurturing me.

Chapter 14: The Strangers

It takes me a while to calm down. Endless waves of emotion seemed to be crashing over me that I couldn't stop crying. Charlotte didn't let go that entire time, and for that, I'm grateful for her.

The electric kettle clicks.

Freddie asks softly, "Coffee or tea, anyone?"

"Tea, please, Freddie," Charlotte says appreciatively.

My counterpart and I say, "Coffee."

Freddie looks at both of us. "Two sugar, one cream, right?"

We nod.

"Charlotte, how do you like your tea?"

"As is, thanks."

He prepares our drinks and distributes them among us, then pours himself a tea and adds milk from the mini-fridge. We all sip our drinks in silence, each of us pondering our situation. I know I am. Right now, I'm trying to figure out who those people in the cornfield were, and why they shot Reeves instead of me. It doesn't make sense. Is there another organization besides the 'Agency' involved in this weird multiverse affair? And if so, why the hell would they save us?

"Well, boys," Charlotte says, her voice still trembling, but much stronger than it was earlier, "it's been a crazy day, to say the least. I'm uh... I'm gonna have a cigarette, and then I'm going to bed. Hopefully I'll get some sleep. I kinda doubt I will, but it's worth a shot, right?"

A thought crosses my mind. "Is there anyone you can call? Family? Friends?"

She gives me a sad little smile. "No one who'd care. And if they did, they live too far way to be of any help. I guess I have my grandma in Detroit, but, well, she's eighty and senile. Not much help, ya know?"

It hits me like a punch in the throat. "Oh... I-I'm sorry."

Her hand caresses my arm with half-hearted playfulness. "Don't be. It's fine."

My counterpart asks, "So who sleeps where?"

Freddie asks him, "Any ideas? I got us two rooms just in

case."

I probably have the same idea my counterpart does. I ask him, "Do you have your gun?"

He shrugs, eyes flicking briefly toward Charlotte looking for a reaction on her face. I don't look at her. "It's in the Mustang," he answers. The regret in his voice is plain as day. Probably kicking himself now.

"So we only have one gun between the four of us. Charlotte? Are you comfortable with me staying in here with you? I-I won't— I'm not going to sleep. I'll be by the window there, keeping watch."

She smiles at my sudden awkwardness. "It's fine."

"Okay," I say with newfound confidence, "it would be easier to keep track of all four of us if we stay in the same room." I gesture toward Charlotte and Freddie. "Since you two are non-combatants, it would make sense if both of you got some sleep while... while the other me and I take turns on lookout duty. Whichever one's on lookout gets the gun."

"Agreed," my counterpart says.

"That sound good to you guys?"

Freddie thinks for a moment. "Where are you gonna sleep while the other you is on lookout?"

"The floor."

"Take the bed. *I'll* sleep on the floor, kid."

"Not with *your* back problem, old man," I reply curtly. "You're sleeping on one of the beds. Charlotte—"

"Hell," she says, "I'm not a Disney princess. I don't need pampering. I'll sleep in the bathtub if it makes you feel better. Just knock before any of you go to the bathroom so that I can pull the curtain."

My counterpart and I chortle at her joke. "Would that make you feel safer?"

"A little, yeah," she admits.

While Charlotte smokes outside the door, I strip the bed closest to the window and pad the bottom of the bathtub with the sheets and the comforter. At the same time, my counterpart runs to the next room over and brings the mattress cover, sheets, and two pillows from one of its beds, and throws them over the bed I just stripped. It's a little warm, so I switch on the A/C in the window. My counterpart and I both ask Charlotte separately if she's comfortable, if she needs anything else, the works, and she refuses any further help.

"It's okay," she says to me for the second time, her patience wearing a little thin. Even now, she's smiling knowingly. "Thank you for your concern."

"Okay. If you need anything—"

"I got it. Close the door, hon."

I wish her good night and shut the bathroom door. As I'm passing the beds to the front, I notice Freddie is already sprawled on the bed closest to the bathroom, snoring deeply. I envy him for that.

My counterpart's sitting by the window. "I'll take first watch."

"Three hours, then we switch."

"Deal."

I hand him the gun, set the extra mags on the table, lie down on the unoccupied bed, and switch off the light. Lying on my side, I close my eyes, doubting I'll ever get to sleep after a day like today.

My doubts are apparently unfounded. I dream of my first tour in Afghanistan. I was famously separated and left behind in the Arghistan desert. I don't know how it happened, except that it was my own fault. Clumsiness got the better of me. I fell and knocked myself out, or I overslept, or *something*. I remember looking up at the sky and seeing a black comet. It was strange, so I stared at it. The black comet grew in size, its otherworldly cobalt aura leaving a glowing trail streaking across the sky. Then I realized it was coming straight at me...

At this point, I can't remember how it happened, only that the 101st went to Takht-e-pol without me. I must have overslept. In the open desert? Someone would've woken me, wouldn't they? Heat stroke? I don't know. What I did know at the time was that I was a lone stranger in a strange land. It was terrifying, thinking that Taliban forces could be waiting behind every dune, watching me from every ditch I walked by. In my dream, the white sands are so bright and over-exposed that my eyes can't it, nor can they find the convoy's tracks; and the sky is a vast, crimson vortex looming above me. Strange eldritch shadows swirl around in it like schools of fish, their groans like distorted, electronic thunder rumbling all around me. Feels like an oven. I'm sweating profusely in my IBA. Feels like I'm melting in it. Head getting light. Mouth dry; I can feel my tongue scaling and cracking.

Then Yusef appears like some sort of guardian angel. A Muslim drifter sporting Ray-Ban sunglasses and a sharp goatee, with a casual air about him. His quilted scarf protects his head from the sun's merciless rays. "You are far from home, my American friend," he says to me.

"I know." Fearing him to be an enemy—I'm ashamed to say that back then I thought they all looked the same—I ask him, "Where are you from?"

"Nowhere in particular anymore," he says. "I was Mujahedeen. But that was a very long time ago. Now, I travel."

"Travel? You're not with anyone?"

He grins at me. It's hard to tell what he's thinking behind those Ray-Bans. "Only I walk alone, but I am never truly alone. Allah is with me, always. You lost?"

"Yeah," I admit with severe embarrassment. "Don't know what happened. I woke up and my company was gone."

"Who are you with?"

"101st Airborne Division."

"Ah," he says, pointing in a direction that seems entirely random. "They went that way. To Takht-e-pol."

"How do you know that?"

"That is my gift. I know things." He shrugs. "The desert is treacherous. Let me take you."

"That won't be necessary."

"Why not? What have you to lose? Except your life, of course. And that can easily be avoided—with me." His grin widens. His white teeth shine brilliantly in the sun.

I wake up to the bedside lamp shining in my eyes and my counterpart shaking the bed and whispering harshly at me, "Someone's out there! Wake up, goddamn it."

I sit bolt upright and switch off the lamp as my counterpart rushes back to the window and peeks outside through the curtains. "Christ, they've doubled!"

"What do you mean, 'doubled'?" I roll out of bed and lumber to the window. Peering through the space between the curtains, I look out at the parking lot and see a row of men and women in IBAs and fluorescent red and blue face paint standing in front of the grassy field. They look like demented versions of the US Marine Corps. Just standing there, watching us. "Jesus Christ," I gasp. I make note of their weapons—they're even *armed* like the Marines! M4 carbines, M16s, a couple M249 SAWs. They look ready to stage a full-scale war, and equipped well enough to win it. Two of them, a man and a woman, turn their weapons over to their closest companions before advancing across the lot. The closer they come, the more oddly familiar they both are. They stop about ten feet away from the window, raise their arms, and rotate slowly. When they're facing us again, the man continues to the door, leaving the woman behind in the open. Even with the bright, ethereal face paint, it's difficult to make out any defining features. Then he disappears from view. We hear his boots scuff the ground in front of our door.

He knocks. Casual, quiet enough as to not disturb any neighbours we might have. It doesn't even wake Freddie, whose snoring sounds like a chainsaw sputtering between life and death.

I peer cautiously through the blinds. The woman is still standing there with her legs spread apart, arms clasped behind her straightened back, chin tipped high.

The man knocks again. My counterpart and I squat down. I instruct him to go wake Freddie and Charlotte and tell them to stay in the bathroom, and to give me the gun so I can handle this. Without question, he obeys, handing me the gun and then moving around the first double bed, keeping low enough that he may as well be crawling on all fours. He shakes Freddie awake and whispers for him to head into the bathroom with him. Freddie groans as his back problems add strain to his efforts to sit up and slide over to the foot of the bed. My counterpart can do little to help him. Eventually he's able to nudge him to the bathroom door, and knocks on it twice. Charlotte answers, but I don't see her answer. I can hear them whispering back and forth with unmistakeable urgency and alarm, and then Freddie is allowed into the bathroom with my counterpart close behind. My counterpart hesitates, looking at me. I wave my hand, gesturing for him to go in with them. He does.

The visitor's rhythm is slower this time, his fist pounding against the door three times every five seconds.

I slide along the wall beside the door, about to call out a warning to leave, or I'll shoot, when the visitor speaks first: "I know you're awake, Michael. You're against the wall, beside the door as I speak."

My blood turns to ice. I can feel an uneasy sensation tingling up to the nape of my neck. I try my best to mask my nervousness as

I reply, "Then you know that I'm armed."

"Affirmative."

"Who are you?"

"You don't recognize me? The others did."

"I'm really not in the mood for games today."

"Fair enough. I wasn't, either. Well, I already know you won't let me in, so I'll do the talking: I'm you. About three years from the future. Sort of. It's complicated. My Charlotte died in 2002. What's happening to you now, I've already experienced almost three years ago exactly—in my time."

"You telling me about time travel now?"

"No, not time travel. Just a delay. The Agency can't try to take us all out at once, so they've been working their way across the multiverse, chasing us out of our own respective timelines, no matter how radically different they are. I'm about four hundred thousand realities away from home." His voice sounds like mine, without a shadow of a doubt, but there's something about him that sounds... lifeless. Empty. Not like the fearful determination of my immediate counterpart. This one has been places I probably can't even imagine—but will probably experience in some form or another—he certainly sounds like it.

"I've done you a courtesy by bringing the old lady up from town. We've added supplies for your journey should you decide not to come to base with us. Whatever you do, if you get stopped, don't let any cops search the trunk."

"Supplies?"

"Everything I know you'll need."

"What makes you think I'll come with you?"

"I'm going to leave the address in special code in your glovebox. You'll either come now or you'll come later. If you're one of the smart ones, you'll come now. If you're a little daft, shaken up from today's events, but decide to come to base later in the day, you won't be a complete waste of time. Two days is too late. I've seen every possible outcome a thousand times over. Trust me. You'll want to pick one of the first two options."

"And if I pick the third?"

"Then you may as well kiss the Charlotte you have in there with you goodbye right now."

I don't reply. My visitor pauses, letting it sink in. "They'll be here around 0800 hours. I suggest you move out at 0700 at the latest." His feet scrape the walkway again, and I rush to the window to watch him walk toward the woman standing in the lot. He nods to her. She flashes me a smile that's given a ghastly quality under all that paint, and gives me a friendly little flourishing wave, telling me without speaking a single word that it's a Charlotte he's become closely associated with. She spins on her heel and follows him, the other counterparts disappearing into the growth outside of the lot's perimeter, uncanny wraiths in the night. The pair follow suit.

I open the gap in the curtains a little wider and search for the Mustang. For a minute, maybe three, I don't see anything, but then I hear it—the familiar purr of the engine as the Mustang's beams streak across the cracked pavement before sweeping around and shining directly in my eyes, blinding me momentarily as the Mustang is parked next to the Impala. The engine cuts out. Another counterpart rises from behind the wheel, shuts the door, and crouches, slipping my keys behind the tire. Then he slips away into the brush to join his companions.

I wait for ten minutes, watching the grass for any signs of movement in the dark. I decide they would know I'd wait that long, and so I wait another five until I realize that it wouldn't matter how long I waited, different versions of me probably tried the same shit. I would just have to chance it.

First things first.

I inform the others of my encounter with yet another version of myself, who appeared to be a leader of some kind of militia made up of parallel versions of myself and Charlotte; and that they left my Mustang here with 'supplies'. I also told them about the invitation to their base, that we should leave at seven, and that he said if we don't go to their base, Charlotte will die in two days—or so he says. Nothing is left out.

"Jesus," Charlotte breathes.

Freddie agrees. "The young lady couldn't have said it any better. What the hell are we gonna do?"

"What *can* we do? It's not like we have many options as it is," I say. "The Agency will be here at 0800. It's four now. That doesn't give us a whole lot of time. He told me he left a coded message in the glovebox pertaining to the location of the base."

"And you think we should go there?" Charlotte asks.

"It seems like the safest option. Why would I lie to myself? They didn't act hostile. They even made a show that they were unarmed before they came up to the door."

"It still doesn't feel right," she says.

"Do you trust me?" I ask her.

She almost smiles. "You're asking me that after everything that's happened?"

My heart sinks a little. "Fair enough."

Now she *does* smile. "Yes, I trust you." She playfully punches my arm. "You're the first man who's actually gone out of his way to save my life. That I know of. I can't think of anyone else who can travel to another dimension."

I'm having a hard time reading her tone. "I can't tell if you're joking or not."

She raises herself on her tiptoes and plants a soft kiss on my cheek. "How about now?"

I stare at her. I can feel my counterpart watching us, trying to hide his conflicted feelings about this. She seems to notice him as well, because she turns to him and asks, "You want one, too? Here." She kisses his cheek. "Mwah. Jeez, I'm gonna have to pick one and stick with him, aren't I?"

I point at him. "He's the original in this universe." I had my chance...

"Yeah, I suppose that makes sense." She locks arms with my counterpart. "Well, stranger, what now?"

The three of us look at Freddie's blank expression. "This is all too weird," he says.

"Agreed," my counterpart and I reply in unison.

"Yesterday you were telling me you had a date. Suddenly you're shooting cops in the street, you're from a parallel universe, and there's a whole army of you?" Freddie practically runs to the electric kettle. "I need caffeine."

"I'm sorry, Freddie. I hate that I involved you, alright? I just didn't know what else to do. I didn't know what they'd do to you if I hadn't taken you along."

"I'm not angry, Michael," he assures me. "Excuse me." He comes through with the kettle, fills it in the bathroom sink, and then returns to plug it in on the table and wait. He sets his hands flat on the table and sighs. "This is all so goddamn overwhelming."

"I know."

"It seems hopeless no matter what we do. We're dealing with a vast multiverse with endless possibilities, right?"

"Right."

"So how the hell do we get out of this situation?"

"I can't answer that."

"Had a feelin' you'd say that."

Charlotte couldn't keep herself from yawning.

I ask her, "Do you want to lie down? We still have a few more hours before we need to leave."

"I don't think I'll be able to sleep now," she says. "Aren't we compromised already? I mean, if alternate versions of you found us, don't you think the Agency would've gotten wise to it eventually? If this has been going on for as long as our visitor said it has been, then…" she trails off.

Michael and I exchange looks. "Good point."

"That *is* a good point." Freddie switches off the electric kettle and starts putting it away. "That is a *very* good point. We should leave. Now. I'd like to go."

My counterpart and I look at Charlotte and Freddie. Both of them clearly want to leave now. "Alright. Guess it's settled." Pausing, a thought crosses my mind. They've impressed me. "You guys are taking this tremendously well."

Freddie says nothing. Charlotte shrugs. "I've had worse dates."

Chuckling, I turn and cross the room, start unlocking the door. "Gun, please. I'm gonna make sure it's safe first."

Michael returns my pistol to my hand. I open the door and peek out, glancing both ways down the walkway. Only two other cars besides the Impala and the Mustang are parked in front of rooms with their curtains drawn, with three parking spots between them. Not a soul in sight. The grass isn't disturbed. I hear nothing but crickets.

I walk out and take my keys from under the Mustang when a thought occurs. I lower myself on my hands and knees and look under the car, searching its underbelly for anything that looks like an explosive device. It's clean. I stand back up, unlock the driver side door, open it. Nothing. I go around and check out the damage made by the Agency van: the taillights were knocked out and the spoiler was heavily warped. The hatchback's panel has a long crack in it, and through the tinted glass I could see a black tarp draped over an abstract object behind the back seats. I lift open the hatchback, then I throw the tarp over the seats and gape at what I see.

Guns. Lots of guns. Cases of ammunition line the back of the seats. Four M4 carbine rifles, a Mossberg 500 pump-action shotgun, six M9 pistols, two sheathed Ka-Bar fighting knives, and a Milkor MGL revolver-type grenade launcher are piled between cases of ammunition that line the back of the seats and a German-made grenade box set on an angle to accommodate the hatchback. I open the grenade box and find ten M67 fragmentation grenades. I gawk at the arsenal—

Charlotte's voice startles me: "Michael?"

Quickly, I close the grenade box, pull the tarp back down, and close the hatchback.

Chapter 15: Driving Miss Denver

"Clear," I call out, signaling for the others to come out. Freddie's the last one to leave and shuts the door behind him.

"Who's driving?" Charlotte asks.

My counterpart looks at me, volunteering without saying anything. I answer: "I got some sleep, so I'll drive for a while." My counterpart nods, understanding. Everyone piles into the car, my counterpart and Freddie squeezed in the rear, Charlotte up front with me. I feel relief when we get off the parking lot and onto the highway, leaving the Impala behind. After five minutes, Freddie's snoring again. I can feel his right foot twitching occasionally under my seat. Half an hour, my counterpart's out, his head hanging forward, chin digging into his chest. I glance toward Charlotte. She's still awake. Looks at me and smiles bravely. I can see from her eyes that she has faith in me. I hope I don't let her down.

I can't take this silence, though. "So," I begin, searching for something to say. After a few seconds, I ask stupidly, "How are you?"

She chortles.

"Sorry."

"No, no. I'm okay. Er... guess that's a strange thing to say for someone who's the target of some weird conspiracy."

"Yeah, I know how that feels."

She chuckles. "I know you do. You're the only one who would understand that, I'm sure."

"You know... I never got your last name."

"I never gave it," she says, "but it's Denver."

"Charlotte Denver." I smile. "I like it."

"You never told me yours."

"Colorado."

She searches my face. "You're joking."

I grin. "Yes, ma'am."

She giggles and slaps my arm. "What's your *real* last name, jerk?"

"Hammond."

"Michael Hammond. It's nice."

"It doesn't sound as nice as 'Charlotte Denver'."

"Oh, please. It's not *that* great."

"It is, though," I insist, "it has a nice ring to it."

"Does it?"

"It does."

"Hm." She grunts.

We grow silent, staring forward at the highway. It stretches far beyond the Mustang's high beams into an abyssal darkness. The sky seems darker than it was before, the stars' speckled light fading into the obscurity of space's vastness.

"Hey," she says.

I glance at her. She seems apprehensive; searching for the right way to word whatever's on her mind. "I'm sorry if this is too personal, but... what happened in your reality?"

"What do you mean?"

"On that hill. The picnic spot."

My heart nearly jumps into my throat. I feel my legs turn to jelly; I have to strain to keep my foot on the gas. Why am I so nervous? "Uh... we uh... you know, we took in the view. H-Herman looks nice that time of night, so I thought you'd like it."

"I did." She's giving me an expectant look, telling me to go on.

"And... and..."

"Don't be shy, Michael. Tell me everything."

I breathe deeply. "We got... intimate."

She seems to perk up at this. "Oh, good."

"'Good'?"

"I'm glad that part stayed the same."

My heart races. I glance at my counterpart in the rearview mirror. He's still asleep. I hope.

She reaches out and touches my shoulder. "It was a wonderful night, Michael. Tell you the truth, I haven't had this much fun in years."

I give her a weird look. "People are trying to kill you."

She laughs before quickly slapping her hand over her mouth and looking behind her. When she sees that she hasn't woken anyone, she gives me a mischievous smirk. She whispers, "I know. Crazy, isn't it?"

"I wouldn't call you crazy for it..."

"It's probably my least favourite part. Well, that, and the lack of sleep. But you know… this is probably one of the best nights of my life."

"Why?"

"Because of you."

"Why me? I didn't do anything. Hell, I might even be the reason you're in this mess."

"You said it yourself. I died. You tried to protect me. It exploded into this big ol'… clusterfuck of a mess that I can barely make sense of. It's really mind-blowing. So you're from *another* reality. It's insane. I wouldn't believe it if I didn't see it. Your experiences with me are the same, but it wasn't with me at the same time."

"No," I say, unable to hide my sadness, "not quite with you."

"What do you…?" It seems to click, because her eyes dim and her voice goes quiet. "Oh… right. I'm sorry."

"Don't be. I'm having a hard time wrapping my head around it, too."

"Look on the bright side," she says. "You still have me."

"*He* does, I don't."

"You're the same person."

"I'm a different *version* of the same person."

"Is there really much of a difference?"

"Yes. We both think separately. We both have our own individual thoughts and feelings. I don't think the other me back there would appreciate it if I did anything with you. I… I had my chance. I let you down the minute I let you walk up those steps. I lost you once already. I won't be doing it again. I'm just here to help. That's all. Once this is all over, and you guys are safe, I'll go elsewhere and leave you be with him. Hopefully it works out… I really like you. I… you make the world a brighter place, somehow. I want it to seem that way for you, too, when you're with m—with him."

It's hard to read the expression on her face. She looks disappointed and sympathetic at the same time, but there's something else there… something I can't make out. "You're too hard on yourself, Michael."

I don't say anything.

"There was nothing you could do. What matters—what I appreciate—is that you didn't give up on me. You know, you're the first guy who hasn't." She chuckles, shaking her head. "One guy left me because I wouldn't have sex with him. Another one left me because he didn't think I should be playing the guitar."

"You play the guitar?"

"Yes. Been playing it since I was seven. I wanted to be a rock star goddess or something." She chuckles softly, shaking her head. "I had this dream to move to the big city, buy an electric, start a band…"

"What happened?"

"I quit high school and took a job as a bartender."

"Oh."

"I sell drawings on the side sometimes. Made a few bucks with commissions. Not exactly steady, but I mean, I was able to get that house. Now it's all there behind us.

"And," she pauses, "*and* there was this other guy who left me because I was too much to handle, apparently. Okay, I'll admit, sometimes I get a little frisky. And… and… eh… one time, this nerdy guy offered me four hundred dollars to draw a self-portrait, and the guy I was with at the time didn't like that."

"Why? That doesn't sound so bad."

She grins. "He wanted my self-portrait drawn getting fucked by a monster."

I stare straight ahead, heart racing, mind reeling from this new info. What do I even *say* to something like that?

Her smile disappears as she takes in my poker-faced reaction. "I'm sorry. If I've made you uncomfortable, I mean. Sometimes I say things… I don't mean to make people uncomfortable. Sometimes I'm a bit of a bitch. People don't always appreciate my attitude, and I guess I can understand that, to a point. I guess…" she falters, then sighs. "I'm rambling. Sorry." She looks at me.

I don't meet her eyes.

"Are you hearing me, Michael?"

"I can hear you."

"Okay." She gives me a kind-hearted smile. "Sometimes you zone out a bit. Had to make sure."

I nod slowly. "I'm sorry. I wasn't sure what to say about the portrait thing. But… getting back to that other stuff, I don't think you're too much. You're not always predictable, but… where's the fun in that? Predictability. Predictability's overrated. I think that's part of what I like about you. You're unpredictable."

"I'm unpredictable, huh?"

"Yeah, I think so." I look at her. "It's not a bad thing, in your case."

She beams. A playful smirk quickly appears. Uh-oh. "So you like the idea of monsters having sex with me, huh?"

I stammer, "Now you're putting words in my mouth. I never said that." She starts giggling even as I continue, "Let's set the record straight right now: I do not find that idea appealing in the slightest. It's just not my thing. Not that I think less of anybody who… who likes that kind of thing. Different strokes… for different folks."

She turns her face to the window, struggling to stifle her laughter.

"There's nothing wrong with you. And I think it was his loss, leaving you for something like that. I think you're the most amazing woman in the world."

Her head swivels back around. "What's that?"

"There's nothing wrong with you."

She leans closer over the center console, her eyes reflecting the light in the dash's custom blue neon trimmings. "Hmmm?"

I cock an eyebrow at her. "Now I *know* you heard me."

She snickers slyly. "I like hearing it."

"I like everything about you," I tell her. "It doesn't matter how you look in anyone's eyes. In my eyes, you're more perfect and real than any other woman I've ever met, and that's not hyperbole, okay? I know it sounds like hyperbole, but it isn't." I can still see some doubt hidden behind her radiant smile. "I'm serious. I mean it."

"Okay," she says, grinning. She plays her fingers along the hairs on my forearm, tickling me, making me tense up momentarily.

"You should get some sleep," I suggest.

"Like I said, I don't think I'll be able to sleep for a while after everything that's happened." Her smile turns sly. "You're stuck with me, stranger."

I shrug. "Doesn't bother me in the slightest." I switch on the radio to FM and tune it to a rock station, careful to keep the volume at an acceptable level without waking the others. "Good?"

"Trying to drown me out, are ya?"

"Never."

"You might change your tune if we're still together in a few months."

I look at her. "Together?"

She hesitates, giving me a look that I can only describe as startled. Then she shrugs, any surprise at herself visibly gone. "Or whatever. You know what I mean…"

"Yeah."

"Sorry."

"No. No. Don't be."

Eager to change the subject, she asks, "So where are we going?"

"There should be a note in the glovebox."

She opens the glove compartment and takes out a small piece of paper and hands it to me. I take it and hold it close to the dashboard lights, but decide it's an unnecessary risk to attempt to read my own handwriting in the dark while I'm driving, so I give it back to Charlotte and ask her to read it.

"Five hundred, south, tree, 1990."

I feel a hot pang of heartache when an image forms in my mind. Has to be *that* place. Why would I choose *that* place as my command center?

"Do you know it?" she asks me.

"Yes," I answer quietly. "It's in Hiawatha."

She senses the hollow sound in my voice. "You okay?"

"I'll be fine."

"I know that's a lie."

"Later, okay? I… let's just focus on getting there for now. Please."

"Okay." She touches my arm affectionately. "I'm gonna try to sleep, okay?"

"Okay."

"Okay." She forces a humorous chuckle, probably for my sake. "Drive safe, stranger."

"Never do."

She pauses. She seems to be second-guessing herself, then deciding against it, then overruling her previous decision. It takes a short while for her to speak her mind: "Is… would you be okay if I gave you a kiss? On the cheek, I mean, because you're driving. For good luck."

I lean a few inches toward her. "I could use some luck."

She gives me a peck on the cheek and then turns over in her seat, back facing me. "Good night, love."

Alexander Engel-Hodgkinson

"Sweet dreams." My heart's fluttering as I stare ahead at the road. Part of me is in pain. Those words ripped open an old wound I thought I'd cauterized years ago.

Chapter 16: The Stranger Corps

"Mother, do you think they'll drop the bomb?"

A track from Pink Floyd's *The Wall* plays somberly on the radio as I drive in silence. It's almost 6 AM. The sky is bright purple as the sun rises to start the day. It's fitting, the song. The message has been repeating in my mind for two straight hours now.

It's a remote camping spot well enough out of the way of civilization that we would have a hard time getting any stations on old-fashioned radios. Cellular phones are useless out there. No reception.

There's a particularly old tree on the outskirts of the campsite which I called the 'Growth Tree'. A weeping willow that seems to coil up out of the earth and hide its mass behind thick veils of pendulous branches. Mom used to have me sit under it. "Don't forget to smile," she'd say from her spot on a tree stump, her right hand brushing fine streaks of colour across canvas that she'd have situated precariously on a shaky easel. Being the impatient child I was, I would often get bored and fidget. "Stop moving," she'd say curtly. "You don't want squiggly arms, do you?"

I smile at the number of memories I have of her getting frustrated with me. She never really showed genuine anger towards me in those moments no matter how difficult I was. I just wanted to run around and play. She wanted to paint me under the weeping willow. Immortalize me. "I want that perfect, gentlemanly smile of yours to last for all eternity. And when you get kids of your own, you can show them what their grandmother did for her special little man."

There's a pressurized tugging in my chest. Please. Not now, Mom. I take a deep breath and push those memories away. Focus on driving.

At around quarter after seven, I turn off the highway onto a side road. We're deep in the forest before I take a dirt trail route through the woods. Pebbles pelt the car without mercy as the car shudders along the trail harder than I'd like. This is not the car for this kind of thing. The jerky movements jolt my passengers out of their dreams. Freddie's deep yawn startles Charlotte awake. My counterpart sits upright, stretching however he can. At this point, all I really want to do is sleep. My eyelids are heavy. My eyes are stinging. It almost hurts to stay awake.

Finally we come upon something I've never seen before: a chain link gate, chained and padlocked to a post, with a no trespassing sign on it. There's a camera mounted nearby, staring us down. I stop the car and look around. The bushes on the other side of a gully seem to shift in a way that feels unnatural to me. I squint and catch a small ray of sunshine poking through the canopy of leaves glinting off a small piece of metal. A rod? No. Looking closer, I see that it's protruding just above a partition that appears to be made of stacks of wood and dead tree branches. A camouflaged barrier, and a lengthy one, it seems, extending into the brush. A sentry in a ghillie suit is most likely behind it. Sniper or machine-gunner. Can't tell. But it's something I would think of, and if we're in the right place, I probably wasn't the first Michael to come up with the idea.

Charlotte sees the surveillance camera but doesn't say anything. She's taking in her surroundings, her body tense, her eyes searching for any possible threat lurking in the woods.

My counterpart's watching the rear through the hatchback window, leaning over the back of his seat. He's curious about the tarp, but doesn't let his curiosity distract him from searching for any potential threats.

Freddie tries to lighten the mood: "Anybody got a key?"

"We're not alone," I tell them.

I feel all eyes on me. I elaborate. "If they were a threat, we'd be dead already."

"So what do we do now?" Charlotte asks.

"Wait here." I hand my counterpart the gun. Then, with the engine still running, I step out of the car and approach the gate on foot, shoes scuffing across dusty gravel. My eyes are fixed on the camera's dark lens.

Twigs snap and dry leaves crunch under the feet of one of the ghillie suit sentries as he rises from the undergrowth with a rifle level with my sternum. I don't move a muscle as he approaches, his eyes fierce white dots in a patch of green and black paint. I recognize the bone structure of his face easily—it's mine. "State your business," my ghillie counterpart grunts.

I hand him the note from the glovebox. He studies it and gives me another look, then glances around me at my three anxious passengers. He turns toward the gate and crosses the path to the padlock while holding the note up for the camera. He unlocks it, draws the chain away, and gives the gate a hard kick, clearing our path. "Enter," he says. "But drive slowly. No more than twenty klicks an hour.

I return to my place behind the wheel and drive slow. The gate is pulled shut behind us. I watch the sentry in the rearview mirror as he loops the chain around and locks it in place, never taking his eyes off us until we go around the bend. It's a straight line for eleven minutes from here on out.

"Was that you?" Charlotte asks.

"At the gate? Yeah."

Countless pairs of eyes watch us from both sides of the path, their owners no longer feeling the need to hide. Dozens of parallel copies of me in green army fatigues sit behind sandbag barriers on stools cut out of felled trees. Not a single man is too far from his rifle; it's always within arm's reach of its possessor.

There's a five-man machine gun nest every fifty feet, their outer walls paneled with parts from scrapped Mustang II Cobra IIs and other vehicles. The muzzles of infantry machine guns and anti-aircraft twin guns bristle above the nests' sketchily assembled T-walls.

We pass through a wide clearing where the tree is—the weeping willow that has haunted my memories all morning since I read the note. About a dozen Charlottes sit around it on folding chairs, scribbling into their sketchbooks. They occasionally flirt and joke and laugh with a few Michaels that are hanging around; they pause what they're doing to watch us pass them by.

"Wow," Charlotte breathes in awe, unable to take her eyes off her parallel versions. Some of them smile and wave at her. She hesitantly waves back. If there were any doubts in her mind about any of this, that sight probably shattered them. "There's so many of me…"

It's hard for me to take my eyes off the tree. It's more weathered now than it was when I last saw it. Somehow the tree itself seems to have sagged. The drooping, elongated branches swirl lazily in the breeze, unable to conceal the memorial from me. A gorgeous, life-size illustration of my mother, which I recognize from her old wedding photo, had at some point been meticulously carved into the willow's trunk. I recognize Charlotte's style in the trunk, which had been stripped of its rough bark to provide the canvas for the memorial. She looks so happy. Charlotte captured her glowing smile with uncanny elegance.

I can't keep looking at it. Something about it causes me pain.

"Who is that woman carved in the tree?" Charlotte asks.

I was afraid she was going to ask me that. "My mother."

Charlotte looks at me, those snow-blue eyes full of questions.

"She died when I was thirteen."

"I'm sorry."

"It was a long time ago. She's resting peacefully somewhere now."

"She's beautiful."

"I know. Her smile could light up a room. But... it's been a long time since I've seen it."

We cross a bridge passing over a muddy canal and descend a small hill into the place that used to be the campsite. One time, it was a forest, full of life and lush vegetation.

Now it's a vast dirt valley upon which the command center for this strange battalion was built. It's just like any temporary military base I'd seen in the Middle East with barracks, a medical center, restrooms and showers, post-and-beam pavilions with rows of tables and chairs beneath them; a mess hell, a communications office, administrative quarters, two large helicopter hangars, three storage warehouses, motor pool filled with Mustangs, Pontiacs, a couple tanks and all-terrain vehicles; a kitchen, a greenhouse, and a laundry station.

Hundreds of copies of Charlotte and I roam the base with purposeful strides alongside a few faces I don't recognize—conscious outsiders sympathetic to their cause, probably. At least a dozen copies of Freddie smoke cigarettes in a smoking area outside of the kitchen. An electrified fence had been erected around the perimeter, stopping where Lake Michigan began. If I had been involved in the construction of this base, I would have considered the lakeshore a major defensive weakness, and I still do despite the wall of machine gun nests and HESCO barriers fringing the shoreline.

Two Charlottes signal for me to stop and I do. One of them comes to the window, which I roll down, and she says with a friendly tone, "Morning, stranger. The Commander would like to see you first thing. Just go straight to the next intersection and take a left. The administrative office is right in the center of the base. You can't miss it."

"O-okay. Thanks."

She beams and walks away with her fellow counterpart, and they resume whatever conversation they were having before they spotted us.

I follow her directions and soon reach the front entrance of the administrative office, a bulletproofed Quonset hut. Another Charlotte stationed by the doorway twirls her finger in the direction of a small narrow alley between the office and the communications office. "Just park around the corner here, love."

I oblige. Then I get out and wait for my passengers to step into the morning sun, and the four of us head around to the front doorway where the Charlotte guard sticks out her hand. "Gun, please."

My immediate counterpart reluctantly gives her Willard's pistol.

She reaches back and raps her knuckles on the door. It opens, revealing yet another version of me in a sleeveless tank top and open Hawaiian shirt just like the one I arrived to Cherry Springs in the other day. He looks at us each in turn behind mirrored aviator sunglasses, and steps aside. "Come on in."

We file inside. Air-conditioned paradise. File cabinets line the walls and vivid drawings that were clearly done by various Charlottes adorn the curvature ceiling. A blue loveseat is set against the wall on my right. A wood-paneled partition divides the front half of the office from the rear, and seated behind a desk in front of that partition is the same Michael I spoke to earlier this morning. He still has that strange blue-and-red face paint. The same Charlotte who had stood in the middle of the lot this morning sits next to him now with her bare feet propped on the desk. Her face is also covered with the same paint which, under better lighting, is now clearly defined as a stylized red heart over the right eye surrounded by ripples that segue from crimson shades directly around the heart, getting lighter as they expand outward, to light-to-dark shades of blue as they reach the jawline. Her gorgeous eyes peek out at me from under a netted M1 infantry helmet. I can only imagine how uncomfortable that paint would be in the summer heat. Perhaps she's the Vice-Commander

"Welcome," the Commander says from behind his desk. The face paint gives his warm smile an unnatural look. "So you're one of the smarter ones. I'm glad."

Vice-Commander Charlotte beams proudly. "Told ya so."

I step forward. "What is all of this?"

The Commander answers: "The Stranger Corps."

I repeat the name, furrowing my brow. I glance over my shoulder at Charlotte, who appears to have been unable to snap out of her awe of this place. She looks totally overwhelmed. I turn back to the Commander. "You're serious?"

"As serious as the situation we've all found ourselves in."

"They're trying to kill her, right?"

"The Agency, yes. You met, uh... Officers... Willard and... and... what was the other one?"

"Cartman."

"Oh, good, you have."

"Yes."

"Then they told you everything?"

"I think so."

"Wrong."

"Huh?"

"They spoon-fed you complete bullshit. Hey, I don't blame you for believing them. I did, too, when I was you. I *am* you, but I mean, I was in your exact position. Years ago. All that shit about maintaining the multiverse and keeping it from imploding, that's all it was. Just bullshit. *Total* bullshit." He studies our faces. His smile returns. "Maybe this isn't the right time to discuss this. If memory serves, you haven't eaten anything since yesterday, right?"

Now that I was reminded of that fact, I realize just how hungry I am. "Yeah, actually."

He stands up and walks around the desk to the partition's closed door. "We'll get you all fed in a minute. Freddie's already on that. We knew you were coming. But first, I'd like you to meet somebody."

"Who?"

"It's a surprise."

"I'm really not in the mood for any more surprises," I say, before quickly adding, "but I guess you already knew that."

"I did, yes, but I also know you'll like *this* one."

Something tells me this isn't the first time the Commander has said this to himself. He opens the door and moves aside, allowing entry for a shadow from the past. A man with brown sugar skin, a sharply pointed black goatee, and the same Ray-Ban sunglasses from my dream.

"Yusef?!" My counterpart and I exclaim in shock. We stand rigidly as we try to process the sight before us.

Yusef grins. "Hello, my friend!"

Neither of us can bring ourselves to respond. How could he be alive? Of course, it's obvious; with an endless multiverse, the possible outcomes are limitless. But at this present time, it just doesn't seem real anymore. Yusef's death has been so ingrained into my memory as a fact—and technically, it still *is* fact—that I never considered the possibility that others would still be alive.

Yet... here he is.

"The look on your faces," Vice-Commander Charlotte giggles. "It never gets old."

Yusef takes my hand in both of his and squeezes. "It's good to see you, Michael. You look well." He turns to my equally stunned counterpart and takes his hand in the same way. "As do you, Michael." He steps between us, taking Charlotte's hand and kissing it theatrically, making her blush. "It's always a pleasure to see you safe and sound, my dear Charlotte." He releases her hand, steps back to take us all in again. "So *two* of you have arrived here today. I welcome you both to the Stranger Corps."

Chapter 17: Talk Over Lunch

Lunch is prepared by the other Freddies and served to us under one of the post-and-beam pavilions. Cheeseburgers and fries with garden salad and steamed vegetables. The Commander and his Vice-Commander are sitting on the opposite side of the table facing the rest of us. Freddie is seated beside me and Charlotte sits across from him, between Yusef and my immediate counterpart.

Once my initial shock wears off, I'm able to focus on a coherent line of questioning while we eat.

"How did you get out of Afghanistan alive?" I ask him.

Yusef shovels a bushel of vinegar-soaked lettuce into his mouth and makes us wait until it's chewed down well enough to swallow. When he swallows, he says, "I understand the Yusef you knew was shot outside what is now known as Camp Nathan Smith, is that correct?"

I nod.

Yusef turns his head slightly to my immediate counterpart beside me. He also nods affirmative. "Well," Yusef begins, "the easiest part of what I'm about to tell you is the answer to your question: *I* simply did not go in that direction. You see, I had angered some people—a small gang of young bandits pretending to be Mujahedeen. They had tried to rob and kill me in Farāh City, but, well, they were not expecting me to be armed. It cost two of their friends their lives."

I glance at Charlotte as she fires up a cigarette. She gives me a quick look before her eyes dart back to Yusef as she listens intently to his story.

"Unfortunately, they had powerful friends with many resources. To stay would be suicide. So I arranged with an old smuggler friend of mine from another life to provide safe passage across Pakistan to a boat, so I could make my escape on the Arabian Sea.

"As a matter of fact, when I had run into you, I had managed to get ahead of them by about two days, as I had not stopped to rest during my crossing through Helmand. Kandahar proved to be very difficult to cross. They had men stationed everywhere, disguised as everyone; United States Marines, Mujahedeen, Hezbi Islami—everyone. Just for me."

"That's terrifying," Charlotte comments sympathetically. "I'm sorry you went through that."

Yusef grins. "It is in the past now."

"All that for you?" I ask him. "Who did you kill?"

He shrugs. "To this day, I do not know. Thankfully, their influence did not extend far beyond the borders of Pakistan." He grins proudly. "After Kandahar, the following months were quite easy in comparison." He finishes his salad and digs into his burger with gusto. "Mmmm," he moans appreciatively.

"It's good to see you in one piece," I tell him. "You know, alive and well."

"Agreed," the Commander says with his mouth, waggling the last third of his cheeseburger in my direction to show his concurrence.

Vice-Commander Charlotte taps his shoulder gently, a knowing, matriarchal smile on her face. "Not with your mouth full, please."

Commander Michael swallows his food, the authority on his face brushed aside momentarily by a dim shade of embarrassment. "Apologies."

Charlotte and I exchange looks. She smiles at me. *Yeah,* her eyes tell me, *I would do the exact same thing.*

Of that, I have no doubt.

Commander Michael hastily wolfs down the last of his burger and comes right out with it: "Now that everybody's fed—or at least comfortable—I think some explaining is in order. Long story short: the Agency has fucked the space-time coordination of the multiverse and we're working alongside other parallel sects to bring everything back in order. Their constant tampering with infinite parallel realities is the reason why nothing occurs in real time anymore; it's why this began at the start of the new millennium, and why it's still a problem five years later. I wasn't affected until 2002, and you're all new to this whole multiverse thing. Right?"

"Right," Charlotte and Freddie answer almost in perfect sync while my counterpart and I nod our heads.

"That's not the way the multiverse is supposed to go. It's not supposed to be a straight line—it never was supposed to be *that* simple—but it's supposed to be like a linear narrative playing out in real time. Right? That's what makes parallel realties... *parallel.* The problem is... thanks to the Agency... it's not. They've created a paradox. Like a sort of time loop, except time is always moving forward, while the same series of events repeats itself. Ironically, this is because of the Agency's attempts to maintain a solid straight line—the same series of events in every universe, without any major alterations in any of the details."

"I kept trying to tell those cops that it's impossible," I say with a surge of frustration rising up again. "They wouldn't listen, even when they couldn't explain it."

"That's just how the Agency got as powerful as it is. If you tell a story that taps into the fears of the masses with enough urgency, they'll believe it. They'll do everything they can to avoid whatever it is that sounds so scary in your story. In the Agency's case... the threat of the multiverse imploding if their rules aren't followed. Nobody wants to implode. It's a fact. Give them something to worry about and offer yourself as the only solution. Bam!" He claps his hands, startling Charlotte. "Sorry, love," he tells her. "You have followers. You have a cause and they'll be damned if they don't give you the resources to protect them from an imaginary threat they can't even attempt to understand."

I notice a group of Michaels sitting in the back of a military transport as it rolls up the road. They look exhausted, covered in soot and mud, their desert fatigues tattered and seemingly held together by bloodstained gauze. Every face on that transport is staring blankly into space. They look like they've just fought a war.

The Commander continues, "But now the Agency's put us all in a box. They've had to stick with the lie all these years, and it's distorting the fabric of reality. Everything's getting folded in on itself and stretched out, contorted."

The transport disappears around the medical center where I assume they're being unloaded and tended to by doctors whose names I'm not yet familiar with. Most of the new faces in this compound appear to be medics or engineers. I was never good at medicating or engineering anything, so it'd make sense for a private army of my own counterparts to gather people with that expertise.

"I've already had this conversation with the Commander Michael before me. I've been through everything you've been through. Word for word, action for action. It's a mind-bender, isn't it? To think that someday you'll be in my exact position a few years from now."

"What makes you think I'll be in your position? There are thousands of me on this compound."

"And all of them are here under different circumstances. No one journey is exactly the same as another, even if the destination remains the same. In the case of the line of commanding Michaels, the series of circumstances that lead them to this moment are the most similar. Very particular."

"But why? How?"

"Two of you showed up today. That's how I know."

My immediate counterpart and I exchange perplexed looks. We glance at Yusef to see if he has any answers. He doesn't say a word.

"You'll get it eventually," Commander Michael says. "Give it time."

Freddie speaks up for the first time since lunch started: "I don't think I'll *ever* get it."

Yusef replies, "I have been here for a while now… and *I* do not get it, either."

Commander Michael chuckles and pats his shoulder. "That's okay, Fred. You look well, by the way. Lose weight?"

"HA!" Freddie laughs, and the Commander and his Vice-Commander laugh with him while Charlotte, my counterpart and I watch them in silence. Yusef just sits there with a big grin on his face.

It's nice to see Freddie comfortable in his surroundings. Still, when the laughter dies down, he asks a question that seems to have been burning in his mind for a while: "What about the diner?"

Commander Michael's smile fades into grim sympathy. "It wouldn't be safe for you, Fred."

"But—"

"Trust me. The Agency knows all about it. They wouldn't hesitate to use it—and you—to get to the rest of us. And I don't want to risk any harm to anyone who doesn't have it coming." His hand falls away from Freddie's shoulder and he turns to address the rest of us. "The safest place on earth is here. If you're going to leave the compound, be careful not to go too far. And of course, don't tell anyone about this place. Anyone outside could be with the Agency. That's the trouble with these guys. At least in Afghanistan, we knew who the enemy was. Here… it's all too shrouded."

Yusef says, "Afghanistan was not quite as simple as you seem to remember, my friend. No war ever is."

"Of course, Yusef," the Commander says. "That was naïve."

"Hardly," Yusef assures him.

"Damn," Freddie says, lamenting his diner. "All those years…"

Commander Michael replaces his grim expression with a warm smile—as warm as he could muster under all that war paint. "All facilities in this compound are free to use. Take a shower, get some rest, eat more food… whatever you want."

"Oh?" Charlotte drops her cigarette butt under the table and squishes it. "Leaving us so soon?"

Commander Michael gives her an apologetic smile. "Unfortunately, I have something to attend to. Please, make yourselves at home."

Commander Charlotte stands upright and the pair salute us. Then they leave us to ourselves.

Charlotte turns to my counterpart and I. "Did… did either of you get what he was saying?"

"Nope," we say in unison.

She perks upright and clasps her hands between her knees. "So! Which one of you wants to tour this place with me?"

I'm about to volunteer when I realize my place in this. She isn't my Charlotte. I'd be interfering with my counterpart's relationship, as strange as that is to me. My counterpart seems hesitant about saying anything. "Go," I tell them, racking my brain for any kind of excuse to avoid going with them.

"Aw, c'mon, Michael," Charlotte protests, making exaggerated pouty lips.

I chuckle appreciatively at her insistence. "I would, but… I have to go to the bathroom."

Charlotte extends her hand. "Give me your arm."

"What for?"

"Trust me." She smirks.

I stretch my arm across the table. She grabs me by the wrist and uses a permanent marker to draw a pair of identical lines parallel to each other on my open palm, then pushes a small dot in between them. I look at her inquisitively. Seeing the question in my eyes, she says, "In case I misplace you."

I smile. "Thanks."

"Look." She holds out her right hand and shows a similar mark on her palm.

Freddie holds up his hand, showing me the same mark. No doubt my counterpart is also marked, but he doesn't show me.

"Hurry up and go," Charlotte says with a laugh. "We'll wait for you here."

I try to look as embarrassed as possible. "It's… it's not gonna be quick."

"Oh." Her eyebrows shoot up. "*Oh*. Well, that's okay. I'll explore with you later. I should know my way around by then." She gives me a sly smile, then turns her head to my counterpart and hooks her arm in his. "Shall we?"

"We shall."

"Freddie, you coming?"

"Nah, I'm gonna go check out the kitchens."

"Okay."

I watch the couple leave and wait until they're out of my sight. Freddie looks at me with concern. "You okay, kid?"

"I'm fine." I guess I should keep up appearances, considering the possibility that any of the Michaels or Charlottes walking around me have been through this exact situation before; the Michaels would be aware of my lie, but the Charlottes wouldn't know unless they saw me sitting here long after my counterpart had left with his version of her. "I'll see you later."

"Alright."

I get up and head to the restroom and showers. I pick a stall and sit on the seat. The restroom and showers building is made up primarily of wood panels, steel framing, and concrete flooring. There's actual plumbing, which tells me that there's serious financing behind this operation—though for the life of me, I can't figure out where just yet. Air fresheners have been left in every toilet stall as a courtesy. A partition wall divides the showers from the toilets. I can hear a pair of Charlottes chatting about the lead guitarists in a variety of metal bands over the hissing of showerheads and the splashing of water on concrete. I can hear their bare feet slapping the wet floor. One of them drops a bottle of shampoo and hisses, "Shit!"

I make myself as comfortable as can be on the toilet lid and think about how none of this makes any sense.

Then I think about Freddie. *My* Freddie. He's still in my

universe, alone and probably wondering if I died after Charlotte's murder. The poor bastard's probably devastated, fearing the worst. I don't want to think about how he must be feeling right now, but once the thought entered my mind, I can't get it out. It gets me thinking about how I thought of home when I first threw myself off that bridge. Is it possible to return to a reality I'd already leaped from? And if it is, should I risk it? Would he be safer without me returning? Would it be better for him to just live on with his life thinking I died the same night Charlotte died?

Goddamn it. I bury my head in my hands. This is too much.

Chapter 18: Options

One could call it a unanimous vote, even if it was just mine. I decided I would save my own Freddie from my universe before the Agency got to him first, if they haven't already.

There are a number of factors preventing me from achieving this: 1) I have no idea how I would get back to this exact universe so that my absence wouldn't be missed; 2) all the rooftops are too low for me to make a successful jump from, and there aren't any trees for me to climb within the perimeter unnoticed; and 3) the risk involved would most likely prevent anyone of authority around here from approving such a dangerous operation. Surely they'd be sympathetic to my mission, though, right?

Maybe not. The number of Freddies here is significantly lower than the number of Charlottes and Michaels. Seems she takes priority over the man who raised me like he was my own father since I was thirteen. Something about that disgusts me, even worse that it's me who's guilty of doing something like that. Talk about biting the hand that feeds you.

It's decided regardless. I just have to figure a way out of here, and secure a sure method of getting back with Freddie. If it wasn't for the surrounding populace, I'd be questioning whether or not I *can* bring someone to a parallel dimension with me. Obviously that's not even a question now.

I head into the men's shower room, respectfully turning down a flirtatious invitation from a Charlotte standing in the women's shower room entrance with a towel wrapped loosely around her wet, naked body. God, it takes everything in me to decline.

Focus. I note cabinets with spare casualwear, uniforms, and hygienic supplies on my way into the locker room and grab a pair of jeans and a white T-shirt before making a beeline through a crowd of half-naked Michaels minding their own business; drying themselves off, sitting on wooden benches in their towels chatting with their fellow counterparts, getting dressed after their showers, or getting undressed. I find an empty locker at the very end of the farthest row, against the rear wall. I strip, stashing my cheesy Hawaiian shirt, sleeveless top, and faded jeans into the locker and step into one of the vacant showers. Standing under a torrent of steaming water feels good, even as I'm reminded of how tired I am. Everything hurts. My joints, my muscles, my heart… feels like there's a piece of shrapnel lodged there.

Charlotte… I can't believe I let her die. I was so careful. It wasn't good enough to keep her alive. All I did was prolong her inevitable death.

On that note… does that mean the 'Stranger Corps.' is also prolonging the deaths of all the other Charlottes?

Fuck. What the hell does all of this mean? It sounds to me like this is destined to go on and on without end.

Anger surges from within. My knuckles crack against the polished oak partition with a solid *thudding* sound. The wall's a lot denser and stronger than it looks. Goddamn, it hurts. My knuckles glow red under the shower's steaming torrent, feeling like wasps plunged their stingers in every joint.

Stupid. What's the point in injuring myself over a little temper tantrum?

Think. This could go a number of ways. Maybe my counterparts would agree to accompany me on a quick expedition back to my own universe to save Freddie. I don't see why not. At least most of them were raised by him—in the universes where my mother hadn't…

Well. I don't see why they wouldn't sympathize with my cause regardless.

But what if the Commander shoots it down? He'll keep a closer eye on me then, maybe even put me under constant surveillance. He'll make it impossible for me to jump then. I would disobey the order to leave Freddie behind and he already knows it.

Damn it. There *has* to be a way! I scour through my memories, anything and everything related to the Agency and this whole multiverse-jumping business for any details I might've missed; a vision in the rift I passed through, a spoken phrase I thought nothing of before…

A spoken phrase…! I remember eavesdropping on Armitage and his squad in the warehouse, their killing of their own, and the strange way that they threw numbers around. Numbers… designations! Of course. The Agency's a type of bureaucracy, isn't it? It makes sense that they would assign every parallel universe with its own number. They were long numbers, too.

I almost leap with excitement after this revelation. It seems so obvious now. That's how they've been travelling! They've associated the universes with these numbers, and so, that's where they go. It seems simple enough.

Now I have a new problem: which one is mine?

The setting sun blazes atop the lake's crystalline high tide that licks the bases of the HESCO MIL units and the sandbag walls of the machine gun nests. Large campfires as well as electric lanterns illuminate the base with increasing power as the sun's light fades behind the black horizon of the trees that guard us. The white noise of community chatter and activity has gradually been fading to a few scattered conversations rendered unintelligible by distance and the crackling fires. Charlottes joke with other Charlottes, speak with other Michaels, seriously as well as flirtatiously; Freddies and the new faces I still don't recognize converse pleasantly with each other and other Michaels and Charlottes. Everyone gets along here.

I'm only able to find my immediate counterpart from earlier because he hasn't changed his clothes yet. He's with Charlotte, who hasn't changed either. Both seated under a pavilion with a lantern between them. Charlotte spots me, smiles, but seems hesitant to call me over in case I'm not the one who saved them. I approach them. "It's me."

"Ah," Charlotte says cheerfully, "but how do *we* know that?"

"Unless you swapped outfits with a different pair, I know I've got the right ones."

Michael gives me a look. "You look different."

"I showered. Shirt's in a locker. Didn't wash off the mark." I show them the slightly faded mark Charlotte drew on my hand.

Michael asks, "So what now?"

"I don't know," I admit, "but I was thinking about things earlier."

"Do tell," Charlotte says.

"I was thinking about Freddie. *My* Freddie. He's probably worried sick right about now. I... I never saw him after I took you—uh, after I took my universe's Charlotte out on our date. The cops picked me up after her murder and tried to kill me next. So... Freddie's still in that universe, probably wondering where the hell I am. Or worse... wondering why I killed two cops. It wouldn't surprise me if they told him I killed Charlotte, too."

Michael says, "You should take this to the Commander. I don't see why he wouldn't be sympathetic to this problem. If I were in his position, I'd greenlight an expedition to that universe."

"Here's the problem with that: we don't know for sure. He's had different experiences than we have. His perspective on the matter might've changed. And I don't know which universe I came from."

"What do you mean?" Charlotte asks.

"I realized earlier that the Agency has assigned each parallel universe its own number. One of the things I overheard at the warehouse yesterday." I watch the realization light up in my counterpart's eyes. Makes sense to him, too. Good.

"That's weird," Charlotte says. "How would they do that, exactly, if there are infinite universes?"

"Just one of those things, I guess. Bureaucracy. Designated for filing and documentation. No idea how anyone, even an organization as far-reaching as these guys, could possibly hope to document everything that goes on in the multiverse, but they do.

"And I think that's how they've been getting around so well. They've been associating these universes with their own numbers, and so, they only have to think about the numbers and the specific locations to get there without accidentally winding up somewhere they've already been.

"I think, since I've jumped twice as far as I can remember, that I've been jumping at random. I'm not entirely sure how it works, but that's my best guess."

Charlotte and my counterpart sit quietly, thinking it over for a moment. Charlotte shrugs. "Can't you just think something like 'the universe where this started' or something?"

"No idea."

"That's helpful."

"I know."

"It's worth a shot, isn't it?"

"Of course it is. This is Freddie we're talking about. There are just a staggering amount of risks involved. Plus, it almost seems like these buildings were designed with jumping in mind... to discourage it."

Michael asks, "What do you mean?"

"Don't you find it strange that none of these buildings meet the height required for a successful jump? I've leaped off the stage at school or off rocks in Afghanistan. I've jumped off things plenty of times. Who hasn't? I think I have to jump from a specific height, because I never wound up in a portal until..."

I hesitate to mention the bridge and all circumstances leading up to it with Charlotte here. So I make something up: "Until I fell out of a tree on my way home. I was trying to save a cat, a-and the branch snapped under me. It was a long drop. For some reason I thought of home, so that's where I suddenly wound up."

"That sounds like a fib," Charlotte teases. "You fibber."

"Uh..."

"What *really* happened?" She leans forward on her elbows, eyes peering deep into my own, searching for the truth. Looking into them now, there isn't a trace of her usual playfulness. They're hard, resolute, determined.

So I just come out with it: "I tried to kill myself."

Her eyebrows shoot straight up. She leans back, staring at me in stunned silence, hands curled into loose fists on the table in front of her.

My counterpart is just as shocked that I would admit to it so bluntly. He's watching Charlotte same as I am, waiting for some kind of reaction, almost dreading whatever's about to come once the initial shock wears off.

When it does, she whispers, "Michael... I..."

"I know. I'm sorry. It was stupid. I was stupid. I lost hope, and I didn't see the point in going on. I figured I should just spare Freddie the misery of dealing with me and my bullshit—"

I'm cut short by the glare she's giving me. There's a kind of wrath brewing that I don't want to fuck with. "Let me tell you something," she says as she reaches out and grabs one of my hands. She extends her hand to my counterpart. "You, too." She takes his hand and looks at us both in turn. "I don't know which is more concerning—the fact that you think like that, or the fact that you actually went through with it already. If it wasn't for your jumping abilities, you'd be dead. We wouldn't be having this conversation. And that... that scares me." Her grip tightens on both our hands. "Your life has too much value for you to just throw it away like that.

"Now... no more talk like that, okay? Or I'll spank you both right here, in front of everyone." She musters a laugh somehow despite making obvious efforts to fight back tears. "I know it's only been a few days since we met, but please... take it from me: your life is worth more than you know." She's squeezing our hands now. "Understand?"

We nod, too guilt-ridden to say anything.

She beams, sniffling and quickly releasing my hand to wipe tears away. "Good. That's good. Now you gotta pinky-promise." Before we can do anything, she twists her pinky fingers around ours. "Good. I'll hold you to it.

"Now, let's get back to it—have you decided on how you're going to save Freddie?"

"If I'm going to."

"Right… if you're going to."

"I haven't, yet."

"What's stopping you?"

I withdraw my hand and heave a deep sigh. "I don't know. Just… all of this. It's all so complicated. So far beyond anything I can really wrap my head around."

"You seem to be doing just fine when it comes to basic understanding. That's more than I can say." Charlotte glances over at a nearby group of Michaels applauding an acoustic guitar-playing Charlotte sitting on a felled log. She's midway through Led Zeppelin's *Over the Hills and Far Away*, pausing to thank her listeners when they praise her skills. Some strange faces in the front row seem to be smitten with her. "It's all still so surreal," she says softly.

"You're not the only one," My counterpart replies.

I rise from my spot, looking around the darkening base as the last of the sun's light fades behind the trees, replaced by the dark blue, star-speckled vastness of night.

"Where are you going?" Charlotte asks.

"I've decided. I'm gonna go have a word with the Commander."

"Good luck. We'll be here when you get back."

"Okay." I'm tempted to kiss her forehead, even though I know I've no right to. She's not the Charlotte I spent the previous night with. In a way, it would be disloyal to my counterpart if I came on to her… if they've even decided to officially become a couple.

I leave them be as the Charlotte on the log strikes the familiar opening chords to another Led Zeppelin song, *Stairway to Heaven*. The street is lit brightly by electric garden lanterns and a naked lightbulb installed above every front door. Every window has adjustable panes and chicken wire screens. As I pass one of the living quarters, a few unmistakable moans filter through the chicken wire into the cool night air. My heart lurches. I pause for a better listen and hear the rhythmic squeaking of bedsprings and Charlotte moaning and other versions of me grunting in the privacy of their quarters. "Oh, Michael... oh! Oh! God, yes... like that."

"Charlotte... Charlotte!"

My face heats up and my heart pounds. I quickly move on toward the center of the base. Memories of my night with my own Charlotte seep back into my conscious mind. My heart sinks. My body instantly feels worn down, my muscles weak and stiff under a torso that seems to have gained a hundred extra pounds with just those thoughts of her.

Charlotte's dead. Move on. The least you can do is try to save the others.

Two Charlottes dressed as marines stand guard outside the Commander's office door. They straighten when they see me and flash me innocent smiles. "Howdy, stranger," one of them says.

The other asks, "What d'ya need?"

"Is the Commander busy?"

"The Commander's always busy."

"You the new guy?"

"*One* of the new guys," the second Charlotte corrects the first with a smirk. "Two of them showed up today."

"Oh? I didn't know that much."

The second Charlotte wags her finger in a mock scold. "I keep telling you, you need to get around the base more. Can't stay cooped up practicing the guitar *all* the time, ya know!"

The first Charlotte says to me, "He might see you if you're one of the new guys. I can't tell if you are, though. Did you shower?"

I nod.

The two Charlottes beam hopefully at each other, silently communicating something that I can't decipher as an outsider. It makes me realize just how little time has passed since I first met her.

"Well," the first Charlotte begins, rotating back and forth shyly, while the second Charlotte fidgets shyly with the zipper on her uniform shirt. "If you'd like, once you and the Commander sort out whatever it is you're here for—if he's not so busy he can't see you—how would you like to spend the night with us?"

"*Both* of us," the second Charlotte elaborates, "at the same time."

The invitation accompanied with their lustful, mischievous smiles sets my heart into a nervous frenzy. "U-uh... I... we may have to put a pin in that tonight, ladies. As tempting as that is... *really* tempting... it's been a bit of a day. And just *one* of you takes a lot out of me."

They both puff their bottom lips out dramatically. "D'aww. Oh, well."

"I understand."

"Give me one second, okay?" The first Charlotte raps her knuckles against the door and waits for the Commander's reply.

"Yes?"

"One of the new boys wants to see you."

"Show him in."

Charlotte opens the door. Both sentries watch me enter the office, and then they close the door behind me.

The Commander and the Vice-Commander are lounging beside each other on the loveseat, dressed casually, their face paint washed off. Vice-Commander Charlotte is absolutely glowing in a half-buttoned blouse and jean shorts. Commander Michael is wearing a plain black T-shirt and jeans. The band Yes is playing at a decent volume on the radio—*Owner of a Lonely Heart*, I think it's called.

"Good evening." Commander Michael raises a glass of beer— as evident by the case of Cruise Light on the floor by his feet. "Can I offer you a beer?"

"No, thank you, it's okay."

The Vice-Commander asks, "What brings you here, stranger?"

"A concern. I was hoping you'd be able to help me."

Commander Michael comes right out with it: "You want to bring back Freddie from your own universe, right?"

Stunned, I barely manage to form my response. "Uh... yeah, that's... that's exactly what I was going to... how did you know?"

The Commander grins. It's like looking into a mirror trying to be confident, only the reflection seems to successfully pull it off. There's something cool about him, something I don't have anymore. Not since the war. Not since Mother killed herself.

"Been there, done that," he says. "The problem with your case is that the Agency might already be there waiting for you."

"The thought crossed my mind," I admit. This isn't off to a

good start.

"The Commander I've succeeded told me that the war changes every time events loop around. Different circumstances dictate each chain of events. Like I said before…"

I finish for him: "The start and the destination remain the same, but everything in between is different, right?"

"Different wording, but yes. My experiences might not be the same as yours."

"And what were your experiences?"

"In this case? I went back for him."

"Did something happen?"

"No. It was pretty uneventful. I convinced Freddie to come back with me, and after some serious coaxing, I got him to jump with me. The stubborn old bastard thought I was trying to commit murder-suicide, gone crazy after Charlotte's death."

"Okay," I reply slowly. "Then why hesitate this time?"

"Because it could be different this time."

"But it might *not* be."

"Always a possibility. But with the day of the assault just days away, it's a huge risk to let you jump into that universe."

"What assault?"

"The day of reckoning, Michael—and you and your immediate counterpart play a key role."

"But why? None of this is making any sense!"

"I know. I didn't get it either, until the day came along."

"If you know now, then why not fill me in on what the hell is going on?"

"I wish I could. I really do. But I don't think that's too smart. Kinda like going back in time and telling your past self not to enlist."

"But aren't you altering history by refusing to let me go back to my own universe? You're contradicting yourself."

"Sometimes a little guidance is necessary, contrary to what I just said. Small-scale changes in the timeline could benefit the bigger picture. Minor guidance to keep the timeline from derailing. Take, for example, when we were lost in Afghanistan. If it weren't for Yusef, we would have trailed off course, and that would have drastically altered the course of our history—and future. That's why he was there, Michael. That's how he knew that the 104th went to Takht-e-pol."

He lets me think it over in my head. I glance at Vice-

Commander Charlotte, who's quietly sipping beer through a straw, watching me. One detail bothers me. "101st."

"I'm sorry?"

"It was the 101st Airborne Division."

Commander Michael laughs through his nose. "For you, maybe. See? It's the little differences that make *all* the difference."

"Let's backtrack for a moment—about the beginning and the end being the same." The Commander sets his beer down and holds his hands in front of his face, palms facing each other. "Our purpose here isn't *just* to fight the Agency in an attempt to save Charlotte and act as the loop dictates. The Agency's actions have forcibly created a timeline that overlaps across *several* parallel timelines. That's a dangerous paradoxical situation.

"So... our *true* purpose is to break the loop. And how do we theoretically break the loop? We play with circumstances. We change the middle until the new middle circumstances we've created alters the conclusion *just enough* for us to change the destination.

"In simpler terms: we're trying to cheat the theoretical butterfly effect."

It's too much for me to take in. It's too goddamn obtuse a concept to wrap my head around. It sounds like the insane ramblings of a madman. And it's starting to piss me off. "So... let me get this straight... you're trying to change the future by changing the past, just enough not to cause a paradoxical catastrophe, but enough to 'hopefully' change the future?"

"That's correct."

"And that's the reason why you don't want to help me save Freddie?"

"If he even *needs* saving. The Agency doesn't want him. It wants us. You, me, and Charlotte. The Alpha is well aware of what's occurred before us, Michael. It's more than likely he's prepared for the inevitable rescue mission—the rescue mission that he may have prepared for in advance this time around. It's extremely possible that he's altering the past as much as we are. He knows what I did before when I was in your position, and because of that, I can't rule out the possibility that what I did isn't necessarily safe for you to do the second time around."

"Wait, wait... the 'Alpha'?"

He nods grimly. "The original."

"Original what? Me?"

"The multiverse had to start somewhere, Michael. He's the first of us. *The* Michael. He's been after us from the get-go. Hell... he killed the previous commander. I owe him for that."

I stare at him, trying to process this new tidbit of information. When it's stacked up on top of everything else he's told me, it gets scrambled again. Back to square one.

The Commander continues: "Don't think for a second I'm not sympathetic to the cause of going back to your universe to save Freddie. You know as well as I do that the man's like a father to me. I hold him in the highest regard. But if we want to win... sacrifices have to be made. And as much as it pains me, we both have to come to accept that we can't save them all."

"I have to sit down."

"Take the chair from behind my desk."

I wheel the chair out. My wobbly legs feel like they're going to give out at any second. When I fall heavily into the overstuffed office chair, it's a relief. "It's insane. It's all insane."

"Tell me about it," Commander Michael grunts, then sips from his glass. "How about that beer?"

"Yes, please."

He pours me a spare glass that had been left out—as if I truly was expected to show up at his door tonight—and he gets up and crosses the gap between us to put it in my hand. Then he sits back down beside the Vice-Commander.

After gulping down half the glass, I wipe my mouth and sit quietly for a moment. "I think I figured out how you and the Agency have been moving around all these universes. The universes are given numbers, aren't they? Labels to differentiate each one from another. Makes travel easier when you want to go to one specific version of a specific location."

"Ooh," Vice-Commander Charlotte coos enthusiastically. "Fast learner indeed!" She applauds me. "Right on the money, my dear."

The Commander smiles. "Seems I was right about you. You're one of the smartest."

Confused, I ask, "Am I not usually able to deduce that much?"

Vice-Commander Charlotte smirks. "You'd be surprised how slow you can be sometimes."

Commander Michael shoots her a look and she giggles. He can't stay agitated at her for long. How could anyone? "Alright, I admit it. Sometimes I'm not the quickest draw in the Old West."

Don't know where that analogy came from. One of those 'differences,' I guess.

"Our options are limited," Commander Michael says. "The Agency knows what we did before, so retreading previous territory is never a smart idea."

"What about the strike?"

"The strike is inevitable. I've seen what happens when we don't act—the Agency finds our camp and wipes us out. And as you can see, we can't just pack up and go without getting noticed. What we *can* do, is approach the strike from a different angle. Last time, we used boats and a bogus oil company. This time... we'll be utilizing different tactics. For the purpose of security, I can't divulge anything now, but just wait... I think it'll work this time."

The strike hardly matters to me. It's a curiosity at most. My primary concern is Freddie, the man who took me in, the man who tried his damnedest to shape me into a 'fine young man'—his words. "So... we're abandoning Freddie?"

"I'm sorry."

And that was that.

Chapter 19: Under the Tent

I wish I can say that I've never been as disgusted with myself as I am in this moment, but I know that isn't true. I've done worse things. Sometimes I look back on those things and cringe or, if they're things I'd done in the Middle East, I force myself not to cry. The things that happened over there are too horrific for words. Too repulsive. I wake up every morning wondering how I can live with myself. Charlotte tells me that my life is more valuable than I realize—how could someone who's guilty of the things I've done have value? What about all those people I murdered, people who were following orders just like I was, who just happened to fall on the wrong side of my scope? What about the people I abandoned? I'm still doing it, even now, apparently.

"Are you alright?" the Commander asks.

"What?"

"You haven't said a word in three minutes."

"Oh."

"I understand how upsetting this is for you—"

I'm tired of hearing myself talk. It's ridiculous and it's pointless. "Are there any tents I can use?"

"Yes. Would you prefer to sleep outside? The quarters are spacious and air-conditioned."

"I don't want to sleep in the quarters."

The Commander makes a face, equal parts sympathy and understanding—after all, I guess no one would understand me better than me. "Second warehouse east of this location, I think. Jerry will be expecting you."

"Jerry?"

Vice-Commander Charlotte stifles a laugh. I don't know what's so funny all of a sudden.

"Oh, right. You haven't met him yet. Nice guy. He keeps track of our inventory. He's also a brilliant engineer. Some of the things he's come up with come straight out of the movies, I swear. You'll like him."

I scoff. "I'll bet." I finish my beer and set the empty glass on the desk. I stand up. "Thank you for the drink." Then I leave.

As soon as I step outside, the pair of Charlottes try again.

"Hey, hon. How'd it go?"

"You still too tired?"

"Yes, ladies," I reply wearily, "I'm sorry. Another time, maybe. Okay?"

"Alright."

"Sweet dreams, you."

"Where's the storage warehouse?"

They both point in the direction opposite from where I came from.

"Thank you." I head in that direction as they cheerfully reply with "You're welcome!" behind me. I pass the laundry facility and the mess hall, then the greenhouse, and after about ten yards, I go by another cluster of Michaels and Charlottes mingling around a dazzling column of flame. When I get to the warehouses, I approach the middle one and find two men I don't recognize, both parallel versions of each other. He's tall, broad-shouldered, with all of his hair buzzed off his head, wearing a black *Playboy* T-shirt and frayed, oil-darkened jeans.

My God. He looks like a bald Jerry Seinfeld.

As I draw near, they both look up from their game of cards, dark narrow eyes fixing on me. They wave. One of them stands up to greet me. "Michael, right?" He chuckles. "Just kidding. Of course you are." He even *sounds* like Jerry Seinfeld. "My name's Barker. Jason Barker. I'm the lead engineer of this establishment. Also in charge of inventory. But the Commander already told you that, right?"

"Sorry, he didn't," I tell him. "I'm looking for Jerry."

"Look at me," he says, indicating himself. "Who do I remind you of? *I'm* Jerry. You always forget my name." He's grinning ear to ear. Either he's used to this by now, or it never bothered him to begin with. "Jason Barker's the name, but you'll forget that."

"Right." I've seen him around the base a few times, never up close.

"C'mon. You want a tent? No problem. I got plenty. Follow me." He leads me inside the middle warehouse, through a maze of racks and metal shelves that only he knows his way around with the utmost knowledge and confidence. I can tell right away that he knows this place like the back of his hand—only he can make sense of all this clutter. And there's *everything* in here: car parts, gun parts, armour plating, building supplies, power tools, canned food, diesel and petrol fuel, boxes of all types of ammunition, water jugs, TVs, tubes of rolled-up chicken wire, books, air-conditioning units, tabletop fans, and a whole catalogue of other stuff I couldn't be bothered to remember.

"Conversation with the big boss man didn't go so well, huh?"

"No."

"Sleepin' outside might help. I guess it's better for the newbies to sleep outside at first. Helps them get used to the situation and the new surroundings. Sleeping in the quarters tends to upset them. You can hear all the other Charlottes and Michaels in those quarters. Tough for the newbies who experienced a certain loss. You know?"

The thought hadn't occurred to me until now, and I quietly wonder why it hadn't. "Yeah, that makes sense."

"What about you?"

"Huh?"

"You one of the… unfortunate ones?"

"Unfortunately."

He grunts. "I'm sorry. Really."

"Thanks."

Eventually he brings me to a row of shelves on which a large supply of tents is stacked. "Any particular size you want? Colour?"

"I'm not picky."

He snickers. "You never are." He selects a blue tent and hands it over. "Here."

"Thank you."

"Hold on." He crosses the aisle and drags a rolled-up sleeping bag off the shelf. "Here. You need a pillow, too?" Before I can respond, he passes me and strolls to the end of the aisle and brings down a large clear nylon bag full of extra pillows, pulls one out, and throws it my way. "Here you go."

"Thank you." Carrying all this stuff is kind of awkward. The tent bag has no strap, looks like it was torn off.

"Need anything, come by anytime. I'm always open. My counterparts an' I have different sleep schedules to accommodate everyone's needs whenever they arise."

"I appreciate it."

"I know you do. Don't sweat it."

I take the tent to a relatively isolated area at the edge of the compound just a few yards behind the HESCO MIL barrier, and set it up. It's a two-man tent. I unravel the sleeping bag inside and throw the pillow to one end. It's late, feels later. My eyes sting with drowsiness. The chatter of my counterparts, their friends, and the Freddies and Charlottes isn't disruptive enough to promise a lack of sleep tonight. A few Charlottes strum softly on acoustic guitars and occasionally add lyrics to the familiar tunes they play. Huh. She's full of surprises, isn't she? Draws... smokes cigarettes... plays guitar. Pretty good at all three, too. Unfamiliar, somber notes that sound a little Led Zeppelin-esque drift across the cool air. Kind of soothing.

Easy to fall asleep to...

I'm startled awake by a loud ratcheting sound and jolt in my sleeping bag. Charlotte softly assures me, "Easy. It's just me." She shows me the markings on her hand. It takes me a second to recognize its purpose before I show her the symbol she drew on my palm. "Okay, good," she says with a smile. "I got the right one."

I stare at her. The flickering glow of a distant campfire outlines her slender form, brightening the fringes of her chestnut brown hair. Her eyes somehow twinkle despite the shadows dancing epileptically over the gentle curves of her face.

I can hear a few Michaels and Charlottes are still scattered about the dimming fires. One parallel version of her is playing Tommy James & The Shondells' *Crimson & Clover* on her acoustic.

"Mind if I come in?"

"I-I... sure... before the mosquitoes come in."

She nimbly bounces inside and zips the door shut. She's wearing a pair of short-shorts and a plain white T-shirt. Her hair is damp. She smells strongly of orchids and fruit shampoo, telling me right away that she came here almost as soon as she'd dried herself off from a shower.

Sitting on her knees at the foot of my sleeping bag, hands on her pale thighs, she looks me over, as if slightly unsure about something.

"You okay?" I ask her.

"Yeah. Yeah, I'm good."

"Where's Michael?"

"He's... off, somewhere. I let him go."

"What do you mean, you let him go?"

"I… I don't know how to say this without coming off as a total bitch, but… I made my choice."

"Huh?"

"I chose you," she says, "before I drew that mark on your hand."

My heart jumps. I'm not sure what to say, or where this is going. "Charlotte… why? But he's from your—"

"I know. But you know, it's my decision in the end. I like this side of you more." She sighs. "I feel like a piece of shit."

"No, don't. Don't beat yourself up. If it's what you really want…"

"It is."

"How'd he take it?" I ask more out of curiosity than concern for him, and it makes me feel a little ashamed that I feel that way about myself. How exactly does one correctly feel about a woman who leaves a version of you for another version of you?

"Well enough, I suppose. He respected my decision. He wasn't *happy* about it, but he respected it. And I mean… I can't believe I'm going to say this, but… it's not like I'm the only one here."

"Yeah," I reply quietly.

"But, personally, as an individual who speaks for me, I wanted you." She's watching me carefully. "You okay?"

"Yeah."

"You looked like you were spacing out again."

"No, no, I was just… I was surprised."

"Surprised?"

"I wasn't expecting this."

"But it's happening, so, how do you feel about it?"

"How do I feel about it…?"

"No, pressure, okay?" She reaches out and touches my knee, smiling reassuringly. "I've told you what I want. If it's not what you want, that's okay. I understand this is probably a bad time…"

"Can I ask you a question?"

"Of course."

"Why me?"

"I don't know, Michael. It's hard to explain. I guess it all boils down to the little differences. Something about you just affects me on a level that… well, that the other Michael can't. Going through the camp, I've seen all kinds of different versions of you.

Some are bold. Some are shy. Some are disfigured. Some are neurotic. Some are closed off. Some are more open. Some are sneaky. Some are kind. Some are rude. Some are short-tempered. Some are composed. Some are crazy. Some are serene. And some are in between or a little bit of everything. Your absolute best and your absolute worst are all here in this camp. There's very little about you that's been left to my imagination. I'm sure you've had a similar experience today."

"Yeah, somewhat." Curiosity overwhelms me. "Where do I fit?"

"Hmm." She touches her pointed chin with a forefinger, emulating deep thought, still smiling. "Well, I wouldn't say you're the absolute *best*… sometimes you're scary and intense. And I think you beat yourself up too much. And you think too little of yourself. You have all these little problems that you gotta deal with— problems I can't fix. Your confidence hit a brick wall at MACH 5. But it feels right to me. You, like this, with all your imperfections. You're not a superficial version of yourself like some of the others, trying to impress any version of me that they can. I've seen the act they try to pull off." She laughs. "Like the De Niro Pose."

"Oh, God," I groan. I can feel my face burning with embarrassment. "Not *that*!"

"That," she says.

"Tell me I didn't do that in your universe, too."

"Oh, but you did, my dear."

I can't stop myself from simultaneously laughing and cringing at the memory of that embarrassing display. I desperately want to purge everything about that moment from my mind. "God, what was I thinking?"

"You were thinking you could pull it off without me noticing, that's what you were thinking." She grins. "But I noticed."

"No… Jesus, no."

"Yes."

"I'm never gonna live that down, am I?"

She shakes her head, still grinning. "No."

We share a brief laugh, but when we fall silent, an awkward air stifles any further attempt to speak. Maybe it's anxiety, or maybe we just don't know how to keep this going. There's still the lingering question…

A bad note screeches from the acoustic outside and the song

stops. The Charlotte who messed up says, "Fuck, I thought I had it that time... hold on, boys, lemme try that again." After a couple notes, she messes up again. "Dammit. I'm starting over." She starts from the beginning. *Crimson and Clover* slowly takes form again, and she plays through the medley without further interruption.

"You play that really well," I say to the one in front of me—the only one that matters to me.

"Thanks," she says shyly. "I... haven't played in a while."

I try to get the conversation back on track. "To answer your question, I feel happy about it. About you being here with me. The others were..."

"The others were...?" she says, hanging on my last word.

"Like... chords on that guitar."

She gives me a look, silently demanding clarification.

"You know, like the version of you out there playing that song on the guitar. *Crimson and Clover*, I think.

"Correct."

"None of them struck the right notes with me, I guess is what I'm trying to say. Does that make sense?"

"I'm sure there's a profoundly more poetic way to say that, but I'll take it."

I chuckle. "Well, poetry was never my strong suit."

"I know." She crawls up alongside me. Just her being this close makes my heart pound. She seems to hesitate at first, pondering something, and then she asks it: "Is it okay if I sleep here tonight? With you?"

My heart skips several beats. "Y-yeah."

She smiles, slipping into my sleeping bag. There's plenty of room in it for the both of us. Her legs brush up against me. My body is stiff, I'm nervous. She could easily sleep away from me, but somehow, I don't think that's on her mind tonight, confirmed when she presses her body against mine, her head on my chest, her hand on my stomach. I can feel her listening to my heart racing. She giggles. "It's okay. I don't bite much." She sighs, slowly rubbing her body against mine, whispering, "Relax."

"I'm relaxed."

"Fibber."

"Somewhat relaxed."

"Slight fibber."

I hold her tight. "This feels nice."

There's a prickly silence for a moment. Then, softly, she asks, "Do you want to feel nicer?" Before I can ask, I feel her hand slip under my shirt and brush across my chest hair. Then her hand slowly glides down my stomach to the waistband of my pants, and I tense up, making her pause, waiting for protest. When I don't say anything, her fingers push further into my pants, and I feel her grip me. It doesn't take a lot for me to get hard. Just her touch is enough. She tenderly kisses my chest and raises her head, pushing herself up to reach my lips. Our mouths touch. I taste her again. Feels like it's been an eternity since the last time. Her fingers tighten around me.

"Are you sure?" I whisper.

"Yes," she whispers back, kissing me again.

<u>Chapter 20: One Last Memory</u>

I'm awake before I open my eyes. All I see is orange beneath my eyelids. The strong smell of sex and sweat pervades my nostrils. It's a sauna in here, my hair is damp, my skin sticky with perspiration, glued to the fabric of my sleeping bag, and to Charlotte, who's still sleeping with her head on my chest and an arm slung over my middle, breathing softly. I don't want to move and disturb her sleep, but at the same time, the humidity in here is making me feel like an egg sizzling on a skillet, sunny side up.

I quickly reach a decision and gently shake her awake. She stirs, moaning sleepily, sweat-slicked fingers sliding all over my torso. She inhales deeply and sighs warmly on my chest. "Good morning, Michael."

"Morning."

She lifts herself off my body, her legs spread across me, her breasts hanging close to my face. She looks down at me and smiles, leaning back slightly to feel my erection with the sensual folds of her flower. "Mmmm. Excited to see me?" She sways back and forth, teasing me, rubbing up against my shaft. It's too hot in here for any sensible guy to exert himself, but seeing her like this, the sleeping bag falling down her curved back to reveal her slightly pale, rosy-skinned nakedness to me, her full teardrop breasts tipped with hardened pink nipples in close proximity with my face; I'm anything but sensible at this point. All I have to do is take hold of her hips and she knows I'm ready for her.

After twenty minutes, we're spent, drenched in sweat and other fluids, and clambering out of the tent in casual clothing that clings to us. Opening the door of the tent and feeling a refreshing blast of the morning summer breeze is like opening a giant Ziploc bag, the fumes inside the tent escaping with an almost audible hiss. I close the screen but leave the door unzipped to air out the tent, because goddamn, it needs it.

We join a group of parallels as they sit around a fire, giving each other shoulder rubs as they wait for a Michael covered in dark blue streaks tattooed all over his body to rebuild the fire from last night. As he does this, two Freddies prepare a large grille and a pair of skillets, while a Charlotte from an apparently far-off dimension (this one has white hair twisted into a triple bun, and an eyepatch blotting a portion of her face covered in scars) brings over loaves of bread, cartons of eggs, bottles of maple syrup, and bins of margarine. Yet another counterpart supplies a nearby tree stump with stacks of plates and tins full of cutlery.

Charlotte and I mostly keep to ourselves, socializing only when our parallels or a few copies of Freddie interact with us about nothing in particular. We eat in silence, glancing at each other and smiling like we're sneaky teenagers again, our minds still fixated on what we did last night and this morning.

After breakfast, we walk together through the base, exploring the greenhouse, familiarizing ourselves with the laundry facility, the showers—stopping there to occupy a stall for ourselves to wash ourselves off, have sex again under the torrent of steaming water before we could rinse the soap away, and then wash ourselves and each other again. Afterwards, in fresh casualwear, we follow the trail to the old weeping willow tree where a few Charlottes are already hanging around, lying on towels in the shade, reading books, scribbling in their sketchbooks. My mom's flawless portrait in the tree has smoothed with time. It hasn't been there long, maybe a couple years. I stare at her angelic smile in nostalgic awe and remember all those times when she used to smile like that every day. She's exactly the way I always liked to remember her: strong, matronly, loving, gentle. It wasn't until after Dad left when she became frantic and smothering, her fears and insecurities chipping away at everything else until it was all that was left of her, manifesting into something she couldn't hope to control. It took me hours before I realized that she wasn't waking up again; an additional hour to notice the pill bottles on the bedside were empty.

"Hey," Charlotte pulls me back. "You okay?"

"Huh?"

"You're spacing out again," she says with visible concern. "You wanna go back?"

I take another look at the tree and see the little notches cut into it next to Mom, each notch a milestone in my growth into adulthood. After age twelve, the notches stop. "Yeah," I tell her, "let's go back."

As we leave, I glance over my shoulder at the tree again, its thick gnarly branches twisting skyward, high above the clearing...

JUMPING FOR CHARLOTTE

*

At lunch, Freddie meets with us at the same table we had lunch yesterday. He shows us the mark Charlotte made on him yesterday as he sits down. "Where's the other one?" he asks.

Charlotte shrugs, trying to look passive. I say nothing. Gravely, he asks, "You wouldn't happen to know, would you?"

I answer, "No." Just to be sure, I glance around the base at the clusters of parallels and other locals going about their chores: splitting firewood for the almost constantly burning fire pits, carrying supplies to various facilities, tending to vehicle and weapon maintenance, patrolling the grounds in dutiful strides; none of their attention is on us—not as far as I can tell, anyway.

"Damn," Freddie grunts, and then sighs. "I'll try to find him."

"Freddie."

He looks at me inquisitively. I ask him, "If I suddenly disappeared with two dead cops, what would you do?"

"I don't know," he tells me. His brows furrow as his eyes search my face for a reason behind my question. "I really don't know what I'd do. I don't think I'd take it lightly. I don't know what I'd do in that kind of situation." He pauses. "What are you thinking about?"

"I'm thinking about getting the Freddie from my world out of there."

Freddie blinks and gives me a blank stare. "Why?"

"Because I think maybe it'd be the right thing. A way to keep him safe, and, I guess, a way to assure him that I'm okay and very much alive. I've been thinking it over since we first got here. All I've been able to think about is how he might be feeling about all this. First I'm going out on a date, and then a few hours later, the cops tell him about Charlotte's murder, and my disappearance. I doubt they'd forget to mention the two cops I killed. Maybe they'd tell him that *I* killed Charlotte and the cops. Went crazy, lost out to... to PTSD or some bullshit like that. I don't know."

"Listen, kid." Freddie straightened out his bulky shoulders, interlocked his fingers in a ball on the table, and looked me straight in the eye. "Knowing me, if I was you, I'd leave it alone."

My heart misses a beat. "What did you say?"

"Leave it alone," he says curtly. "When you went to Afghanistan, you kept a good schedule when it came to sending letters. Some weeks, I never got any. I had to assume the worst and try to move on. In my mind, you were dead until I got another letter. It wouldn't've been healthy to lean too far in either direction. Dead. Alive. I knew that as every day passed by, the odds from my perspective maintained a steady fifty-fifty until you came home. In your last letter to me, you said you were coming home for good. Hadn't heard from you in the following weeks since. I assumed you changed your mind and went on your way to some other life, or died shortly after.

"It may be disrespectful to some degree, but in my own way, I was mourning you the minute you left to serve. After that, I kinda got used to the idea that you may never come back alive. That I'd open the door to some army personnel with a folded flag and a sullen look on their faces. I know how I would've felt if that'd ever happened—I would've wanted to have been able to see you alive at least one more time. I know this, because I've seen it from several parents and significant others I'd been acquainted with—many of whom were my parents' customers back when they ran the diner—during Vietnam. A third of my schoolmates from junior high never came back home. I was deemed unfit, and so… it took a while for them to get over that fact.

"My point, Michael, is that you'd given me, my parallel, right; one last time to see you alive. The last time he saw you, he saw you happy, asking for a bit of cash like a teenage freshman determined to take a girl he likes out on a date. Ever since your mother passed on, that's all I wanted from you, kiddo." He squinted and wiped his eyes on a large, hairy arm. "It always made my day during those rare times I saw you actually, genuinely smile. And you were so full of energy and excitement when you gave me the news about your date with Charlotte, like yesterday had never happened, like you weren't a wreck trying to live with yourself after all the horrible things you saw out there." Freddie couldn't stop the tears from flowing down his puffy cheeks. "It wouldn't be easy, not in the slightest. But at least… the last time I ever got to see you alive, you were happy."

He starts sniffling wetly and hides his face in his arms, trying frantically to wipe away the tears. His face flushes with deep sadness, a kind of remorse for something that never happened directly to him. I don't know how to soothe him. I wish I could. "Freddie…"

"Just leave the old man that one last memory."

JUMPING FOR CHARLOTTE

Charlotte and I exchange glances, unsure of what to do. Charlotte leans forward, trying to soothe him with a matronly tone in her voice. "Hey, now... don't cry. We're still here, big guy."

His voice cracks. "I know. I... I'm grateful for that."

"Is it true?" I ask him.

"Is what true?"

"That's what you would want?"

"If worst came to worst, yes."

"You're not just... *saying* that, are you?" I feel guilty just for thinking it a possibility, but it flies out before I can stop it. I freeze, watching him carefully.

He gives me something of a glazed stink-eye, anger showing through his sadness. "No. If the police came up to me and told me you disappeared after murdering three people, I wouldn't want to remember you as some sort of psychotic serial killer; I'd want to remember you as the boy I took in when he had nowhere else to go, and the man who left the diner with a spring in his step on his way to do everything he could to give Charlotte the best night possible. Just leave it alone. Nothing you do now can make things better for him."

Even if I wanted to, it would be impossible to argue with his logic. Nobody knows him better than he does.

Chapter 21: Yesterday

I'm still conflicted. What Freddie said probably made more sense to him than it did to me. I understand the reasoning behind it perfectly fine, but his logic bothers me. He can only tell me these things from a theoretical point of view. It's not like he himself had to deal with the cops telling the version from my universe... whatever it was they told him after I jumped. The one I'm concerned about is still out there somewhere in the multiverse, wondering what the hell happened. I have no idea how to get there, but I've had theories on how to get *back*. Looking at the notches on the weeping willow, a thought had crossed my mind: if I carved a specific mark or crude drawing on the tree, somewhere no other parallel versions of myself or Charlotte or anybody else could easily spot from the ground, I could go anywhere and simply remember the mark on that one specific tree to get back to this dimension. It's just a theory, as I've never tried it, but it seems like it could work.

The problem is that I can't think of anything in my own universe that is specific to just that one universe. After all, anything I did would have been replicated thousands to tens of thousands of times over in other parallel universes, and just thinking about an object or a place or a thing would be damn-near impossible. Even now, with that marking, other versions of me might have done the same thing in their universe, and some of them would probably put my theory to the test. It seems oddly cold, waiting for some way of confirmation that a parallel version of myself actually tried it and either failed or succeeded in proving that theory. And if they succeeded, what if they wound up in a different universe that also had the same marking?

This is such a goddamn mess. I want to yell out my frustration. I don't care how many other versions of me or of Charlotte are present. This is bullshit. Every minute I spend on this base feels like another minute wasted.

Yesterday, 'Seinfeld' provided me with an air freshener to keep the tent smelling clean. Charlotte was embarrassed, hiding her face from his knowing smile.

"No need to be so modest," he'd said. "Happens all the time

here. It's normal."

After that, we strolled out along the wharf where at least a dozen gunboats are stationed. A tanker with the Moonoco Gas Company logo on it is apparently kept near the boats at all times, providing fuel for the boats and the trucks and various customized Mustang IIs and Dodge Challengers kept in the motor pool. The Mustang IIs are similar to my own, although there are a few Challengers occupying spaces as well. Their customizations are interesting, if a little unconventional and ugly: the Mustang IIs' hatchbacks were replaced with machine gun or grenade launcher turrets, somewhat downsized to maintain balance with the strengthened axis and armour-plated bodywork; the Challengers' roofs had been replaced with removable sunroof panels to accommodate the machine guns and grenade launchers mounted on the roofs.

"A little overkill, don'tcha think?" Charlotte had asked me when we were perusing through the garage, passing several rows of the sleek, gleaming vehicles, all similarly painted and striped.

"Unconventional," I'd said, my eyes slowly taking in every familiar-yet-unfamiliar shape and curve, every modification, every addition. Most of them have been kept the same, only bulkier, less compact. They're still sleek, but not like before. "A little impractical. Kind of hideous." Teasingly, I'd asked her, "Want me to upgrade my own car like this?"

She laughed through her nose. "No, thank you. I love it just the way it is." As she said this, she was sliding her finger across the hood of a dark blue Challenger with rose-coloured racing stripes front-to-end. I'd noticed right away that something seemed to be on her mind. She only spoke when I said something to her that required a response. Otherwise she would just smile or nod.

"You okay?" I asked her.

"Hm? Yeah, I'm fine."

"You sure?" I asked hesitantly.

"Well," she said, breathing a discontented sigh, "I guess I just don't know what to think about all this. I mean… this is all about me? This is *because* of me? Because I died?"

"It's not like it's your fault. You're not to blame here."

"This whole situation is so fucked up."

I paused. "Yeah, that's true."

"No, I mean it's *really* fucked up. I die and people go to war to make sure the other versions of me don't die." She turned to face me. "I don't want this, Michael. I don't want people to die because of me. If it's my time, then it's my time."

I'd closed the gap between us and held her delicate, oval-shaped head in my hands tenderly. "But it *isn't* your time, Charlotte. That's the point. That's the problem. So one version of you dies in a distant universe. What gives them the right to start killing the rest of you when it has nothing to do with the other versions of you? That's a completely separate life from yours. For them to bunch you all together into one kill order is beyond insane, not to mention unjust."

"They're too big, Michael." Her face screwed up with a pained expression, framed in my hands. "They're too big for us. Yes, it's unfair, and no, I don't want to die, either. I know you want me to stay alive, too. And I want to stay alive for you, live *with* you, hell, until my last day, but… but what's more important: allowing hundreds of people to die just to keep me alive, or letting me die without undue casualties? I'm not *that* important, Michael. I don't want anyone else to get hurt because of me." She took hold of my wrists and gently lowered my hands, then interlocked her fingers with my own. Her eyes were trying to reassure me that this was the right thing. "Maybe it's better to end this now. Look at all this. Really *look* at it. It's already been dragged out for five years. That's too long to fight for just me. I don't know how the others here think of it, but I don't like it. I can't in good conscience go along with something like that."

"No. You're wrong. The only casualties in this will be the ones who come after you. The ones who—who would follow such an illogical, bullshit ideology. It's impossible for the multiverse to just 'implode' because some random parallel version of a human being dies in one universe and lives in the other. It's a stupid over-estimation of—"

She snapped, "I don't care! Michael! I don't care if it's logical or not. I don't care if their plan makes sense. People are *dying* because I'm alive!" Tears beaded in her eyes and streamed down her face. "It doesn't matter if it makes sense to you! It doesn't matter!" She was crying, no longer able to fight back her tears. She fell against my chest and sobbed, wrapping her arms tight around me. I wasn't exactly sure how to console her. I held her there, told her it would be alright, everything would be alright.

But she was never the same after that incident. I ate dinner and showered by myself for the first time since we officially became a couple. She disappeared in the communications shack, deciding to occupy her time with the other Charlottes operating these 'cross-dimensional communicators.'

"That's what they call them," she'd said excitedly when she returned to me. I was sitting with other Michaels and 'Seinfelds' and Freddies around a campfire near my tent at around 2100 when she'd run up to us and checked each Michael for the mark she'd made until she found me. "It's the coolest thing," she said. "They're actually able to have full conversations with other versions of themselves in other bases just like this one. I had this thought. It hit me when I was talking to myself on the other side of the communicator. While we're having this conversation, two other versions of us probably worded the same conversation differently, or it branched out into multiple different directions. I mean, that's the coolest thing!"

A Charlotte sitting on her left turned and said enthusiastically, "Right? It's so weird."

"I know!" she replied.

"Are you okay?" I asked her. She seemed so excited and happy at this time that I hesitated to ask, but last time I saw her, she was distraught, almost hysterical.

"Yep! I'm good." She kissed me, and when she broke away, she waggled a piece of flame-cooked chicken a few inches from my face and tossed it in her mouth, chewing gratefully. "Thanks, honey."

"Want some more? You need to eat." She took another piece of my chicken off my plate. "Hey, thief!" I exclaim jokingly. "You're stealing all my food."

She giggled and kissed me again. "I'll be back." She turned and bolted back to communications, high-spirited once again. I couldn't help but smile at that. I glanced at the other Michaels in turn, most of whom were grinning with me.

"What?" I asked.

"Nothing," one of them said.

Another said, "I just love seeing her in a good mood, that's all."

"Agreed," I replied.

"Agreed," the others repeated in unison. It was a strange thing to try to grow accustomed to.

I'd half-expected her not to join me in the tent that night, but she surprised me by letting herself in a little after midnight. I noticed that the cheer and wonder from earlier was all but gone, replaced with something almost expressionless, a bit somber. I couldn't quite place it.

"Hey."

"Hey," she replied. She undressed and crawled into the sleeping bag with me, pressing her warm body up against mine. "I'm sorry."

"What for?" I asked. But she was already asleep.

Chapter 22: The Dream

I dream about Mom again; the way she used to smile before Dad left us behind (*she had a smile that could light up a room*); the way she told me to sit still and be patient when she tried to draw me under the weeping willow (*"I said, sit still, Michael! Do you want squiggly arms or do you want normal arms like all the other kids your age?"*); the way she would point out a gentlemanly act in a TV show or a movie as we watched it together (*"See that? That's the kind of man you should strive to be."*).

All of those good memories are wiped away. Her face darkening, her smiles cracking, dissolving beneath a mask giving way to wrinkles, to anguish that warp her features. Her face shrivels like a pumpkin rotting at an accelerated rate. The wails, those horrible banshee-like shrieks I remember waking up to in the dead of night, jolting upright in cold terror thinking she's being murdered by an intruder. It's all happening again.

"Mom!" I scream as I dart through the pitch-black halls the way someone who's lived most of their life could without the need for lights. I burst into her room and see her thrashing about in an uncontrollable panic, kicking the sheets up toward the ceiling fan, flailing her arms, smashing the lamp and the digital clock on the bedside table. "Mom!" I practically have to wrestle her, barely able to hold her back as she screams. She shatters a glass of water across the side of my head above my right ear. Despite the lancing pain shooting through my skull, I don't back down. "It's all a dream," I tell her. "It's all a dream."

But of course, they aren't just dreams. It's like she's repeating the last time she ever saw Dad before he left us, every single night. Sleep medication doesn't work. Drinking herself stupid doesn't even work. It's always the same.

In a cruel twist of irony, all those loud, horrifying episodes contrast the overwhelming silence that oppresses our house the day she dies, the day I myself keep repeating in my dreams. Dreams like this one. Dreams that I can't stop. Dreams that I'm helpless to relive again and again and...

It was normal for her to sleep long hours, sometimes whole

days at a time, so I hadn't bothered her. It isn't until I wake up in the dead of night to the total absence of her usual wailing that I realize something's wrong.

My dream is the same as the memory. Waking up to the silence. The unbearable, crushing silence. But the room seems smaller. The moon's silver light filtering through the windows feels brighter, without actually brightening up the rest of the room despite its harshness.

I step out of bed—is the floor on an angle?—and walk out of my bedroom into the corridor with its single window overlooking the backyard. The backyard is an empty void. The moon fails to illuminate the grass or the deck, but the maple tree in the center of the backyard is well-light, shimmering as its branches curl and twist, its leaves stretching and stretching and stretching into long rods pointing downward; it slowly morphs into the weeping willow.

I move down the hall, passing the stairs. I look down the staircase into the foyer, its floor spinning while everything else stays in its place. The bathroom up ahead is empty. I turn, follow the rail above the stairs to Mom's bedroom door, which opens itself automatically as I approach, and enter to find her lying prone in her bed, just like in real life. The empty bottles that once contained her medication are scattered on the floor. Died in her sleep, but for some reason her eyes are open, and she's staring at me, the whites surrounding her dilated pupils piercing the darkness like the severe moonlight in my room.

"You left me," she says.

An electric current jolts through my body and I stiffen fearfully. Her eyes paralyze me, her head still resting on her pillow, her hair fanned out across the bed, crawling up the headboard and the walls like an expanding colony of centipedes, shimmering unnaturally in the silvery slats sieving through the window blinds. Her hair extends further, slithering across the ceiling and the floor, spilling over the sides of the bed toward me, swallowing all the clothes and furniture and trinkets in the room, consuming them in black, glossy tendrils.

Then her body, limp and lifeless, is dragged up toward the ceiling with it. Her feet dangle above the bed, her body twists back and forth from a neck that appears to be a broken, rubbery limb of pale flesh under a head that is simultaneously lifeless and alive, her hateful gaze never leaving me, eyes boring into me…

I choke back a scream.

She shouts, "You left me!"

"No!" I scream. "I was coming right back!"

Strands of her hair lift her right hand by the wrist like it's the will of a sick puppeteer's command. "Your father said the same lies, fed me the same bullshit you did. Like father, like son."

"No, Mom, I was—"

Her corpse bristles, eyes flaring angrily as she grows larger, crushing the bed under her bent knees, the frame giving way with a reverberating snap. Her head rolls to the side as her widening shoulders touch the ceiling. A low moan in her throat rises to that of a furious wailing that distorts further, changing into a scream that shakes the house and brings down flakes of paint from above.

"Michael!?" I hear Charlotte scream. "Michael!"

Mom's torso splits down the middle. I see Charlotte entangled in Mom's hair, struggling to get loose, trying desperately to wriggle free from the shifting confines of Mom's torso. A fly in a spider's web. "Michael!" she shrieks. "Michael!"

Seeing Charlotte in danger is enough to make me spring out to save her—but I can't. Mom anticipated this. She has me pinned to the floor with thick tangles of hair constricting my ankles. I can't move. Panic takes me. My heart roars like a thunderous cacophony of thunder. I have to save her. I have to...!

Long needles sprout from the fringes around the window in Mom's torso, turning her into a Venus flytrap from hell. Its needle-teeth close in on Charlotte, puncture her. The deeper they perforate Charlotte, the louder she screams, her face distended in wide-eyed agony as the needles bore into her.

I wake up screaming her name.

There's something maternal about the way she immediately tries to comfort me, even though I startled her from her own peaceful sleep. "It's okay, it's okay. Shhh. I'm here. I'm okay." She holds me against her in the protective way a mother would comfort a small child. I hyperventilate into her bosom, shaking furiously as the dream's last aftershocks rattle in my mind. I'm drenched in a cold sweat, my hair mottled and damp.

Just a dream.

Just a dream.

"It was just a dream," she assures me. "It's okay now." She kisses my forehead and holds me tighter, strokes her fingers through my hair. "It's okay, sweetheart. I'm here. I'm okay."

I heave a sigh. The shakes have gone away. My tense muscles begin to relax until I reach around her and hold her.

"You're gonna be fine."

"Yes." I fight back tears.

She gives my head another tender kiss, ignoring the wetness of my hair. I finally notice the cold air of the late summer night and stiffen against it. A shuddering sigh escapes my lips. "God, it's cold tonight."

She slides down slightly so that she can look me in the eyes, and smiles, pulls the sleeping bag cover up to our ears. "Is that better?"

"A little. I'm sorry."

"Don't be." She presses herself against me and I feel how warm she is compared to the cool fabric of the sleeping bag. Her hand slides around me and squeezes my buttock. I feel her nipples graze across my sweaty chest. Her smooth thigh touches me further down, makes me tingle with a sudden pang of excitement. "How's this?" she asks with a knowing, playful smile.

I hold my palm against the side of her head. My thumb caresses her cheek. "You did that on purpose."

"What do you mean?" Her face is a mask of innocence. "I'm just trying to keep you warm."

I give her a knowing smile. "You're very sly."

She shrugs the shoulder she's not resting on, feigning innocence, and fluttering her big brown eyes at me while continuing to rub her thighs against me. "I don't know what you mean."

Chapter 23: Stratofortress

Thunder from helicopter rotors startles us awake the next morning. The cyclonic rotor wash whips hurricane-like winds across the camp, nearly rips our tent's pegs out of the ground. Any closer and it will. I scramble out of the sleeping bag and peer through the screen, squinting against the waves of dust blowing at the tent. Charlotte's asking what's going on as I look up at the bulky, almost caterpillar-like fuselage of a Boeing CH-47 Chinook helicopter as it touches down on a helipad about thirty yards from Commander Michael's office building. As the twin engines power down, a crowd gathers to witness the disembarking of ten Commander Michaels and their accompanying Vice-Commander Charlottes, all wearing similar war paint to what our Commander had when we first encountered him. They line up single-file and are immediately greeted by the Commander and the Vice-Commander of our respective base.

It's still dark outside, the sun's first rays hardly brightening the horizon.

I retreat from the screen to dress myself. Charlotte asks again, "What's going on?"

"Looks like a bunch of parallel Commanders have flown in."

She looks at me and then hastily pulls on her own casualwear. Together we crawl out of the tent, her first, then me, and then we slip into our footwear and join the crowd of spectating parallels.

The Commander's eyes seem to pick me out of the crowd with ease. He strides toward me, takes my hand, briefly inspects the faded mark on my palm. Then he glances at Charlotte with a look that I can only describe as conflicted and says to me, "The situation's changed." He slips a folded piece of paper in my hand and closes my fist on it. "The old PBR. *Brando*." He holds his fist in front of my face, his forefinger curls outward, points in what I almost immediately understand is the wharf's direction. "One hour. Yusef's in charge. He'll take you where you need to go."

Something about the way he's talking to me; like the details of this conversation shouldn't be discussed outside of the two of us. Something about it doesn't feel right. Matter of fact, everything about this feels wrong. No one knows me better than I know myself, and I know that the Commander is nervous about something, maybe even outright scared shitless. But why? What did he mean when he said the situation has changed?

Once we'd packed a few changes of clothes and some food, I lead Charlotte down the wharf past the refueling station and boats of varying size and type moored along its side, and then up a lone jetty to our assigned boat.

Freddie—*our* Freddie—is tagging along, wheeling a mini-fridge onto the United States Navy Patrol Boat, Riverine known as *Brando*. No surprise. I recognize it as the boat from *Apocalypse Now*. Figures a version of me with three additional years of combat experience would name it *Brando*. I was never much of an original thinker.

Yusef is already on board with two other Michaels and a 'Seinfeld,' all cross-trained to operate every crucial duty, I'm sure. With those four, and Freddie, Charlotte and I, the boat's filled over capacity by us three tagalongs. A back supply of fuel in six 20-litre jerry cans is tethered in a cabinet in the cabin alongside the fridge, which is hooked up to a solar-powered battery pack, and an old-fashioned radio setup is stands against the rear wall. There's a hatch in the floor leading to a cramped storage space in the hull where backup ammo and weapons, first aid, non-perishable food items, toilet paper, and cases of bottled water are kept. Dual Browning MCHB machine guns are mounted in the forward tub turret while a pintle-mounted M60 loaded with an armour-piercing incendiary ammunition belt occupies the aft.

Yusef answers the question in my eyes. "Auctions are wonderful things for war enthusiasts, my friend. A former Navy official was going to scrap it. The Commander cut him a good deal about the price. When I saw this, I said, ah, 'scrap it, get rid of it,' but he said, 'no, no, my friend, it's a good boat. I checked it myself.' Sometimes there is no swaying you."

I get straight to the point: "So what's this mission about? Where are we going?"

"Canada."

"Come on. Be serious, Yusef."

"I am perfectly serious. We are going to Canada. I have never been there myself, but I remember that you mentioned you were from Ontario, which I believe is not far from here, correct?"

"From here? It's a week by boat, maybe more. But why?"

"Why what? Why are we going to Canada?" Yusef shrugs. "Rendezvous."

"Rendezvous?"

"Yes."

"With *what*? Who?"

"Calm yourself. I cannot divulge such sensitive information just yet." He puts his arm around me and leads me away from the others, his voice low, his eyes narrow warning slits. "Unfortunately, we must flee. The essentials in the cycle must live. And so, we are going to a rendezvous point in Canada where we will hopefully be safe for a few days at least, from the Agency."

"What about the assault the Commander was talking about?"

"There has been a change of plans. Something has altered our course. This is uncharted territory now, my friend. Not even the Commander knows what to do except to have you sent to one of our safe houses in Southern Ontario to await further instructions."

"*Southern* Ontario?"

"Yes, Allah willing. Keep your voice down."

"I don't understand." I look around, watching the activity on all the other boats. It's like the whole base is being picked up and loaded onto them. "Are we evacuating?"

"Yes. Our location has been compromised."

"Why the hell didn't you just *say* that?" I hiss in frustration. "Why are we evacuating?"

Yusef adjusts his sunglasses with a frown. "I do not know much more than you do. Parallel versions of the Commander apparently did not come bearing good news. That is all I know. We must go now."

We cast off into Lake Michigan. I keep by the aft M60 watching the other boats depart from their moors, scattering in different directions. Five tugboats drag barges containing the Stranger Corps' few tanks (hidden under tarps), and shipping containers full of goods from the storage warehouses across the water. A car ferry loaded with twenty modified cars including my own unmodified Cobra II glides not too far off, having just left the shore. Four motor launches and five cabin cruisers outfitted with .50 calibre machine guns and anti- air and sea weaponry escort two passenger ferries carrying most of the Charlottes, non-combatant Michaels, Freddies, and sympathizers whose names I either forgot or was never told in the first place. The ferries look like legitimate commercial boats, and their crews probably have the false papers to prove their 'legitimacy' to any law enforcement that they may run into during the journey.

Three Black Hawks buzz angrily over us, accompanying the Chinook, their rotors whipping veils of mist into twisting frenzies.

It isn't until we're about a klick from land, the crudely constructed wharf and the strip of buildings behind it with the lush green forest beyond its boundaries; that I start to hear a faint sound that immediately kicks my senses into overdrive before I even know why. As it builds in my ears, this high-pitched, electronic shriek, a banshee's cry echoing across the dull morning skies—I start to realize what it is. I can hear it clearly over the guttural roar of the patrol boat's engine with disturbing clarity, as if it's right on top of us. My eyes search the grey clouds; the gloomy, bland canvas that dulls the sun's light. There's shouting from the other boats. A siren wails a distant warning, resonating across the water. The undeniable deathly howl of a Boeing B-52 Stratofortress easily overpowers it, forcing everyone on the patrol boat to clamp their palms over their ears as it rises to ear-splitting decibels. Yusef and I (and my two parallels on the other end of the boat) shout almost simultaneously, "Get down!"

Then it happens. Huge orange blots pepper the shoreline, spires of flaming earth and debris shooting skyward like a billion rockets launched simultaneously. The base disappears under a carpet of destruction. I can see a separate ball of flame blossoming brightly where the jetty starts—the fuel tanker at the station spilling burning fuel in all directions, the concussive impact blasting the jetty into a mist of splinters. A motor launch that didn't make it out far enough is ripped apart like wet cardboard. The choppers wobble uneasily as their pilots struggle to maintain control.

It isn't until the shockwaves sent tearing across the water reaches us that the reports of the explosions rend the air hard enough to crack Yusef's sunglasses with a pop that nearly implodes our skulls. Freddie and Charlotte yell out in horror and surprise, their hands over their ears doing little good against the violent, rumbling thunder. 'Seinfeld' must have hidden himself in a compartment below deck, because I can't see him anywhere. My two counterparts huddle in the cabin entrance, trying to shield Charlotte and Freddie with their bodies somehow. The mist is momentarily swept out of existence by the shockwave before gradually returning to shroud the surface of these disturbed waters again. I can hear screams coming from the ferries and can only imagine how much louder the explosions were for them, as they're two hundred yards closer to the shore than we are.

The screech begins to fade, the B-52's massive shadow sweeps over us as it ascends back into the clouds.

We're left stunned, shaken, gaping at the apocalyptic orange wall of smoke, fire, and dust erected in the Stratofortress's wake. The base is gone now; the Agency's strike is a crippling success.

Overcoming my initial shock, I run across the boat to Freddie and Charlotte, both of whom are curled up on the floor in the cabin. My counterparts are asking them the same questions I'm asking: "You alright?"

"What?" he gasps, visibly shaken.

"Are you hurt?"

"Are you okay?"

"You alright?"

"N-no, I think… I think I'm fine."

'Seinfeld' pops up from a hatch down below. "Is it over?" Everyone ignores him.

Charlotte's looking worse than Freddie is, so I rush to her side. My counterparts do the same. I tell them impatiently, "Back off! Stop crowding. Please. Give her some space. Hey. Hey." She reels when I touch her cheek, her tearful eyes wide with terror. "Hey, hey, it's alright. It's gone. It's gone, Charlotte. Honey." I frame her face in my hands and look straight at her, trying my damnedest to comfort her. "It's gone."

She reaches out, grips my arms, her fingers digging into me. She's trembling like a leaf clinging to a tree branch despite the efforts of a strong autumn wind.

"It's gone," I tell her again.

"God… oh, God…"

Yusef is almost eerily calm, as if he's totally unaware of the destruction that just unfolded, even as he takes off his glasses and studies the cracks in the lenses. "God has nothing to do with this."

I look at him, notice his cool demeanour. "Do you know something?"

His brown, piercing eyes flick down at Charlotte. "I know what caused this."

"What? Why are you looking at her like that?"

"She may know why."

Charlotte looks up when she hears this, her eyes wide with confusion and fear.

Yusef decides to give her memory a jolt. "The communications room. You spoke to parallel versions of yourself via the interdimensional frequency."

Just then, the radio in the cabin squawks. Commander Michael's voice crackles through its speakers. "Yusef. Yusef! Do you copy?"

Yusef slips by me, steps over Charlotte, and pauses in front of Freddie, who's sitting between him and the radio and is far too large for Yusef to step over. "Excuse me, please."

Freddie nods and crawls out of the cabin, prompting Charlotte to do the same if only to get out of Freddie's way. There isn't enough room in there for the three of them. Charlotte falls into my arms and begins to cry into my chest, clinging to my shirt and trembling furiously.

Yusef picks up the receiver. "This is Yusef. We were unharmed by the shockwave." Yusef glares at me across the deck— or maybe he's glaring at Charlotte. "It was too close."

"They may be circling back around for another pass. Continue to Mackinac Island and then proceed straight across Lake Huron to French River. No detours. No other stops. If there's an emergency that may force you off the water, let me know first—otherwise, don't break radio silence."

I'm running the route through my mind. We would never be too far from land. How does the Commander expect us to get all the way into Ontario from here without being found out? We would be safer on the roads. Out here, we're sitting ducks to any Agency aircraft that might be flying around. Hell, they already know we're here. The mission screams 'suicidal desperation'. We're equal to a colony of mice scattering anywhere we can to get away from the big, scary human that discovered us, hiding in every corner of the human's house in the hopes that the human won't notice. But no one knows the human's house better than the human.

Yusef hangs up the receiver and sees the apprehension in my eyes. I think he knows how idiotic this plan is. The Commander may be a parallel version of me, but that doesn't mean I know what he's thinking. What *is* he thinking? How could he think this is a good escape plan?

"What did you mean when you mentioned the communications room? You're not seriously blaming Charlotte for this, are you?"

"Not exactly," Yusef replies coldly. "*She* may not have done anything at all. But we know that even a small idea can have big consequences. I know she had such an idea. Whether or not *she* acted on it, or a parallel did, is yet to be determined."

I ask, "Would the Agency use that Stratofortress if we were on land?"

Yusef sweeps his hand, indicating the shore. He asks curtly, "What do you think?"

"No, I mean in populated areas."

"They have a tendency to avoid casualties whenever possible."

"So they wouldn't, then?"

"Not if we were in populated areas. But they can clear the highways. Evacuate towns under some pretense or another. They have the power to take unwanted casualties out of the equation. Land. Sea. Air. It would not matter how we went about it."

"But there are enough towns up here where we can avoid strikes from the Stratofortress if we kept moving," I tell him.

"Sure. But then there are all the ground troops and police who can corner us on land. Then where would we go? Michael, trust me." Yusef squats beside me and places a firm hand on my shoulder, careful not to touch Charlotte, who has gone stiff and silent. "If there were some other way, surely the Commander would have chosen it."

Other boats are beginning to pass us toward a small family of islands. Smoke from the burning shoreline thickens the air, joining the mist. It's almost impossible to tell the difference between the two; one is grey, the other a slightly darker shade of grey.

"We have to go." Yusef retreats into the cabin and throws the engine into a guttural snarl; it roars to life. The patrol boat starts moving at a synchronized pace with the other boats.

The Beaver Archipelago ahead of us could easily be avoided. I wonder why the Commander decided to build a fort within Hiawatha instead of settling on one of these islands. None of the surrounding towns are occupied, nor have they been in years, some even decades; but it seems like setting up shop on one of these islands, even if it's just a small spit like High Island or Gull Island, would be the smarter thing to do.

The more I think about where we are, the worse our situation seems. The only way off Lake Michigan by boat is by passing under Mackinac Bridge, which seems the most likely and advantageous for an Agency ambush. We would have to destroy that bridge, but that would block our paths, and there's no way in hell we'd survive the journey under constant hellfire from an Agency battalion stationed on it. If we travelled by land, at least we would have a fighting chance.

Goddamn it! I went back to Michigan to escape the hell of war. Now I find myself back in the middle of it all because a woman was nice to me during a time when I couldn't even be nice to myself. And now she's as good as dead, another victim of circumstance in another nonsensical war that's gone on too long, like the rest of us sorry, heartbroken bastards. When it's put like that, it sounds like the most pathetic thing a man could resort to.

Yusef breaks the silence: "You are probably wondering about why we never settled on the islands there." I turn my head toward him as he continues. "Technically, we did. We built a communications center and a series of bunkers. Nothing is finished as of yet. Ironically, they were being built for just such an occasion as this—to detect inbound threats and provide shelter from them—and we cannot even use them." He scoffs, nearly breaks into a fit of angry laughter. "We should have been paying attention."

The stabbing points of Gull Island's balsam and white cedar trees materialize as we approach, becoming less of an eerie mirage and more of a solid black outline against the sunrise. Fiery ripples sent across the sky by the rising sun that gradually sweep the blues of night away makes for a strange, psychedelic picture. The misty shroud and curls of smoke swirling around our boats have an otherworldly golden shimmer to them, their edges tinged with red and purple.

I hear shouting in the distance and look around at the other boats as they divert course, banking in different directions. My heart jackhammers as a horrible realization creeps its way into me.

The radio squawks again: "Yusef, do you copy?"

"Copy," he says into the receiver.

"The B-52 is coming back around. We're ordering all boats to fan out. Repeat: fan out!"

JUMPING FOR CHARLOTTE

We're in the outer left flank. Yusef immediately banks further out with the neighbouring boats following suit. All I hear is shouting and terrified screams over the guttural roars of motors. Then the motors get louder as dozens of propellers desperately churn the water into conflicting little hurricanes. Every boat zigzagging chaotically, each threatening to spill all of their passengers overboard. Hulls collide and scrape. The ferries blow their reverberating horns in warning.

Then that horrible shriek overpowers them all. The horror unfolding around me becomes this silent movie with a distorted, unimaginably hellish version of György Ligeti's *Requiem for Soprano*. Every Michael scrambles to protect their Charlotte. Every Freddie throws himself to the floor of his respective boat, trying to protect any versions of me closest to them. I threw myself around Charlotte, *my* Charlotte, doing my damnedest to protect her from this, as if I could. She asks me something, screaming, but I can't hear her over the roar of the plane.

Then it all happens at once. The water erupts on the far flank, towers of it shooting hundreds of feet skywards, erecting themselves in erratic patterns all over the surface, decimating smaller boats and obliterating portions of the ferries. The concussive force of the pounding explosions slams our boat off its belly. Our ears pop. The air is sucked from our lungs and Charlotte is ripped out of my arms as we all spill into the water. The boat rolls on top of us, and then the water's depths echo with vicious thunder, hurling shockwave after shockwave into us.

Before I know what the hell happened, I'm out.

Chapter 24: Gull Island

When I come to, I'm lying on my side in something soft and grainy. When I turn over, pain shudders through my body like a shimmering heat wave in the desert. Sand. I'm on sand. My eyes are burning beneath their lids. I'm afraid to open them for fear of going blind should I expose them to whatever bright light may surround me, so I listen instead: distant cries, a few scattered screams that pierce the white noise of the waves crashing on rocks and splashing up the beach. The occasional pop. There are no birds that I can tell, only people shouting; some crying, some wailing further down the beach, a few others chattering angrily to each other. A low reverberating droning noise fills the sky above us, the looming presence of a manmade bird watching the confusion from a safe height.

"This one's awake." I feel a hand touch my shoulder. The voice sounds like mine. "Hey. You okay?"

Their hand shoves me back and forth. More waves of pain ripple through me. I moan in protest. "Yes. Yes. I'm up. God, stop." I raise my arm—God, it feels so heavy—and I swat weakly at the owner of that hand. I don't strike anyone, but the hand eases back, so I guess the gesture did its job. Jesus, my head's killing me. Like it's being crushed.

Charlotte.

I bolt into an upright position, terror overcoming pain, and I open my eyes and look around for her. There are a few Charlottes scattered about the beach under the cedar trees, some missing limbs and lying down, being tended to by distraught Michaels and Yusefs; while others stride aimlessly in shock. Various other Michaels, Yusefs, and combatant versions of Charlotte and Freddie hastily build machine gun nests in a freshly dug-out trench under the treeline. On the other side, beyond the beach, I can see a vast layer of corpses and debris from the destroyed boats floating on the water, gradually following the tide to shore. Half of the Chinook juts awkwardly from the shallows among the wrecks. A single motor launch with a .50 caliber machine gun mount sits askew on the beach, with a man perched behind it, another Yusef from the looks of him, pointing the gun at the field of debris. Turning my head to the fringe of the cedar trees I can see the smouldering, fire-gutted wreckage of a Black Hawk lying on its side behind a sand dune.

The owner of the hand that shook me is another me, this one in combat fatigues and mirrored shades. His clothes are almost completely dry, from the looks of him. Probably one of the lucky crew members from the beached motor launch. He says, "I thought you were just about done for."

"Charlotte," I ask, "and Freddie, and Yusef—"

"Breathe. Take it easy."

"Where are they?" My legs are numb. I'm weighed down by this horrible dread. Christ, I already know what happened to the rest of them…

My alternate self confirms it with a grim shake of his head. "I'm sorry. I couldn't find them."

No…

I lost her again. And Freddie. Yusef… I failed them all.

"Hey," my counterpart pats my shoulder. "You alright?"

"No," I answer numbly. "No, I… are you sure…?"

"I wish I could say I wasn't."

My eyes well up with tears. Christ. No. Not again

"The commander's gone, too. And his Charlotte."

I don't respond. I'm staring at the sand, half in shock.

"They have the island completely surrounded." He cocks an M1911 pistol and offers it to me, holding it by the barrel. "Keep your head focused. You can still save her."

"But she's dead."

"No, she isn't."

"She's *dead*!" I exclaim, tears causing my vision to shimmer and sparkle. I wipe furiously at my eyes.

"She's *not* dead," he counters, "not for as long as we do our best to protect her from them, whatever the hell *they* are."

I will never be able to piece together just what the hell the Commander was saying about time loops and event loops and all of that. It made my head hurt worse than it already did, just adding to the pressure building inside my skull.

I notice something's shading my eyes from the sun and glance up at a pair of binoculars in my counterpart's hand. I take them from him and through the magnified lens I can see a barrier of forty-five-foot U.S. Coast Guard patrol boats with bow-mounted .50 caliber machine guns, coalescing with ominous clusters of what looks to me like night-black cyclone-class U.S. Navy patrol boats armed with 25mm autocannons and .50 caliber machine guns. The cyclones look like hideous wraiths gliding through the wreckage left in the Stratofortress's wake. Something about them is off. They aren't flying the American flag or the flag of the State of Michigan. They aren't flying anything. But the Coast Guard boats are.

Four Black Hawks buzz above the approaching onslaught, their wing-mounted machine guns and rocket pods jutting at the beach.

I magnify the lens further, squinting at a lone figure standing beside an autocannon on the leading cyclone's bow. He's familiar somehow. Middle-aged, with greying short hair. Something about his structure and posturing seems tailored for maximum casualness to put one at ease. Yet, even at this distance, dressed in combat fatigues, he has the clashing air of a businessman.

A businessman. It clicks together.

"Armitage," I growl as my internal organs seem to come to a boil. Everything still hurts, but now the aching pain only fuels my growing rage. "I killed that son of a bitch already."

"So did I," my counterpart says. "It doesn't matter. There're infinite versions of them all. Watch out for Zona and Reeves, especially. Unless you've dealt with them before...?"

"Zona may have been in the van that nearly ran me and Charlotte off a cliff," I tell him, "but I can't say with a hundred-percent certainty. Remembering my close encounters with him in Charlotte's house on two separate occasions turns my fingers rigid, my knuckles whitening as the binoculars' mechanical joints groan in protest.

Someone else emerges from the cabin of the leading cyclone and salutes the 'Sarge,' who salutes in return. I've seen enough versions of me to recognize the familiar build of this stranger standing on the other side of the autocannon across from Armitage; the way he carries himself topside—it's me. I stare at him intensely, noticing the weathered look of his face behind mirrored aviators. I can tell he's seen a lot.

But what the hell is he doing on an Agency ship?

"There's always one," my counterpart says, as if he already found out somehow.

I turn away from the binoculars. "One what?"

"One who leads them right to us. The Alpha."

"Yusef said Charlotte might've told them."

"Yusef likes to speculate, doesn't he?"

"Yeah, but—"

"I noticed he's not too fond of her."

"Yusef? Come on…"

But my counterpart's face is hard, eyes thinned in a bitter squint. Behind us, the other combatants are propping their machine guns and sniper rifles on the bank of the trench. The armaments that survived the Stratofortress are damn-near pitiful, and I realize right then and there that we don't have a chance in hell of surviving a direct confrontation with the enemy, especially if *I'm* leading the charge. No one knows how I'll react in a desperate combat scenario better than me. Of *course* they have a version of me leading the charge!

My counterpart shouts over the din of work and worry: "Any snipers see a shot, you take it!"

A rifle barks immediately, its report echoing across the water, startling various Charlottes.

Quickly I consult the binoculars. There's a brief delay between shot and impact, as the potential targets on the leading cyclone are still talking to one another when I look at them. One, two…

Sparks explode between Armitage and the cyclone Michael as the round glances off the cabin's armour plating. Both lucky bastards flinch instinctively before ducking down out of sight. "Shit!" the shooter yells from the trench. Just about every other sniper down there starts shooting in a vain attempt to peg at least one of them in their retreat—the Agency's Michael ducks behind the autocannon while Armitage rushes around the cabin out of sight.

The machine gunner on the beached motor launch opens up on the boats, shaking the air with a rumbling staccato. Tracers flash across the wreckage on the water, strafing the bows of the boats. I watch as Coast Guard officers hit the floors of their boats while those on the machine gun mounts bravely stay at their stations to return fire.

The autocannon's muzzle flashes like a light signal on the leading patrol boat's aft. The sound hasn't traveled here yet, and the rounds will be here in less time than that. I scream, "DOWN!" as I throw my arm around the nearest Charlotte's waist and dive head first into the trench with her. The beach violently heaves gouts of sand into the air as the autocannon's fire pounds everything left on it to oblivion. Tracers from other boats rake over the beached motor launch, causing its gunner to flinch behind his M60E3 as he continues firing. Every Michael, Yusef, and Charlotte with a machine gun in the trench responds with their own volley, accuracy be damned. It's mostly the debris field floating between the two parties that absorbs most of our fire.

I scramble into a squat and help the Charlotte I dragged down the slope with me to her knees. "You okay?"

She nods. "Thanks, love."

Seeing her intact stabs me with a confusing kind of pain I've forced to familiarize myself with. Sure, she's alive right in front of me, but... it's not *her*. It's not the Charlotte I fell for. The Charlotte I fell for is...

I rip my eyes away from her and peek over the bank as machine gun and autocannon fire continue to churn the beach's sands like the raging waves of a stormy sea.

The four Black Hawks ascend; the two outer helicopters fan out in opposite directions while the pair in the middle end their ascension sooner and dip their noses toward the beach, wing-mounted armaments strobing and spewing curls of black smoke. Four rockets shriek through the air. Someone yells, "Incoming!"

The trembling earth shakes hard enough to send me sliding back down to the trench floor as the beached motor launch and its gunner are blown apart in a bright orange wall of roiling flames. The day darkens around the explosion as it swells outward, searing across the sand, hurling pieces of the motor launch into the cedar trees. An intense wave of heat rushes over us all. Feels like my hair is burning off my arms.

More rockets whiz from their pods and blow portions of the treeline into burning splinters. The shockwave tears through the trench, slamming us to the earth. The sound is deafening. My ears ring loud enough to drown out almost all sound. Tracers fly over our heads—Christ, they're getting closer—while probing machine guns rattle high above us. Cedar needles and branches pepper us endlessly. A headless Michael slumps down the bank and three Charlottes shriek in terror. Many of us return fire. I just have the M1911 in my hand. May as well be wielding a rock in this scenario.

We're pinned down by helicopters and patrol boats with

enough ammunition to level a city block and then some. Cedars tumble to the earth, which is alive with tracers and 25mm rounds. Explosions crash around us, on the beach and in the trees behind us. A constant, heavy downpour of sand and dirt threatens to bury us alive.

I crawl along the ground to the nearest Michael still breathing. He's lying with his back against the bank hugging an M24 rifle. "We have to retreat! Into the forest!"

"To hell with that!" he shouts back. "I'm staying right here!"

"If we don't retreat, we'll die here, you understand?"

His expression says it all. Resigned. He says, almost too quietly for me to hear over the roar of battle, "We're already dead."

Other versions of me clearly have the same idea I came up with, however—I glance up in time to see a knot of Michaels running with a trio of Charlottes into the woods, the Michaels shooting toward the beach as they raced for the other side of the island.

I flinch when a Black Hawk whooshes above us, so close my ears pop. A blanket of ridged bark and needles covers the trench combatants. A second group consisting of Michaels and Yusefs, with two Freddies and one Charlotte, attempt to follow the first group's example and are immediately shredded by autocannon fire. I twist away from the horrific sight of them decorating the nearby trees with pieces of themselves. More screams than gun reports sound off in the trench. They're wearing our numbers thin. Fast.

Hopelessly, I glance past the gory remains of the second group and search the trees for the first. They're mostly just distant shapes in the gaps now. They're making it. They're actually making it. But if the island is surrounded, it doesn't really matter, does it?

No sooner does the thought cross my mind that the entire forest lights up, blinding me and others, but I turn away before anything permanent happens. The sudden rush of air is so hot it makes everything that came before it seem like a warm summer day. The air becomes swelteringly hot, cooking us in our clothes, as a great wave of liquid fire pours across the forest, consuming it and the first group with unparalleled greed, filling the scorching air with a strangely sweet gasoline smell...

Napalm! They're dropping napalm on us!

A storm of that liquid fire incinerates the trees and everything around them within fifty yards, ripping Gull Island apart from end to end. Fireballs as bright as the sun fill my vision and rise high above the blazing trees. It's hell. This is hell and I'm stuck right in the goddamn middle of it. It's so hot it feels like all the moisture in my skin is getting sucked out. The air is suffocating. Alternate versions of everybody are falling to the ground, choking, gasping, trying to scream. Our resistance ends in dying whimpers and—

No.

I can't watch her die again. Not again.

The Charlotte I dragged down with me is curled up in the fetal position, retching from the smell and the lack of oxygen, covered in soot and needles. I fall on my knees beside her and gather her up. She flails weakly. "Hold on… hold…"

"Listen. Listen to me." I frame her face in my hands. My thumb wipes a streak of tears across her cheek, smearing the soot covering her skin. "I'm getting you out of here. Okay? I'm not gonna—"

The booming roar of an explosion directly in the trench a few yards behind me causes me to instinctively jump forward, covering her from the resulting hail of debris. I do my damnedest to ignore the renewed set of wails from injured or dying combatants. "I'm not gonna let them hurt you. Not again. Not ever again."

"I can't do this," she gasped. Her hands latch onto my shoulders, her nails digging into my arms. "I never wanted this."

"I can fix this."

"*This*?!" she screams. A 25mm round whistles above her head. I pull her closer to the ground. "People are *dying*, Michael! For me! I never wanted this. Not at this cost. How can you possibly expect me to?"

She's just scared. Have to soldier through this. I take her hand and she yanks it away. "No!"

"Charlotte, I'm getting you out whether you want me to or not!" I grab her wrist again and she wriggles in my grip. I jerk her forward and she stumbles after me. "Let's go! Now! Run!" I turn and bolt along the length of the trench with her staggering behind me, the M1911 in my right hand; keeping my head low as I dash over corpses and zigzag around parallel versions of us during their losing fight for our lives. The cedars above us are caked in sticky flames. A tree topples over and hits the tops of the banks, forming a burning bridge across the trench. I have to stop momentarily to assess its strength and decide to drag Charlotte under it, coming out the other side before it splits in half and falls inward between a pair of Yusefs praying to Allah. It's like they didn't even notice the tree falling between them. We don't stop despite Charlotte's resistance to my pull, but self-preservation keeps her ducking, dodging bullets and flying debris, holding out her free hand in case she suddenly trips over something and falls. But she doesn't fall. I won't let her fall again.

Through the roiling haze of smoke we press on through toward the end of the island. More bodies collapse off the bank. Explosions continue to boom oppressively all around us, closing in on the trench. Different sections of the trench explode, launching bodies and armaments and tree branches into the blazing napalm-soaked treeline. Deadly stalactites of fire plummeted into the trench. Dodging them iss like trying to dodge the rain. Charlotte's coat catches fire and she screams. I whirl and rip it off her and throw it over the top. Then I check her for burns. "You okay? You okay? Jesus…!"

She's okay. Still telling me to let her go. There's nowhere *to* go. Fire is all around us. Fire and death. Closing in. Suffocating. Getting harder to breathe with every passing second we stay in this goddamn trench. The joint army of Coast Guard and Agency soldiers continue to fire on our position with an overpowering roar while our resistance dwindles to a couple of feeble pops and metallic clanks, which are quickly silenced by another explosion, an exclamation point that rumbles through the smoking earth. We're done for. All I can do now is get her out of this hell before it consumes us.

We reach the end of the trench. Dead end. I yank Charlotte forward against the slope. "Careful. Be careful." She's coughing, retching from the smoke, struggling to breathe. I'm being conservative with my own air intake despite my racing adrenaline and absolute terror. How the fuck do I get her out?! We can't climb the trees because they're all on fire. Can't hope to launch a counter-attack with just us. All I have is a pistol. I look around and see an AKM with an under-barrel GP-25 grenade launcher on the ground, clutched by a lifeless Freddie whose torso stops halfway. I tuck the M1911 into the waistband of my pants and gently pry the AKM from his rigid fingers, staring at Freddie's wide, dull eyes reflecting the flaming canopy above us. I check the launcher, and to my relief it's still loaded with a 40mm caseless grenade. I reach down and close his eyelids. "I'm sorry, Dad."

I turn back to Charlotte. She's curled up against the bank, coughing violently between sobs. I search our immediate surroundings for an idea, anything to get us the hell out of here. A tree groans as its trunk crackles and gives. I watch it fall into the ditch. Then I crane my neck, scanning the trees for one I could climb. When I turn and look beyond the smoke and flames, past the dead end, I see a towering white cedar right on the beach—big enough to possibly conceal us from our attackers, and isolated in such a way that the only way for the napalm to get to it is if the wind carries it over.

And in this dry weather, with the wind picking up, our window of opportunity's closing fast.

I gather Charlotte in my arms. "Can you stand?"

"W-what?" she asks weakly.

"Can you stand?" I shout over the roar of the flames and the Black Hawk buzzing over us.

"Yes. Yes." Her legs wobble under her, and she needs my support, but she can manage standing, at least.

"Okay, baby. You see that tree? We're gonna climb it."

"Tree...?"

"I need you to keep it together just a little longer."

"Michael..."

"I need you to stay strong for me, okay?" I push her up the ditch and then follow her behind the last of the shrubbery and trees not yet fully alight by napalm. The smoke seems to be hiding us from the enemy for the time being. "Keep your head down." Gently I nudge her forward, guiding her to the big white cedar tree. It's ten feet of open ground between the fringe and the base of the tree. Ten feet out in plain sight, with nothing but a shroud of smoke to protect us. We reach the fringe and I squint, peering through the smoke, looking for dark shapes moving around in there. Coast is clear.

"Go!" I grab her arm and haul ass across the sand, lunging forward in a running crouch to compensate for her disoriented stumbling. "Go! Go!" No shapes, nothing close enough to be a threat, nothing that can see us. I can see the outlines of boats on the water, their metal gleaming as the sun reflects off them. I can hear the helicopters in the sky. Their rotors are sending the smoke away from the forest, but not with enough intensity to expose us. Not yet.

We duck under the tree's low-hanging branches and reach the

base. That's when I take her by the wrists. "Climb onto my back and hold on as tight as you can."

"Michael, I—"

"What?"

"I can't."

"Yes, you can."

"I can't do this anymore!"

"*Yes*, you can! Hang on to me!" I pull her body against my back and press her hands together. "Hang on!" I wait until she's locked her fingers together before testing how sturdy her grip is. Good enough. Now to climb this tree with only one hand and a 110-pound woman draped over my shoulders...

I strap the AK across my front so that the butt stock is dangling between my legs. Then I take hold of two lower branches and heave myself off the ground. The entire trunk is bristling with endless little branches for me to grab onto; more than enough to make a climb to its peak a cinch.

I feel her slipping. "Hang on *tight*, Charlotte!" The overpoweringly sweet gasoline stench of napalm invades my lungs, forcing me to retch as I cling stubbornly to the branch. Her arms around my neck don't help my breathing much, especially when she gradually puts further strain on me as she struggles to wrap her legs around my middle, feet kicking the AKM and trying to manoeuvre awkwardly around it. I lean forward, swinging the rifle against the tree until she can lock her feet in front of me. My biceps are already screaming in resistance. Drive out all pain, all fatigue. The intense heat of Afghanistan was a lot worse than this. Move! *Move!*

One branch at a time, I drag us up the white cedar tree's rough, furrowed bark, through endless sprays of its scaly green leaves. Napalm smoke prickles my nostrils and stings my eyes; somehow getting worse the further I ascend. Charlotte coughs into the nape of my neck, her grip weakening until she becomes aware of it, then tightening up again out of fear of falling. After three painstaking minutes, it's a long way down and we're not even halfway up the tree yet.

That's when a Black Hawk whirls around the tree, its powerful rotors whipping the branches in a frenzy around us. I hold very still, as close to the trunk as I can, wishing I could will myself invisible. Gotta get higher. Don't stop.

I climb on. As far as I know, it was just a mundane act on the pilot's part, a swoop in the continued search for survivors on the *ground*, not in the last of the unburned trees. Or so I hope.

Charlotte whispers, "Michael!"

"Shh. I think we're okay." I feel her limbs constrict around my body. Somehow it's comforting, if only because she's still warm with life. "I love you," I tell her.

"I'm sorry," she replies.

The Black Hawk makes another pass, its spinning rotors roaring deafeningly in our ears. I keep climbing. After another minute, the foliage thins out. I pause and look out through a wide gap in the rustling scale leaves at the smouldering blackness that used to be the forest of Gull Island, now a monstrous, sky-high mountain of black clouds. The pocked beach is teeming with Coast Guard and Agency personnel, dotted by the still-flaming wrecks of the motor launch and the Commander's downed helicopter. Boats both Agency and Coast Guard fill the teal waters between patches of overturned hulls and scrap, as well as the emerald shallows lining the shore. There doesn't seem to be an end to them, with more boats and helicopters coming in from Canada, from the looks of things. Jesus. You'd need an army of at least a thousand just to stand a chance in hell of getting off this island. But of course, with napalm involved, that's debatable.

The afternoon sun is in the early stages of setting. Has to be somewhere around three or four by now. I can't tell for sure. Its glare is harsh and bright, though its heat is nothing compared to standing in that trench.

"Look at them all," I gasp, indicating the horde scattered across the beach. I see Charlotte's face turn toward the view in my peripherals. She doesn't seem to have any kind of reaction to them. "There's so many of them," I continue in awe, consciously searching for the cyclone-class patrol boat where my doppelganger manned the autocannon, and finding it resting in the shallows with only two sentries posted on deck. The superiors don't seem to be anywhere near it.

A Black Hawk hurtles past us again. My head swivels urgently toward the deafening noise. There in the open bay is the whole goddamn rat pack—my Agency counterpart the 'Alpha', Armitage and his entourage; Zona, Mason, Chow, and the one with whom I have a personal bone to pick, Reeves. They're all cramped in the helicopter's bay, and all of them except Armitage and Reeves have rifles pointed right at us. Reeves stands behind the door-mounted M60 machine gun, ready to fire. Armitage is braced between my counterpart and Zona with a loudspeaker, his scarlet-red tie whipping against his cornflower blue dress shirt in the wind. He addresses me through the loudspeaker: "It's good to see you alive and well, Michael." His voice is calm and strangely casual. It's surreal just how smoothly he speaks through the loudspeaker after all this chaos. "This is it. This is the end. You've reached the top of the tree and now you can't go back down, can't go left or right. There's no 'up' for you to ascend to. Your only options are to surrender peacefully or die."

"Michael," Charlotte whimpers. "Just let me go."

"Stop talking like that," I hiss. I raise my voice over the roar of the helicopter's engines. "Bullshit! We're dead either way! You're gonna kill her just like you killed all the others!"

"Yes, Michael, we will kill her," Armitage replies so coolly it has the opposite effect on me. It just pisses me off. "We're going to kill her and there's nothing you can do about it. In the end, the outcome will be the same. All you're doing is prolonging the inevitable."

"What gives you the right?!" I shout. "What gives you the goddamn *right* to decide?"

"The same principle that apparently gives *you* the right to decide: the preservation of life."

I glance over at my counterpart. He seems passive about the whole thing, like maybe he's done this a thousand times before, *lived* this exact same situation a million times already. It's aged him considerably. He looks ten or twenty years my senior. But that isn't right, is it?

"Give it up, son," Armitage continues over the loudspeaker, "we can only continue this charade for so long before implosion becomes an inevitable fact."

"Implosion, my ass! This is a vendetta. This is straight-up sanctioned *murder*! And for what? To 'stop the multiverse from imploding'? Really? Is that the best you fuckers have?" I feel Charlotte's arms and legs loosen around me. "Don't let go of me, baby."

"It's over, Michael." I turn my head and stare straight into her eyes. Pleading eyes glassy with tears that stream down her cheeks. "Please. Let me go."

I feel her slipping and quickly take hold of her wrists, pressing them together. "Charlotte, no!"

"Let her go, son," Armitage says. "Release her or we'll be forced to open fire."

"You can't do this!" I howl. Blood rumbles in my ears. My heart pounds. I can feel her wrists sliding apart in my rigid, sweat-soaked fingers. "You goddamn bastards!" I turn my rage-filled eyes on them. All of them. The bastards. They all look indifferent and tired. They just want this to end so they can go home to their comfortable fucking lives. But Charlotte... she's everything to me. She's all I have. What right do they...?

My counterpart shifts to the side, a seemingly casual gesture if not for the fact he's also lowering his rifle and cocking his head ever so slightly over his shoulder. Something about the way he does it registers as a signal to me. I look past his shoulder into the bay, but I don't see anything except the wall on the other side. Then I look down between his legs. A pyramid stack of three long metal cylinders strapped together under the passenger seats, barely in my line of sight. Cylinders...

The napalm! But why the hell is he showing me that? Unless...

"I'm sorry."

Charlotte's hands pull free, wrenching me from my thoughts, dropping me back into the present. "CHARLOTTE!" I whirl to see her falling. A minute frozen in time. Her face a tragic smile, clear streaks of skin shining through the layers of soot and dirt caking her face where her tears had rolled. Armitage barks something but I don't hear him as I brace myself against the tree and spring out into space after her. Reeves opens up with the M60. Zona curses loudly and fires her rifle from beside my counterpart.

My AKM swings up...

I'm flying through a hail of bullets...

...swings up in an arc and I fire it...

...My leg takes a hit and I scream...

...I fire it one-handed at the helicopter.

At the bay.

Between my counterpart's feet.

At the napalm.

The Black Hawk's bay belches a huge plume of liquid fire that incinerates all onboard instantly. Flaming gouts catch in the rotors which sweep the napalm in an orange whirlpool, floods the entire sky like the world's first midair hurricane. The napalm whirlwinds bellow with untapped fury as the helicopter comes apart within the firestorm's eye, its fuel and armament systems exploding simultaneously, feeding the raging sky. As the helicopter begins to fall, so, to, does the napalm. I twist in the air, wind squealing in my ears, as I reach for Charlotte with the wrath of heaven crashing down around us. The white cedar tree is greedily consumed in the bright orange downpour. I can feel the heat searing into my clothes, boiling my blood under my skin, burning me up. Almost there. Almost…

And I see Charlotte looking up at me, the burning sky reflecting in her eyes and shining on her soot-tinged skin. She's reaching for me, as if by instinct, as the beach's sand rushes up to meet us both.

I take her hand. Clamp my eyes shut. My mind races as the flames descend upon us, burning us; as the ground shoots up to flatten us.

And it wanders back home.

Alexander Engel-Hodgkinson

Chapter 25: Separate Ways

The impact slams the air out of my lungs. I find myself deflating in three feet of water, my eyes clamped shut, with images of fire dancing around me. Something—or some*one* thrashes under me, kicking my legs, my stomach and chest, then my head. Almost knocks me out cold. I float through a warm space, weightless, as fluid fills my lungs, and then two sets of claws dig into my shoulders and drag me out of the water and pull me onto a hard, uneven surface. Feels like dusty old scales. I can sense the dust clinging to my wet palms. I retch and water gushes out of my throat. My head's swirling. Vision's blurred and my sense of balance is out of whack; the earth and sky trade places with the trees and each other. Somebody lifts me into a sitting position.

"Here. Give me your arm." Charlotte? "Give me your arm." I can barely move, let alone obey. I feel my arm being lifted and slung around her shoulders. My eyes are still closed, stinging from the pressure. She seems fine. Maybe her Michael—wherever he is—jumped her around before I found her. Who knows. This is the first time I tested it out myself. It was a dumb, desperate gamble that paid off.

She carries me to a bench and flops on it beside me, breathing hard. I open my eyes and see a figure immortalized in stone looming high above a sheet of fire, his wings aflame in an incredible display of eternal strength while he pours a stream of water from a vase balanced on his mighty shoulders into the scorching pool. He looks like God sent a lone angel down to put out the fires of hell with a single vase. Kinda laughable when you think about it that way.

I recognize this place. The park. We're in the park. The gazebo is there. The gardens and the cobblestone pathways. Only difference here is that there's now a wide spattering of napalm burning around the fountain and shimmering on the water's surface, though it's dying fast in the pool, dissolving, as smoke hisses into the mid-morning air, patches of it will be burning for quite a while on the path and the grass.

Morning...? All I know is that we're back in Cherry Springs. I don't even know if the Michael and Charlotte of this universe are alive and well, or if they're long dead by now.

"Here," she gasps, peeling her wet shirt off with great effort. She's wearing a tank top underneath it. "Hold still." She twists the shirt, wringing out the excess water, and then ties it around the bullet hole in my thigh with the tender yet firm expertise of a nurse's touch, to my surprise—and agony, when she tightens it around my wound and I feel the knotted fabric biting into my torn flesh.

"Agh...!" I lay my palm across my stomach. A thought crosses my mind. No gun. I look down. The M1911 isn't in my waistband anymore. I look at Charlotte. She's sitting just an arm's reach from me, chest heaving, looking pale. But she has the gun in her right hand. She slides to the far end of the bench.

"Don't try it," she cautions.

"Try what?"

"You were going to make a move for the gun."

I say nothing. Too busy breathing. Everything hurts. My right leg oozes hot fluid down my eviscerated calf where the bullet got me, though her shirt is definitely helping in keeping my blood from flowing freely. Just can't feel my leg now.

"Weren't you?"

"What reason do I have... to... take it from you?"

She sniffles and forces herself up to her feet. "I'm going now, Michael." I make a move of protest, but I'm immediately halted when she points the pistol at me. Her finger's on the trigger guard. It's just another warning, maybe the last one she makes before she touches the trigger. "I can't live like this anymore. Not like this. Not at anyone else's expense. I love you, Michael, really, I do. You have no idea how much this breaks me." She wipes water from her eyes, backs away two paces down the path toward the gazebo. "But this isn't... I can't... *we* can't live like this."

"Don't you understand?" I gasp. "This was... this was for your protection, Charlotte. From *them*. I love you, Charlotte, please... this... it was all for you."

"No," she says, "it was all for *you*."

Somehow she makes a .50 calibre round straight to the heart seem like a better alternative to what she just said. I stare at her in shock, unable to get a reply out. I have so many things I could say. Enough arguments to fill a dictionary. If only she'll listen.

But she won't.

"Goodbye, Michael." She turns and runs. No matter how

much I scream for her, how many times I yell her name in a fit of manic desperation, she doesn't stop. She doesn't slow down. Doesn't even turn her head. Just keeps on running.

"CHARLOOOOTTE!" I lunge off the bench to pursue her, but my freshly injured leg gives under my weight and I collapse on the cobblestone path in a heap. Tears sting my eyes. My heart's going through a shredder in my aching chest. She's leaving me. She's leaving me.

I look up. She's just a shape now, shrinking into the long shadows of dawn, disappearing behind a myriad of trees and the gazebo and street signs.

She's gone. Somehow her leaving me hurts worse than any of her deaths that I witnessed. Something about this is much more final than death. Nothing can undo this.

So I lie there on the cobblestone path and cry into the dirt in a way I haven't since the full realization of what Mom did to herself finally caught up with me. The woman I failed to protect has abandoned me.

Chapter 26: Worlds Apart

Don't know how long I was out. I'm jolted awake by a pair of hands that lift me off the path. "Here. It's okay. It's okay." The voice is rough, grating, an aged parody of something familiar. Whoever it is, they sit me back upright on the bench. I'm still in the park. The fires have been put out. I look up in a daze, up at my own face, but it's not my face. It's worn like crinkled leather, with small cuts and scars covering it. It's the doppelganger from the helicopter. An alternate version to the Michael I'd killed. The Alpha. He's wearing plain clothes, a Judas Priest T-shirt, and frayed jeans, with an unzipped hoodie to protect him from the morning chill. Mirrored aviators adorn his hair above his forehead like some kind of urban crown.

"Easy, now," he says. "Easy." He notices my glare and backs away slowly, showing his palms. He sits himself down on the ledge of the fountain's pool, sets his hands flat on his knees, staring across the path at me. "Just me and you."

"I don't have time for this."

"Let her go."

"Why?"

"I think deep down, I knew why. I was in your shoes once."

"The fuck you were," I spit venomously. "Why the hell would I *join* the Agency?"

"Because up until this point, I didn't understand it."

"What's to understand?" I wince when I shift my leg and feel heat rising from my wounded calf muscle.

"Well, first off, the Commander was wrong."

"Bullshit."

"It's true." He raises his hands. "Would I lie to you?"

"I don't know what I'd do to me at this point. But I know what I'll do to *you*."

"Right. That reminds me." He draws his gun and I stiffen at the sight of the Beretta 92F in his hand. Then I flinch when he tosses it into my lap. Flinching only provides me with another painful reminder of my calf. I look down at the gun in my lap, then glance back up at him suspiciously. He doesn't say anything. Just watches me with an unusual serenity. I pick up the gun and check the magazine. Full. I slap it home and pull back the slide. There's already a round chambered. What the hell?

"Can we continue?" my doppelganger asks me, dropping his hands to his thighs.

I point the gun at him. "Speak."

"There is no paradox. There never was."

"Then what was all this?"

"Just history... repeating itself. But I changed it. The other Michael, the one she chose you over, he's dead now. I made sure of it. After he provided us with the coordinates, I made damn sure I put a hole in his head. He *was* to be my replacement if the Commander didn't, and you... you would have become the new Commander if not for the fact that I changed everything. I did what he did three years ago. But *that* Michael didn't kill me. The future Commander killed him in the assault and took his place in the Agency as their new uh, *consultant*.

"You see, the current Commander of just a few hours ago got it all wrong. For starters, I didn't kill the previous Commander. I *am* the previous Commander. And he misunderstood the concept of time travel. Of everything. Jumping from dimension to dimension doesn't do anything to time itself, although the event of traveling to another dimension in 'real time,' so to speak, is surprisingly rare.

"Sad saps like you and me... we're only human. We have needs. And Charlotte, love of my life, believe it or not, fulfilled that need. She made life worth living again. The best days I ever had were spent with her, brief as they were.

"Or so it seemed. Problem is, when she—when Alpha Charlotte—died... she was a rock star. She pursued that life and that life killed her. Too much cocaine, I think. Well, her manager—you, me... he could jump, too. And he got the crazy little idea that he could save her if only he got into that change room a little bit sooner. And the more often he did this, the wider the shockwave. That's how other Charlottes died. That's how other Michaels started developing crazy little ideas..."

Silence falls between us. I have a million questions. One succeeds above the rest: "If *you're* the previous Commander, where's the real Alpha?"

"He's dead. The only reason, I suspect, that the Agency keeps me around is because of you. And others like you. What better way to deal with a complication, an anomaly like you and the other parallel versions of us, than by using one of us as a consultant? After all, no one knows me better than me. When this is all over, I've no doubt they'll drop the act and kill me with the rest of us. You and I aren't casualties in this affair, not like Yusef or Freddie. Their Alphas are still alive. But *ours*, and Charlotte's, they're long gone. That's the difference."

He pauses, then, letting this sink in. Somehow it's making a scary amount of sense, and I'm hating every goddamn thing about it. "Like I said... time isn't looping. We're just living by the very definition of insanity: doing the same thing over and over and over again and expecting a different fucking result each time. But we keep making the *same* stupid decisions, and so, history—not *time*— keeps repeating itself."

I stare at him, long and hard. For a while, the only sounds we hear are the wind blowing through the trees above us and the trickling of the water fountain behind my doppelganger.

"How do we stop it?" I ask him. "If you know so much about it, then..."

"The only way to stop it is to do something we wouldn't do."

I get a sinking feeling in the pit of my stomach. Still, I feel compelled to ask: "What's that?"

He stares at me for a long stretch. It's just the sounds of nature I hear. They're strangely overbearing until he speaks again: "Let her go."

I don't speak. My heart's going down like one of the ferries on Lake Michigan when the Stratofortress made another pass— blown to shit, with whatever's remaining of its structure and passengers sinking into the water's cold, indifferent depths. My mouth is dry, like all the moisture was somehow sucked in behind my eyeballs. I can feel the pressure building there, forcing me to blink continuously as my tears press through and roll down my face. "I can't do that."

"Yes, you can."

"I *can't*!"

"*Yes*, you can. You just won't. We never do. And the longer this goes on, the more often she'll get hurt."

"Bullshit."

"'Bullshit'? 'Bullshit', huh? I wish it was. But then again, if it was, would I be here talking to you?" Before I can answer that, he does it for me: "No. I wouldn't. Because this whole thing would be resolved."

"What is the goddamn *point*?!" I roar in a surge of frustration. "It doesn't matter what I do," I tell him—myself, whatever he is, "because a new timeline will be created for every possible outcome I *don't* choose. How the fuck do you *stop* something like that?"

"You don't," he replies calmly, "you simply alter it. Before, there were always two of us left. Both would have different experiences of the same cataclysmic event like the one you just went through, and both would have different grasps of the situation. From there, only three options would remain: replace the me that served as a consultant for Armitage and his platoon, replace the Commander in the Corps, or walk away from the whole thing.

"But I've already told you that history repeats itself, because we only choose one of the first two options—never the third. Because we just can't bring ourselves to let go of the one woman who was a shining light in our lives when we hit our absolute lowest.

"So instead of expecting a different outcome by allowing the exact same thing to occur, I changed it. I killed the Commander and the second Michael. Now it's just one with three options to make on his own. And I'm here to guide you in the right direction."

"You can't make me do anything," I snap at him.

"Of course not." He gives me a tired look. "After all, you're the one with the gun. We both know if you thought I was bullshitting, you would've shot me already. That's what I did. But I remembered everything my successor said, and I know where he went wrong. He didn't change a goddamn thing. He thought simple logic and reason would get through to me. It didn't. I took the gun away from him and emptied the magazine in his... face." He pauses, eyes going dark, staring past me at an oak tree standing next to the sidewalk, though I know that's not where his mind is.

He snaps back in fifteen seconds. "Then I followed her." His eyes drift lazily to mine. "It was a mistake I should never have made. But you still have time. You still have time to set things right."

I'd be lying if I said this whole clusterfuck situation makes sense to me. All I'm getting out of this is that this experienced version of me has done everything he can to change the future without traveling through time.

Traveling through time. God, I don't know how I got here. A

week ago, if someone told me I'd be jumping into parallel dimensions and struggling to stop myself from saving the woman I love from constant, repetitive death, I would've probably answered with a blank stare, or told them they were crazy. Not even the introvert in me would've kept me from saying something about that.

Yet here I am, pointing a gun at my doppelganger who's apparently experienced everything I experienced earlier in the 2000's, as he tells me that alternate versions of me keep making the same mistakes to the point where it's a goddamn threat to the *multiverse*. 'Let her go,' he's telling me. How the hell can I possibly do that? Life finally gives me a break—someone who actually cares about me, who loves me, and then life tells me to go fuck myself, that I can't have her, that my *existence* in her life is what's killing her.

That *I'm* the problem here.

"I'll do it differently," I tell him.

He looks disappointed. "No, you won't."

"No?"

"No."

"How could you possibly know that? After telling me everything you've told me. I know where I went wrong."

"No, you *think* you know where I went wrong. Trust me. You don't know what you did wrong until it's too late to change it."

"There has to be a right way."

"I already told you what that is: let her go."

"How would you know that's the right way?"

"It's the only way I never bothered to try."

"I can't give up on her like that."

"It's the only way she'll survive."

I shake my head. The tears are flowing freely now.

"Move on," he says. "Live your own life, free from her. Let her live her life free from you. You had some good times, but it's over now. It can't be salvaged. Move on, man. Seriously."

My hand trembles. The gun rattles quietly in my quivering fingers.

"Move on," he says calmly. "Focus on yourself for a while."

A disturbing thought crosses my mind. "If I let you go... will you continue to pursue her?"

"Only the ones affected by our disruption. But she'll still be around, prospering, enjoying life, finding new love, growing old...

worlds apart from us.

"But we have no future with her. We tried, goddamn it, we tried, and it just didn't work out. That's life dealing us a shitty hand. It happens sometimes. There are plenty of other fish in the sea. Just have to look for ourselves. It took me three years to understand that for myself."

I wipe my eyes on my sleeves. "Some things were never meant to be, huh?"

He shrugs sluggishly, like his shoulders are too heavy for him. "Some things were never meant to be.

"Now," he adds as he bends forward, reaches over his knees, and picks up the AKM I'd dropped before I passed out, "I have somewhere to be."

"No—stop," I tell him.

He racks the bolt.

My finger closes on the pistol trigger. "Hey! Hey!"

He points the AKM at me and I instinctively unleash a three-round beat into the center of his chest. He convulses on the fountain ledge, the AKM's muzzle tracing erratic spiral patterns in the air between us. His eyes are still locked on me. The AKM barks in his hands. The side of the bench erupts into splintery chunks beside me, startling another shot from me—this one higher, desperate, yet, through arduous training and a handful of years of service in the Middle East, intuitively precise—that lances a 9mm round right between his eyes. His head snaps back and his body follows, limbs flying upwards as his torso crashes into the fountain.

And there he stays with his legs draped over the fountain's ledge. Pink-tinged water trickles over the side and down to the weed-infested cobblestone.

For a while I say nothing, do nothing, feel nothing but shock and the throbbing pain in my leg.

I just killed myself. But... he drew on me first. He broke the rules of engagement, not me.

God, that sounds crazy. I'm crazy. Losing my mind. All this time-travel-not-time-travel-dimension-hopping shit is tearing my head into shreds. She was all I could have ever wanted. I never meant for any of this to happen. I could never have turned out like this.

I grit my teeth, groaning against the pain as I grind off the bench and put a little weight on my bad leg. Pain shoots up from my thigh, but I can stand—barely—and I limp pathetically to the fountain to look at the corpse of my future-past self. There he floats, partially submerged, in water that more closely resembles sparkling red wine, eyes closed, the corners of his mouth curled ever so slightly upward in a peaceful smile. He looks serene. Like this is all he wanted in the end. Like he died knowing he succeeded. Did he succeed? I don't know for sure. There's gotta be a universe where he does, right?

I don't feel their presence right away. They're like ghosts, or figments of my imagination, showing up at random, always lingering in the background. Now they're front and center, surrounding me and the park benches that ring the circular cobblestone path around the fountain. The Agency people, whoever they are, *what*ever they are. Their guns are drawn but at their sides, pointed at the ground as if I'm no longer a threat to them despite the pistol in my hand and the AKM within my reach on the fountain's bottom. Armitage is the only one on the path, standing five feet away from me. I could easily shoot him. Hell, I could kill them all before they had a chance to raise their firearms in retaliation.

But what's the point? Charlotte's done with me. Everything that's happened is a testament to our co-existence being a very bad idea. I love her more than anyone in the world and every world I go to tells me it's unhealthy for us both—her especially. Do I really want to keep this going? Chasing her through countless realities, fighting off endless waves of Agency forces to 'protect' her from them? If what my Agency self has told me is true, this could end if only I stopped the cycle. If I stopped, she could live on and flourish.

"I found a beautiful dahlia in the Afghanistan desert once." Armitage's calm voice snaps me out of my thoughts. The bullet-chewed bench creaks in protest when he sits on it. He leans forward, elbows on his knees, hands clasped in front of his face. "I don't know what kind of dahlia it was, but it was this... this little neon blue anomaly in the red sand. I thought it strange that this fragile little thing would grow so splendidly in the harsh conditions of such an unforgiving land. I thought it would surely die if I left it there, so I took it with me. Took it home and watered it regularly; I gave it plenty of sun in the window of my apartment, where it... quickly withered... and died. It died... I thought I could help it live a long life. I just loved it so much. The idea of such contrasting beauty blossoming there, of all the places on this earth to blossom, it chose to be there and nowhere else. Sometimes I wonder if it would still be there if I hadn't uprooted it. Perhaps its fragility was all in my head."

I watch him for a while. He stares unblinking at the ground, his mind elsewhere. I glance up at each face in turn: Zona, Chow, Mason, and finally Reeves. They look worn out. There's no hint of anger or malice on their faces, just fatigue and a little sympathy.

I look at Armitage again. "It still exists, doesn't it?"

"Yes," Armitage replies, looking up. "I suppose she does. But she and I are worlds apart now."

I have to take weight off of my bad leg, so I sit down on the fountain ledge next to my last kill. The gun in my hand feels heavy, the oiled metal grimy against my skin.

"What about you?" Armitage asks.

I set the gun down on the ledge and heave a deep, shuddering sigh. "I'm done."

Afterword

Originally written for a collaborative indie author anthology entitled *Reality Glitch*, *Jumping for Charlotte* was something like a 30-page love letter to chase movies, or romantic thrillers, or... whatever.

Truth is... it just came to me.

See, about eleven authors (including myself) got together to create an anthology of short stories—a collection that would eventually be called *Reality Glitch*. 'Parallel universes' was the theme. We would exchange drafts and proofread them. I'm ashamed to say that with a combined fourteen hours of school and work in a shitty factory five days a week, I neither had the time nor the energy to proofread anything. I barely had time to write my own contribution, and even then, I submitted the first and second drafts a couple days past their deadlines. I really am sorry for that, guys.

Anyway.

I was hurting at the time for someone whose feelings for me weren't nearly as strong or as straightforward as my feelings for her. So on top of being an exhausted wreck, I was an emotional wreck, as well.

I asked her once about her opinion on the concept of reincarnation, which she believes is true. I'm not of the type to immediately believe or disbelieve one thing or the other—unless it's something stupid, like Scientology (LOL). But I would toy with the ideas I stumble upon, and my brain would get to work, even when I don't want it to.

Eventually, brainstorming the concept of reincarnation led to double lives, then triple lives, then alternate lives; imagining myself in Michael's shoes and the woman I cared for so deeply in Charlotte's shoes—without the death and mayhem or other disturbing qualities contained within this story. I imagined a world where she actually cared for me. Being the messy, romantic sap that I was, I got to work on the first draft just a week before the deadline after nearly a month (as I remember it) of coming up with nothing. I would shirk my school assignments, stay up late on the rare nights when I could actually keep my eyes open and focused; just to work on

Jumping for Charlotte. Appropriately, I wrote it in the first person, which the other collaborators weren't too thrilled about, thinking it was just a cheap gimmick.

Responding to their suggestions and notes plastered in my drafts was difficult, and not just because of my tight schedule. I like criticism. I encourage it. I want people, especially fellow authors, to point out the flaws both real and perceived in my work so that I can fix them. But sometimes, the questions they came up with were near-intolerable. "What is an RV?" for instance. One of them even asked in a note "What is a 'rock bench'?" I couldn't believe it. I never responded to him, directly, but I responded to the note: "It's a fucking bench made out of fucking rocks."

Despite some frustrating moments (one suggestion was that I delete exposition dialogue and follow the "show, don't tell" rule at the beginning, only for that same author to suggest I explain more of what's going on in the dialogue at the end concerning the exact same thing), it was a good experience. I'd dare say it was vital to my growth as a writer. The original draft was very over-the-top with propane tank explosions, constant *Groundhog Day*-style segments where Michael would go to a world, find Charlotte, attempt to save her, only for her to die—rinse, repeat—and a stampede of robots; creating a jarring, tonal mess that conflicted not just with the darker, more serious aspects of the story, but also with the group's target demographic and the tones of the other authors' stories. Consistency is key, you know. I know I didn't do a very good job as a collaborator (again, sorry), but I still learned a thing or two.

Although I kind of dedicated the story to that person, I never told her, because she would have probably never read it anyway, and in the 0.01% chance she would, I doubt she'd like it. She would probably be disturbed by it. She had a problem with the darker side of my writing to the point of being concerned for my sanity. Maybe she was even afraid of me, which was and still kind of is upsetting to think about. She laughs at the very idea of me having a romantic side, because all she saw was a dark-minded individual with a violent sense of humour and concerning traits in his personality.

That side of me does exist. Honest.

I was doubly discouraged when *Charlotte* wasn't

mentioned in the subsequent reader reviews for *Reality Glitch* as a highlight, and was instead, in one review, noted as the only story that one particular reader would never want to read again due to its morbidity. It takes a lot to offend me, but within the frame of time it was published, in the state of mind I possessed, that one kind of stung.

I'll take it with a grain of salt. It's fair criticism, after all.

It's unfortunate how all of that ended. Two years and then some later, I'm right back where I started—out of a different relationship that seemed to be going so well, promisingly well, even beautifully, it *was* my life and I was happy and I wanted her to be as happy as I was... but I guess it wasn't meant to be. It was all knocked off the track by a curveball that came out of nowhere. Sigh.

Then someone else came along. Life does that sometimes. And I guess that's what this is all about.

This is a definitive, fleshed-out version of the short story; much like *I Keep My True Love in the Basement/REMIX* is a definitive version of its respective short story. Unlike *REMIX*, which mostly expanded upon the ideas of the short, extended the short's already existing material, and added about two hundred pages of plot and side characters to tell a larger-scale, more coherent version of the story; *Charlotte* is a complete retelling. I find the original short unsatisfactory, so now I'm making it better. I doubt *Charlotte* will end up being as long as */REMIX* turned out to be, but who knows what could happen? *Cobalt Christmas* was only supposed to be 200 pages, and its paperback format hits about 475. If a book is good, there are no page limits.

Alexander Engel-Hodgkinson

Works by Alexander Engel-Hodgkinson

Clockworld (One-Shot)

The Tea Party Affair

I Keep My True Love in the Basement (One-Shot)

Reality Glitch ('Jumping for Charlotte' segment)

No Bounds ('Cranston & Layman' segment)

I Keep My True Love in the Basement/REMIX

Cobalt Christmas

She Watches Me Bury Her

Jumping for Charlotte

The Laughter in the Woods (*COMING SOON*)

The Final Apocalypse Saga (First two volumes previously published as 'Dark-Boy')

Cobalt Rogue, Vol. 1: The Dead Blue

Cobalt Rogue, Vol. 2: Sky Japan Welcome Party

Cobalt Rogue, Vol. 3: Cemetery Rumble, Part I

Cobalt Rogue, Vol. 3.5: Hell Week (*COMING SOON*)

www.ingramcontent.com/pod-product-compliance
Lightning Source LLC
Chambersburg PA
CBHW021034130626
46552CB00005B/1842